The
Dark Space
Between

Also By Cassandra Stirling

Space Between Urban Fantasy Series

The Tidal Space Between
The Deep Space Between

Merryton Mews Cozy Mysteries

Poisons and Pens
Holly and Havoc

THE DARK SPACE BETWEEN

CASSANDRA STIRLING

T/W: Mild violence in an enclosed space

Cover designed by MiblArt.

For more information and to sign up for my newsletter, visit
cassandracstirling.com/spacebetween-book2.

THE DARK SPACE BETWEEN

ISBN 979-8-9867520-2-0 *Paperback*

ISBN 979-8-9867520-3-7 *eBook*

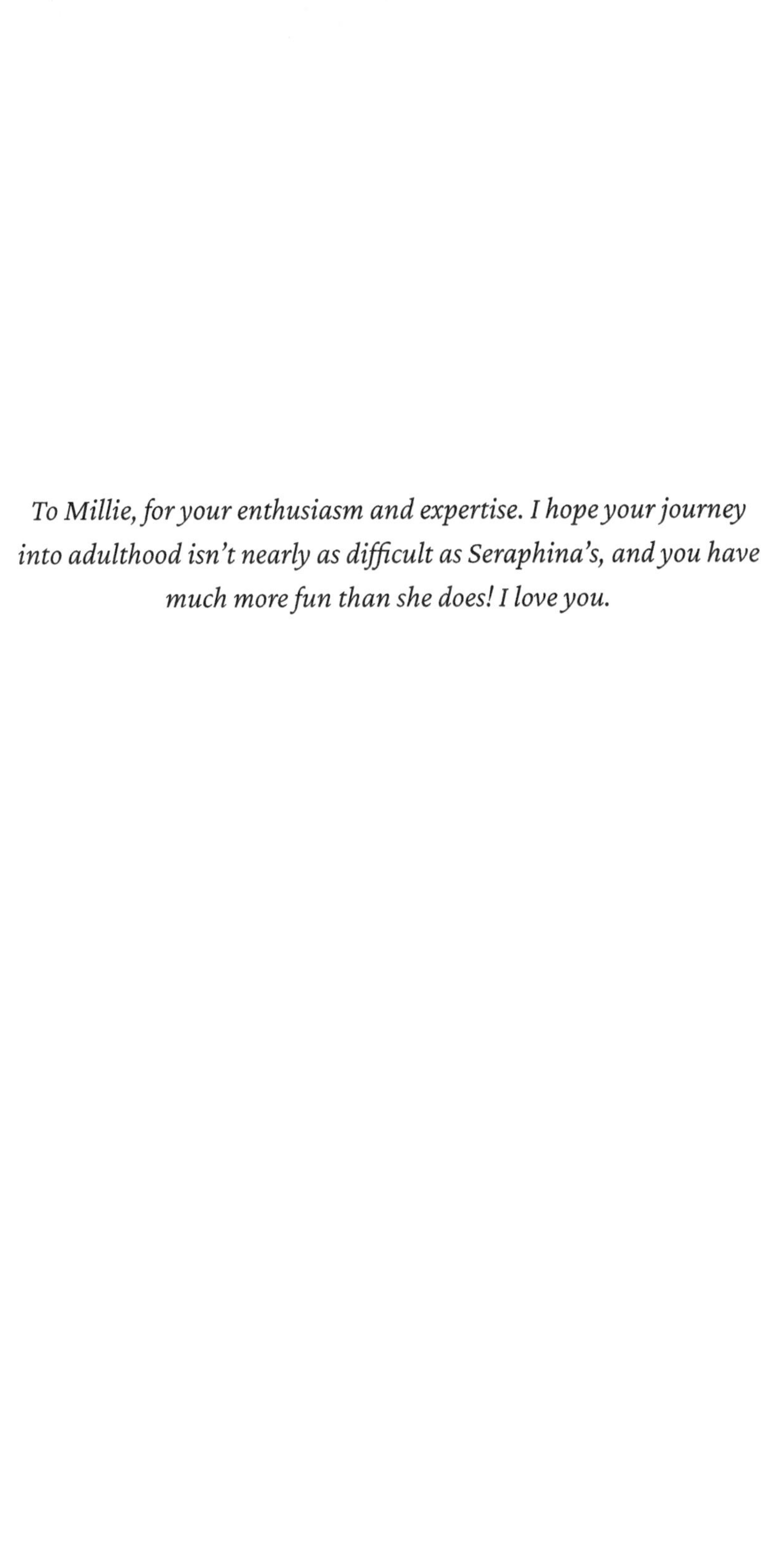

To Millie, for your enthusiasm and expertise. I hope your journey into adulthood isn't nearly as difficult as Seraphina's, and you have much more fun than she does! I love you.

CONTENTS

TO CATCH YOU UP

(There Is Too Much)

At twenty-five years old, Seraphina Lastra Covington graduated with her Masters in Book Restoration from Columbia University in New York City and expected her life to begin. Without a job and a place to live, however, it stalls before it starts. Seraphina has no option but to go home to the Magic Community of Merricott, New Hampshire.

There are several problems with this scenario. The first is that the good people of Merricott still haven't forgiven her family for the magical terrorist attack that occurred twelve years before in a Big Top Tent; an attack initiated by Seraphina's grandfather. It doesn't matter that Seraphina lost her mother, father, beloved uncle, and grandfather in the incident. Or that Seraphina had nothing to do with it, since she's human and unable to wield aether or shift to another form.

Or rather, her humanness is also a problem. The Magical Community takes their invisibility in the human world seriously. There is a large magical ward covering all of Merricott to discourage humans from stepping even a toe in it. This allows the Wielders, Shifters, Trolls, Elves, and whatever other beings roaming the area to live without having to wear their human faces, or as Seraphina calls it, their "game faces." Even though Seraphina is technically a member because her parents were Shifters, she is a human anomaly no one can explain. Including her.

Seraphina thinks her biggest hurdle will be to face the ghosts of the past and learn how to cohabitate with an aunt who doesn't seem to want her there. Her aunt dropped her off at a human boarding school mere days after the Big Top Tent incident twelve years before, and their relationship is tenuous.

But she's wrong.

Within hours of being alone in the house, Seraphina's not-so-imaginary friend, Angwyndith, resurfaces to renew their bond. Angwyndith is a Bodach (aka Judge) of the Magical Community. Her purpose is to enforce the rules of the Coda—the rules that govern them all. She shares the body of Seraphina, her Host. While currently separate, the goal of Bodach and Host is to reach Harmony, or the ultimate merging of both the Bodach and the human.

Angwyndith is the reason the incident at the Big Top Tent only took forty-two lives. She, and by attachment, Seraphina, stopped the being responsible for the attack, a Guide by the name of Rozag. But Seraphina has little to no memory of it and finds Angwyndith pushy, manipulating, and condescending. After she finds out Angwyndith nudged her as a child to read more books, Seraphina also questions her identity and her love of books.

At the same time as Seraphina's return, a Wielder child has gone missing. When he isn't found by the most powerful Wielders in the town, one of whom is Seraphina's aunt, the town points their fingers at the Lastras, or rather the last of their Shifter clan, Peter Jensen. Peter is the slightly crazy Shifter who lives in the woods behind Seraphina's house. He, however, has also disappeared.

When the Security Forces of the Free Folk (SF) arrive in town to assist in the investigation, the stakes rise. The SF are the CIA and FBI of the Magic Community, doing their part to police the community, while gathering knowledge and conducting research as well. The SF still don't know what happened in the Big Top Tent and they hate being in the dark about anything. With time running out, Seraphina races to find Peter. She needs to stop the town and the SF from blaming her family for something they had no part in, at least this time.

Unfortunately, Seraphina is too late. She finds Peter, plus a host of other missing pets and smaller Shifters, dead in her favorite clearing behind the house. Her aunt panics and sends Seraphina away, hoping to put distance between the town's distrust of her and the missing. But Seraphina can't hide from her past, her present, or Angwyndith any longer.

She returns to town and figures out who is responsible for the deaths: the town's High Master of the Cunning Folk and her aunt's boss, Sean Harriman. Seraphina and Angwyndith interrupt Harriman in the middle of a powerful spell, initiating the Inquisition of Hearts (a review of all that Harriman did in his life) and the final Judgment—death. However, they can't stop the spell Harriman is casting. Upon his death, the spell is released and Harriman's house blows up. Unfortunately, the SF agents witness it occurring. With nothing left to hide, Seraphina introduces Angwyndith to her aunt and the SF, which leads to this book. The SF wants her to train with them so that she is never a liability on the field.

The question that remains is: does she really want to train with them?

"A real decision is measured by the fact that you've taken a new action. If there's no action, you haven't truly decided."
~ Anthony Robbins

1

HER HUMDRUM LIFE

(SHE WASN'T LIKE THEM)

Seraphina's back stung as it hit the mat and her breath whooshed out as Moira's knee pressed against her windpipe. Panic clawed at her as her feet struggled to find purchase on the slippery surface, Moira easily pinning Seraphina's flailing arms to the ground.

Her lungs on fire and black spots appearing in her vision, Seraphina went limp. "Yield," she said. The pain in her throat increased for an eternity and then disappeared as Moira moved off of her. Seraphina lay on her back, sucking in air like a drowning man.

"What did you do wrong?" Moira asked from her crouched position near Seraphina's head.

"I panicked."

"Yes, you did. Stop thinking so much about what hurts, where the pressure is, or what I'm doing. Focus on you and what you can do. You can't break free if you don't act." The intensity of Moira's gaze increased with every word.

Seraphina pushed herself up, her muscles screaming in protest. Ballet had prepared her for some aspects of Krav Maga, but nothing could prepare her for having her own body used against her. "I know, I'm trying."

"Are you? Or are you wasting my time?"

The words struck like a blow to the chest. Moira was one of the few instructors who talked to her. The last thing Seraphina wanted was for it to end, even if she knew she'd never measure up to Moira's exacting demands.

"Well?"

"I'm not wasting your time. I'm just not a fan of close combat." That was an understatement. Seraphina had avoided all contact sports at boarding school for a reason. "I'll get it."

"You better. Your opponent won't give you the chance." Moira glanced at the clock. "Time's up. I'll see you on Wednesday."

"Thanks," Seraphina said as she heaved herself off the floor.

She scooped up her badge from the battered wooden bench along the wall and pushed through the doors leading to the rest of the Facility, the unending white of the hall broken only by the combination locks built into the lockers on either side of her. No matter what else the Security Forces did below ground, they couldn't alter the above ground building enough to remove its original function as a high school.

But then the SF did nothing without a reason. They picked this building in the middle of nowhere Virginia for its strategic location: two hours away from the nearest city, close to a working airfield, but far enough away to train the combat teams of Shifters and Magic Wielders without the humans noticing. Not that the humans would. The 9,000 acre campus had overlapping wards hiding it from prying eyes, the heaviest of them covering the building. As they did everything, the SF took separation and invisibility from the humans to the extreme.

A laugh brought her gaze up from her study of the floor. A squad of Shifters and a battle-dressed Wielder emerged from the steel doors at the other end of the hall. The Shifters' broad shoulders and combat armor took up most of the space, but the pads of their feet made no noise, not even from the claws extending from their hairy toes. The leader of the group, a Shifter in Warrior form, stood taller than her Uncle Patrick, but while imposing, his eyes were kind and a smile played around his lips.

The Wielder paced a step behind the leader of the group. Her hair was cropped as short as Aunt Tristana's, but dark instead of speckled with gray. The Wielder's presence dominated the space as if she'd thrown out aether to appear larger than she was, even though her form was slight compared to the others. Her silvery eyes locked on Seraphina, and while her face stayed calm, the fingers of her left hand weaved a pattern, watching for any reason to use the spell she readied.

Seraphina felt like she'd been punched in the gut. Aunt T had looked at Seraphina like that three months ago, in a kitchen full of people who could've crushed Seraphina like a bug, just like this group. Was she really such a monster?

The Shifter in front flicked a glance over his shoulder, a subtle shake of the head causing the Wielder to relax her fingers. Seraphina gave him a small smile and flattened herself between two lockers to let them pass. He nodded in thanks. The Wielder watched her like a virus under a microscope, but her fingers remained loose by her side.

As the group walked by, a Shifter said, "Hey, Chief Gabriel, can Sarge drive the truck this time? We may get there in one piece if he does."

"Only if I get to pick the music," a deep voice replied. Groans and hoots followed this proclamation.

Seraphina's smile warmed up to a grin. She missed the banter of friends, the easy laughter, and the connections and shared history.

The last Shifter in the group caught sight of her and his step faltered. Eyes wide, he slid sideways to put as much space between them as possible.

The small pit in her stomach, her constant companion since she first walked through the front doors, flared and the smile slid off her face. She wasn't like them, and she never would be. She peeled herself off the wall and continued to the elevators, which were sandwiched between two sets of steel doors. One set led to the gym and the other to the lobby. If there were any incursions, an alarm would ring out and the doors would lock down, but Seraphina couldn't imagine anyone being stupid enough to attack the most lethal and powerful organization of the Magical Community.

The wait took less time than normal; the ping coming mere seconds after she pressed the button. Seraphina swiped her badge on the scanner and punched the floor to her room. Her feet moved automatically once the doors opened again, her thoughts churning in rhythm. There had to be some way to make friends among the thousand or more people who worked here. Not everyone would fear her and Angwyndith, right?

A badge wave and her security code got her in the cell they called a room. Between the metal desk, the twin bed, a small bookcase, and the trunk she had brought all her things in, she had approximately one foot of walkway. She could stretch out her arms and almost brush the gray cement of either wall with her fingertips.

She checked the time on her phone and grimaced. If she didn't get a move on, she'd be late for class. She threw her towel over her shoulder, picked up her caddy, and a clean set of clothes. Swiping her badge off the desk, she left her room and hustled for the bathroom down the hall.

If she didn't know better, she would've said this place was a prison instead of the law enforcement arm of the Magic Community. No cellphones allowed, but no cell signal either. No laptops allowed, except in her room or in the cafeteria. All mail, email, and messaging services monitored and censored. The list went on and on. They hadn't told her she couldn't leave the grounds, but she wouldn't put it past them to stop her if she did.

Her life legitimately sucked now, as barren as the stone floors, walls, and ceiling she currently called home. And worst of all, the coffee sucked, too.

2

ONE DOOR CLOSED

(AT LEAST THERE WAS FRO-YO)

A few hours later, Seraphina's feet jiggled against the thin wool blanket on her bed, doodles filling the notebook next to her instead of the code sections she'd been trying to memorize after her last class. She shoved the book away from her. How would any of this help her on the field?

An image of the combat teams' leader, Master Chief Benchley, calling out code sections across a bloody field like a quarterback at a football game crossed her mind, and she snorted. None of it seemed to matter and yet codes of conduct, regulations, and history were all they were teaching her.

The cold from the stone seeped through her hoodie as she bumped her head against the wall. Each day blurred into the next, and she didn't think she could take much more. The decision to come to the Facility had made sense, but then she'd have jumped at anything that got her out of Merricott, especially after the death of Peter and the incident with Sean Harriman.

She couldn't escape being haunted by her summer, though. Peter's ghost followed her around the Facility every time she saw a Shifter that looked like him. And she still had nightmares of the day they had Judged Harriman, his eyes floating above a miasma of writhing orange and black flames, as Angwyndith pronounced death the sentence for his crimes. Goosebumps feathered down her arms as the room filled with too many memories.

A beep from the laptop broke the chilling silence, and she jumped. Heart pounding harder than a notification required, she glanced at the screen, hoping it was more than just another assignment from her instructors.

Ro: Hey. What's shaking?

The last of the cold receded as Seraphina smiled and pulled the laptop to her to respond to her best friend's message.

Seraphina: Nothing. Nada. Zip.
Ro: Is it really that bad?
Seraphina: I just spent an hour memorizing code for an exam in two days.
Ro: Blech.
Seraphina: It could've been worse. I was supposed to be at the lab getting pricked by the evil Dr. Pianail, but a sign said it's closed for Alban Efled, the fall equinox.
Ro: I know what Alban Efled is.

Seraphina rolled her eyes.

Seraphina: 'Sup with you?
Ro: I got the job!
Seraphina: CONGRATS!!! That's awesome!

Ro: I know, right? Who'd have thunk? Me, a marine biologist... in training.
Seraphina: I did. I thunk it. What are you and Simon going to do then?
Ro: Move to North Carolina. He's been looking at jobs there and figures he'll be alright.
Seraphina: You're leaving NYC.
Ro: I know. :(

Seraphina's heart sank as her loose plan to return to New York fizzled out. But it wouldn't be the same there without Ro. If she was honest with herself, it also wasn't where she wanted to be anymore, but it beat going back to Merricott. Again.

Seraphina: When?
Ro: A week.
Seraphina: :(
Ro: I just wanted you to know.
Seraphina: I'm thrilled for you. You deserve it.
Ro: You can visit!
Seraphina: Yep. I'm a lot closer to NC here, if they ever let me leave.
Ro: You're not a prisoner, Fi.
Seraphina: Feels like it.

Three dots rolled on the screen and Seraphina waited to see what would come next. When they lasted longer than normal, she bit her lip.

While she and Ro chatted every week, their conversations were still littered with the minefields from the fallout of their last fight and the big Angwyndith reveal. The first few weeks she'd been at the Facility, she'd thought they weren't even doing that until an overheard conversation reminded her of the security controls. A quick IM later, and they were back on track, even if Seraphina had nothing to talk about.

Ro: I gotta dash. I'm meeting the gang for coffee. Wish u were here :(.

Her stomach sank. She'd done it again, poked a soft spot and drove Ro away. When would this get easier?

Seraphina: Me too. I'm jealous of the coffee. Have an extra one for me.
Ro: Will do. Love ya.
Seraphina: I love you too! Congrats again!

Seraphina closed the laptop lid with a soft click. She was happy for Ro, but they were moving further apart. Ro had made progress in her life—new job, a new place to live, a boyfriend—while Seraphina was stuck in training mode.

Again.

She just wanted to be done with all this already. While she enjoyed training with Moira, she had no hopes of winning a battle against a Shifter, no matter what Moira said. She'd give anything to go back to the way it was before she left New York, the recent grad student who restored books for the local bookstore.

Except she wasn't even doing that right now.

The box of books she still owed Finn mocked her from under the desk where she'd shoved them. He hadn't pushed her to send more in his email confirming the delivery of the last book she'd sent him, but he had to wonder why she'd only sent three books back in ten weeks.

It would be four books soon, as the restoration of *Jane Eyre* was close to completion. The book stood clamped in the wood rack on the desk, its new spine gleaming. The glue on the spine should be dry by now, although she could give it another few hours.

Her stomach grumbled, and she drummed her fingers on her thigh. She could mail the book to Finn and hit the cafeteria right after grabbing a quick snack and a refill of coffee, re-energizing her to study. Two birds, one stone. Before she could talk herself out of it, she scooted off the bed and laced up her sneakers.

The wooden-handled crank on her book rack turned easily, and she caught the book before it fell out, careful not to jar the new spine. She inspected the spine, pleased with how she'd merged the old and the new without it being obvious. A quick glance at the paste down end papers attached to the inside front and back covers showed them well stuck, but the glue was still slightly damp. She blew on it to speed up the drying process.

A small twinge of guilt assaulted her. Finn paid her for the quality of her work, and he took a chance on her when he didn't have to. She *could* send it tomorrow, but it was already late and if she got more behind, Finn may tell her he didn't want her to do the work anymore. She snapped the book shut. The still damp paste didn't matter. It would finish drying in the post, since the book would travel closed.

She grabbed a shipping slip from the stack she'd filled out when she thought she'd be more productive and left her room. She'd be gone twenty minutes tops, and she'd get right back to studying, and the next book project, fueled with a little frozen yogurt.

Food made everything better, right?

***

Once the elevator reached the top floor, Seraphina rounded the corner and stepped into the mailroom, which had once been the high school's main office. The SF had kept the long wooden counter but had gutted the rest of it and had bricked up the windows. They gathered all the mail here and then brought it to the gate guardhouse to be sent out. Yet one more layer between the MC and the human world.

The younger Wielder who normally sat there sulking like her ability to wield aether had died was nowhere to be found. Instead, Seraphina could see the backside of one of the Guards bending over a bin.

"Hey there," Seraphina said.

The person jolted upwards and hit their head on the counter above the bin. "Dammit. Don't sneak up on a Shifter like that."

"I didn't think I could." Seraphina frowned. When he just stared at her, she continued, "Sneak up on Shifters. Isn't your hearing supersonic or something?"

He snapped his teeth at her. "I had an incident. What do you want?"

The force of his anger surprised her, and she stepped back. "I need to send this out."

"Do I look like the mail guy?"

"Well, you are behind the counter where Ambrosia normally is, so yeah, you do," she fired back.

"I'm a Guard," he said, tapping the Slándála badge on his arm. "I'm checking packages, not mailing them."

"Fine." She kept her hand on the book, not wanting to let it go as he moved toward her. "Where's the diva who works the counter?"

"Diva? Who you callin' diva?" A squeaky voice behind her piped up. Ambrosia ambled toward the counter with half a sandwich in one hand and a soda in the other. Her short hair, with its purple, blue, and pink swirls, looked like birthday cake frosting at a tie dye celebration.

Seraphina sighed. "You. The last time I was here, you got a paper cut and made it sound like you were dying."

"I was. I was eating a salad with lemon vinaigrette, and it stung like a mofo. Who are you to judge my pain?"

"No one. Obviously." Seraphina rolled her eyes. "I need to mail this out."

"Where's it going, and is everything here?"

"Merricott, as usual, and yes, it's all here. It's delicate, so I need you to be careful with it. Throwing it around will damage the new spine."

"I don't throw things unless they're in an envelope. You want to watch me put it in one, 'cause it'll take a minute. I want to finish eating and have a few in front of yours." She waved her sandwich at a group of packages stacked up near the computer terminal, the corners of each aligned to as close to ninety degrees as they could get.

Seraphina bit her lip, a hunger pang hitting her as if on cue. "No. It'll be fine. If you promise to be careful with it."

"Stop harassing the staff," the Shifter growled at her. "If they said they'd be careful, they will be. Or they'll answer to me."

"I'm not harassing Ambrosia. It's my reputation in that book. If it gets messed up, I can't ship another one and expect to get paid." If she didn't pick up the pace on getting books to Finn, she'd go home for the holidays and face the ire of an eight-foot Troll. She grimaced. "I have a lot to ship out over the next few weeks."

The Shifter squinted at her for a moment, his mouth half open as if he meant to say something but thought better of it.

"It'll be fine," Ambrosia said around a mouthful of sandwich. "Go away now."

Seraphina tapped the book one more time, shrugged, and left it on the counter. As she moved toward the lobby, she heard Ambrosia say, "Thanks for covering the desk while I grabbed lunch."

"I wasn't covering anything. I'll need to review that book before it goes out," the Shifter said.

"Whatever, dude. Just put it on the pile when you're done."

"Have some respect, Wielder," the Shifter snapped back.

She moved too far away to hear Ambrosia's response. At least it wasn't just her; he was an asshole to everyone.

3

BLAST FROM THE PAST

(She Was No Longer Hungry)

The smell of homemade bread wafted down the hall, and Seraphina's mouth watered. She hadn't eaten since the protein bar and banana she'd had before class. A full meal would be better than just frozen yogurt.

The cafeteria doors at the end of the hall opened and a pair of Shifters walked toward her, their voices low. "No idea, but if they don't find out who's doing it, heads will roll."

The shorter Shifter grunted. "Who would be stupid enough to piss off Sawbones?"

"Someone with a death wish, like that wisp."

"Most likely. Gabriel would've had it out of her in minutes." The snap of his claws sent shivers down Seraphina's spine.

"Why he signed up for Eventon is beyond me."

"Two words: Crater Lake."

"Mark my words, the frackin' Aetherheads will get them all killed." The slam of the stairwell door cut off the reply.

Seraphina dissected their conversation as she entered the cafeteria. They'd not studied Crater Lake or Eventon in Fairchild's history class, so those must be recent missions. "Wisp" was a slur for something, but she'd not heard it before.

"Aetherheads" she knew meant Wielders, and she had learned that "cockroach" was a slur for a human when a guard called her that as she'd entered the gym on her second day. Moira had ripped into him about codes and respecting the other phyla. He apologized, but the damage had been done.

If they weren't scared of Angwyndith, they thought she was a pest. Either way, no one talked to her, and no one would.

The murmur of conversation and clatter of trays swelled as she wandered over to the meat station, her hunger increasing the more the tantalizing scents came her way. The different buffet sections held an overwhelming variety of dishes, depending on the time of day, alongside a wood-fired pizza and sandwich section, a hot plate section, an ice cream station, and the usual drinks and silverware fare. As she wavered between grilled lemon chicken or fried chicken, a tray snapped down on the runner next to her, piled high with raw beef.

"Fried chicken," said a gruff voice.

Seraphina's eyes slid sideways at the Shifter standing next to her. He wasn't talking to her, was he?

"That's what you want if you're wavering. I can smell the fake lemon juice from here."

He loaded his plate up with enough mashed potatoes to feed a small army. A muscle-bound arm squashed a laptop to his side, looking like a tablet in comparison. A cupcake sticker covered the brand name and almost swallowed another sticker with the bottom end of an S and another letter intertwined.

She tilted her head to get a closer look, but he twisted away to pour gravy on his potato mountain. He didn't look like a stickers guy, especially since he was shaped like a bouncer, all top heavy and bulgy.

"Thanks. Fried chicken it is then." She smiled at him, but he was already moving away toward a table full of other security guards, sliding his laptop down next to him.

Seraphina sighed. At least he had spoken to her.

After filling her tray, she found a table furthest away from everyone else and sat down. Her gaze roamed the room as she ate. Small clusters of Shifters lingered at large round tables, their voices carrying across the cavernous space.

At smaller tables, Wielders in lab coats read or leaned across the table for quiet conversation with their colleagues. Solo diners were rare, even during busy periods. Today, one other person sat by themselves, hunched over their laptop at the opposite end of the cafeteria, a bright pink headband all Seraphina could see of them through the thinning crowd.

"Hey, Agent Summers," a Shifter called out across the cafeteria.

Seraphina's fork clattered to her plate; her gaze following Summers' every move. He surveyed the room, his eyes passing over her as if she were invisible. Once he found his prey, he moved across the room with quiet precision, stopping by a rowdy table of Shifters. He leaned in and said something. The table erupted in laughter, and several of its members pointed at the guard who had recommended the fried chicken.

The Guard said something sharp back. Summers shrugged, still chuckling, and walked away, a laptop under his arm. His exit cued most of the others as chairs screeched back, leaving their trash behind and the object of their mirth to wolf down his food alone.

Seraphina breathed out as Summers left without talking to her. The last time she'd seen him, he paced in her backyard, a phone planted to his ear. Her aunt had just woken her up from her nap on the kitchen table, telling her to go upstairs. As she stood, he had faced her, claws out, every cell in his body ready for a fight. She didn't blame him for his paranoia. Meeting Angwyndith in all her Bodach glory could terrify the scariest of monsters, and he had just sat across the kitchen table from her.

No longer hungry, she pushed the tray away. Her half-empty glass of lemonade tilted, and she swiped at it. Her fingertips brushing the plastic gave it the momentum it needed to tip over and spill its contents all over the tray and table.

"Crap."

She grabbed her napkin to mop up the mess, but it quickly soaked through. She hurried to get more from the dispenser, but when she came back, an Elf was already there. Fresh blue booties covered his feet like the ones she'd seen on a crime show on TV, and the doll-sized mop in his hand swished over the surface of the table. She'd seen this Elf before in the halls, always cleaning.

"Oh gods, I'm sorry," she said, swiping the wet table with the napkins in her hand.

The Elf bobbed its head and, in a low grumble of broken English, told her it would manage. She smiled, thinking of Demi, her little Boobrach friend from home, who caused nothing but trouble. They might both be Elves, but there the comparison ended. Demi was half the size of the three-foot Elf before her, and his voice had a higher pitch. He also ran around naked, while this Elf wore a small toga wrapped around the main parts of his anatomy, for which Seraphina was grateful.

This Elf also had a snubbed nose, with large, cavernous nostrils in the center of its face and little beady eyes peered out from under a heavy brow bone. But its lips were beautiful. Lush and full, they looked like a 1940s starlet's, but painted with purple lipstick instead of red. Until its black spiked tongue appeared, spoiling the effect.

Her little cleaner finished wiping up the mess. With a swish of a cloth and a low bow, it disappeared, appearing at the table with the still eating guard. It moved to pick up the trash, and the guard growled at it. She scowled when the Elf cringed away from him, but she couldn't fix that behavior any more than she could fix how her hometown treated Demi.

Different channel, same show.

She shoved her debris into the trash and slammed her tray on the pile. Grumbling under her breath, she filled her giant travel mug with coffee and tucked it under her arm. She wasn't leaving without her frozen yogurt.

As she approached a junction in the hall, a Wielder wearing a lab coat and a heavy face mask crossed her path, their pace quick. She'd never seen a Wielder with a face mask, even in Dr. Pianal's lab, where noxious fumes were common enough to warrant a sign warning anyone coming in. Curious, but also delaying the inevitable, Seraphina followed them away from the elevators.

Her adventure ended before it began. The Wielder reached a door, did a series of hand movements and a badge swipe, and then disappeared behind it. She saw a less-than-tantalizing glimpse of metal and white stone on the other side before the door clicked shut, the scanner light turning red. With a gasp, her toes a hair away from breaching the ward, Seraphina rocked to a halt.

When she first arrived, she'd almost stumbled into a doozy of a ward when she made a wrong turn on the floor housing Dr. Pianail's lab. Only Angwyndith's warning had saved her from getting propelled into a wall. After that, and to avoid a lecture from Angwyndith, she spent a Sunday wandering around the floors she had access to and examining the ones she could find. It took her a while to figure out what to look for and just how to tilt her head to see them, but once she did, she no longer missed them.

The ward in front of her had a scarlet hue shimmering in between its rune symbols. According to her made-up color-coding analysis, red for danger and green for relative safety, that made the area behind the door high security. She could ask Angwyndith if her color chart was accurate, but all Angwyndith would say was to read a book and figure it out—her go-to comment these days.

As if sensing Seraphina's thoughts, Angwyndith's warmth ignited from her inner core, sliding up her torso with comfortable familiarity. Seraphina took a bite of frozen yogurt, savoring the mix of sour and sweet on her tongue, to tamper the irritation that simmered beneath her skin. Angwyndith had abandoned her to the SF after the first week, bored with their teachings and the books in the library. She only showed up to lecture and nag; something Seraphina could do without. The warmth splayed out and then stilled like a cat arching its back inside of her.

She doubted Angwyndith would appreciate the comparison, though, and kept it to herself, like a lot of her thoughts these days. The imaginary chest of unsaid things got more stuffed the longer she stayed at the SF.

The only real question was what would happen when it burst.

4

KNOWLEDGE SAVED LIVES

(Diligent She Was Not)

Angwyndith rose up the twinkling ladder from the Deep Space Between, connecting to her Host's senses. The Child's nervous system showed low levels of distress, as it had since their Judgment of the High Master Wielder, but nothing concerning. The sounds that invaded the Space Between as she came to that part of the ladder were no more exciting than usual; footfalls on stone and the crunch of something the Child ate muffled and yet deafening at the same time.

The Child was almost always eating. If she applied herself to her studies as diligently as she did to food, she would have been much further along. Even worse, she relied on Angwyndith too much. Angwyndith's purpose was not to be the means of skirting educational responsibilities. Mayhap it was time to teach the Child a little self-sufficiency, even if the tools she had at her disposal were rudimentary.

A pang of disappointment hit Angwyndith as she passed and connected to the ladder point for sight. She had come expecting great things from the library of the Security Forces of the Free Folk, especially since it had been created in 1895, just as she began her Dark Rest. Had she known an organization such as this one was forming, she mayhap would have pushed for an earlier awakening.

However, based on what she had seen thus far, it would have been a waste of time and energy. She had expected a much more expansive book collection and a more cohesive foundation in the organization. Instead, she found only discord, and a library filled with tomes only a child would find relevant.

Luckily, that was what her Host was.

Careful not to peer out of her Host's eyes until fully connected, Angwyndith soon reached the last connection point on the ladder. It no longer took the same effort to reach as it had once done. The shift to the Harmony between them had begun, but it lagged compared to the speed with other Hosts. And that ever draining of Angwyndith's aether when they were as one still fatigued and annoyed her, but at least it had shifted to a lesser degree.

She shook off her thoughts as she completed the last connection to her Host's consciousness, catching the last whiff of a thought about sweet and sour. The amount and color of the luminous aether in the ward before them caught Angwyndith off guard. While the Facility had excellent wards protecting its structure, this ward was at a level like that guarding the High Master of Cunning Folk's library, whom they had recently Judged.

How could the Child be thinking of food when something so glorious awaited her study?

The Child's feet inched forward as she leaned over to study the marks etched in the floor, her toes almost overlapping the protective barrier.

"I would not step closer to those symbols if I were you. Not only would it hurt, but it might also propel you to the far wall," Angwyndith said in the Space Between.

"Hello to you too."

Angwyndith ignored the bite in the tone, focusing on the ward before them. *"It is fascinating how they have twisted the natural ways of magic to their suiting here. This is not a traditional arrangement and yet it is very effective in what it does."*

"How can you tell what it does? I know it means keep out, but all I see are symbols on the floor with an ominous glow."

"Taken individually, it is nothing, but if you piece each rune together, the meaning is clear." Angwyndith stopped before she gave away anything more. Mayhap the moment for teaching was at hand. The Child needed to become more familiar with the properties of wards, and Angwyndith would not always be around to stop her from walking into them.

"Individually, if you view each rune on its own, you will see nothing of concern. However, if you connect each rune where they touch, you will read the warning they give and the spell they contain. Try it, my Host."

"I recognize Isa, which means ice or block. And there's the Z one... um, Algiz, I think, which means protection. Berkana for birth." The Child paused as one rune escaped her memory. Before Angwyndith could prompt her, the Child blurted out, *"Raido! For journey."*

Angwyndith's view shifted as the Child tilted her head.

"How does that create a ward strong enough to keep me out?"

"I already mentioned how. See where they connect to read their story. You missed one." How this Child survived this far without her, Angwyndith would never know.

"I didn't miss one. I don't get how Partho—magic and mystery—fits into an overall ward of protection." The Child's voice bordered on peevishness.

"You can go no further in your understanding until you figure that out."

"Duh. How am I supposed to do that?"

Angwyndith sighed, her warmth puffing out at the Child's throat. *"That is what I am here to teach you. Or rather, I will fill in the knowledge not gained through studying the simplistic texts to which you have access."* Angwyndith added a touch of emphasis on the last phrase, hoping the Child would glean her meaning.

The resulting quietness of her thoughts made it unlikely.

"I understand each rune's meaning, but how does a rune on protection connect to a rune on femininity to create a 'keep out' ward?"

"You are looking at it too linearly, my Host. You cannot dwell on the individual connections, so much as the connections between all the runes instead."

A popping sound filled the Space Between as the Child removed the spoon she was sucking on. *"What does that mean—the physical connection? The symbols touching?"*

"The runes are not just symbols. They are the whole of the magic in and of them. It is not just their meaning that is at play here."

The Child sighed. *"Nope. Still don't get it. What do you mean by 'of them'?"*

Angwyndith leaned back from the metaphysical ladder on which she stood. How could she explain something that was inimical to her world purview? *"You understand what aether is, yes?"*

"Yes, Angwyndith, I understand aether."

The sarcasm in the Child's words pounded against Angwyndith's fragile hold on her patience. *"Bear with me, please, my Host.*

I do have a point." Angwyndith took the silence that followed as acquiescence. *"Luminous aether surrounds us, fills us, is us, so to speak. Each item it imbues takes on a unique form, coalescing into the tree in the forest, the bird on the branch, the drop of water on the leaf, and the leaf itself. While each form is separate, they connect at their base level because they comprise the same thing—aether."*

"I've heard that before. We are one; one vibration, one love, blah, blah, blah. How is that related to the runes?"

Angwyndith's frustration overflowed. *"If you cannot be respectful of what it is I am attempting to teach you—,"* she bit back the rest of the sentence before she caused a rift. They had just gotten over the previous one. *"One moment."*

Time for yet another approach.

An infinite shelf housing every scrap of knowledge Angwyndith had learned since she came to be, including the memories of every Host in which she inhabited, appeared before her. She pulled out the volume when Magdalene, a particularly slow Host, was seven years of age and had learned about aether, magic, and everything in between. Angwyndith recalled learning patience and how to see the world through Magdalene's simple viewpoint. Mayhap she could use it for this Host.

"What makes an orange an orange? Is it the flesh? The peel? Or both?" Angwyndith asked.

"The fruit flesh is the orange. The peel just protects it."

"But without the peel, the flesh would not survive, so are they not one and the same?"

"The peel just protects the flesh. You don't eat the peel, at least I don't. Except you can add it to a recipe. Well, the zest, anyway."

Angwyndith waited, her patience stretching thin as the Child's thoughts dithered, flitting here and then, and finally, came full circle, the penny dropping with a loud metaphorical clink.

"*Oohhhhhh. I get it,*" the Child said. "*The peel is as much a part of the orange as the flesh inside. Which means the runes' symbol is the flesh and the circle around it is the peel.*"

"*Without the peel, there is no flesh to be eaten. Without the flesh, the peel would be nothing,*" Angwyndith replied. "*Each exists because of the other; the orange is an orange at that point when both exist in the same space, when the aether of peel and the aether of flesh connect and merge. You can get to the soft flesh inside by peeling the outside of the orange. It is the same with wards.*"

"*So instead of looking at them individually, I need to look at where they connect and what that combination means.*"

A surge of triumph filled Angwyndith. They were once again making progress, even if Angwyndith had told the Child exactly that not moments before. "*Yes, my Host. See the thread that runs between them, and you will see how to unravel them as well.*"

The Child stabbed her spoon in the cup she held.

"*Is there a problem, my Host?*"

"*Finding a thread through runes that Wielders learn from birth seems impossible.*"

"*Study the texts. They will show you the way.*"

A heavy quiet filled the Space Between as the Child called to mind all the books she'd read so far on this topic. It did not take long. "*I need a* Runes for Dummies *book.*"

The triumph Angwyndith had had only moments before withered to a sharp pang of annoyance. "*Do you not already have that in the texts in the library?*"

"*Oh, burn, Angwyndith. Don't be a book snob. I'm learning a lot from those books.*"

Only you could.

The lights on the ladder, muted moments before, flared in warning. Angwyndith ignored them and focused on what the Child said next.

"Besides, reading isn't the be all end all. There are lots of ways to learn." The Child pivoted and walked away from the door.

Her disappointment palpable, Angwyndith severed the connection to sight to avoid the disorientation that always followed the Child's movement, although walking was not as intense as that infernal contraption she drove.

The Child sighed again. *"It's going to take some time."*

Everything took longer with this Host.

"I understand, my Host. I will help you where I can."

The weight of teaching her pulled Angwyndith down a rung on the ladder. She wished to skip to the Harmony but could not. It was as if the Coda was punishing her, placing her with such a novice Host.

As if she conjured it, twinkly lights pulsed in the Space Between and a chill breeze swirled around her, lights streaming by as the Coda called. Angwyndith remained still, studying the pattern. The Coda, the living rules that governed them and the reason for her existence, had not visited since they had arrived at the Security Forces' domain.

There had been no interruptions or interference in Angwyndith's duties as it had done before the last Judgment of the High Master Wielder. The Coda behaved as it had always behaved, quiet and in the background. As it should.

The lights pulsed again, this time brighter, each coming closer to the other, almost removing the darkness in the Deep Space Between.

I apologize. I did not mean to suggest you did not have the right to be here. I only question the need to do so.

The cold contracted, drawing some of Angwyndith's warmth with it.

It is unusual, your presence here. My purpose, my role, is to question everything. If I did not, I would not see what I needed to see.

It returned in a rush, a biting wind consuming all Angwyndith's warmth. She clung to the ladder, confused by the unwarranted assault. The lights merged and blasted her with their solidarity, appearing brighter than the outside world's sun on a cloudless summer day. She could not escape it; it enveloped her in its grasp.

She heard the Child speak, but the words did not penetrate the prison of ice and light. With a snap at her warmth, the chill dissipated. Angwyndith felt like the Child did when her Wielder family member chastised her for doing something wrong, when nothing wrong had been done.

She did not like that feeling.

"Hello? Earth to Angwyndith?"

"You do not need to summon me in that way, Child," Angwyndith snapped.

"We were talking. You stopped talking, which is impossible for you to do when you have the microphone," the Child said. *"What's going on?"*

"I have other duties besides talking to you or teaching you the basics of magic, which you should already know," Angwyndith said, still smarting from the chastisement of the Coda. The surrounding lights flared in warning.

"But I don't." The Child enunciated each word.

"Then learn them. You have the books, you have the mental capacity, it is not nearly as hard as you claim it to be."

"Easy for you to say. You're a part of the Magical Community and have been forever."

"As are you."

"No, I'm not."

Oh, for the love of the Coda. Not this again.

Angwyndith did not understand the Child's continued focus on her biological form. The Child's form said nothing about her worth or her capabilities. Only the Child's mind mattered here. *"Stop using your humanity as an excuse. It is not. I have inhabited many Hosts and their phylum did not define them."*

The Child's posture changed, all her muscles tensing up. *"My phylum doesn't define me. Everyone else does."*

"Child..." The lights blazed at her, causing her to stop speaking.

"Angry Death?"

"I dislike that nickname, as you are well aware."

"Huh, imagine that, being called a derogatory name is insulting."

This would not end well if Angwyndith responded in kind, no matter how much she longed to explain why the term "Child" applied to her. *"This is not helping, my Host. I will return when you are in a better mood."*

Before the Child could respond, she yanked her connection free and fell into the comforting darkness.

5

THEY KNEW NOTHING

(Neither Did She)

Class had already started when Seraphina slipped into her seat. It had been five days of silence from Angwyndith and Seraphina wasn't complaining, even if she'd love to talk to someone other than the walls. Dust motes danced in the projector's light as its hum filled the room.

She pulled out her textbook and notebook and then hung her heavy backpack on the chair next to her. Instructor Fairchild paused at the interruption, twenty heads swiveling her way in reaction. In the darkened room, some eyes glowed, like small animals peeking out from under a bush.

Except none of the people in the room were small.

The ticking of the clock sounded like a bomb about to go off. Fairchild stepped into the light, and said, "Nice of you to join us, Cadet Lastra. Care to tell me what happens if you're late on the field?"

Seraphina gulped. "Someone dies."

"Exactly that. You're lucky all we're covering today is history."

"Sorry."

"You would be if your actions affected another's." He resumed his lecture and the eyes of the other students that were pinning her down swung around to face the front.

Queasiness slopped across her belly, his words churning up the guilt she still held from the summer. Peter had died because of her. It wasn't her actions, but her inactions that were the problem. Had she paid attention to what had been going on in Merricott, it wouldn't have happened. He had always looked out for her and yet the one time she could've returned the favor, she hadn't.

"Cadet Lastra?" Fairchild's voice broke through her memories.

She sat up, her brow furrowed, and glanced around at the pairs of eyes staring at her. Again. "Sorry, could you repeat that?"

The deadened eyes of a combat-hardened soldier stared back at her. "What were the three main reasons they created the Security Force of the Free Folk?"

"Um, to police the Magic Community. Research and development." Her brain stalled on the third. Palms clammy, she threw out a guess. "Economics, like taxes."

"Cadet Larson," Fairchild said, pinning his gaze on some other poor victim, "why do we need to police the Magic Community?"

"To stop threats before they get out of hand." Larson stumbled to a stop, but Fairchild motioned for him to continue. "Any internal matter that could spill over into the human, I mean, the Multitude's notice puts us at risk of being detected. The Security Council mandate is clear: remain undetected by the Multitude."

"Any other reason?"

"To save lives, sir, of those phyla affected."

"You've missed one, Cadet Larson."

Larson flicked a glance at Seraphina over his shoulder, and her stomach flipped. When she'd done the reading for this class last night, one sentence stood out more than any other, the one Fairchild just asked about. She had scoured the book for more references, but found none. The one thing she wanted to know only Angwyndith knew, and Angwyndith wasn't talking.

About anything. Her knee bounced under the table.

"Uh, sir, to ensure the services of the Bodach were not needed."

"Cadet Lastra, care to elaborate?"

Seraphina's cheeks burned, and she slapped a hand on her leg to stop its movement as, once again, all eyes swiveled in her direction.

Fairchild's eyebrows rose. A Wielder in the row below her sniggered and whispered, "She probably doesn't know."

Her gaze snapped to his as anger beat back the anxiety. "It's all about power. No phylum wants someone walking around who could wipe them out with a thought."

Fairchild nodded. "That and the randomness with which the Bodach gets involved. There were multiple times throughout history where a Bodach Judgment seemed in order, but none came."

The whisperer's hand shot into the air.

"Cadet Spotini."

"Sir, why was that?"

"Be specific, Cadet Spotini. Your life may depend on it."

A small chuckle rippled through the class, but Seraphina didn't join in. She had a bad feeling about this.

"Sorry, sir. What I mean to say is, why does the Bodach choose to appear for some and not for others?"

And there it was. She slid down and pulled her hoodie over her head to hide in its depths, but it was clear Fairchild wasn't letting her get away from the question.

"The texts on the matter are unclear, but why not go straight to the source? Cadet Lastra, what is the reason you Judge some, but not others?"

She had no idea. In fact, she knew almost less about it than most of the people in this room.

Angwyndith's warmth splashed across her torso.

"Good morning, my Host."

"Angwyndith. Perfect timing. Care to elaborate on why we Judge some but not others?"

"I cannot share what I do not know, my Host. And you cannot share any of what you know. It would put you in a weak position."

Seraphina kept her face as neutral as possible. *"You don't know why we Judge the ones we do?"*

"I do not. I have a supposition, but there is no need to share it."

The silence in the classroom broke through their conversation, tension thick in the air as twenty-one pairs of eyes waited for a response. Seraphina pressed her lips together and said, "Sorry. That's classified."

"Is it?" Fairchild held her gaze in a game of chicken. She blinked first. "Shame. Let's move on." Fairchild clicked the button, and a slide showed the earliest war fought within and between the phyla predating the SF.

Seraphina hunched over her desk, the pen digging into her knuckles as she took notes. What difference did it make that the phyla fought a war nine hundred years ago? The information was as useful as the regulations they shoved down her throat.

"From all situations can we learn, including those from multiples of your lifetime ago," Angwyndith said.

"Maybe, but there are no wars between the phyla now, the whole reason the SF was formed." The images of the combat team in the hall filled Seraphina's mind. *"Nor are any likely. They even have mixed combat teams to ensure it."*

"One organization does not create cohesion across disparate groups. The Security Force may have made inroads, but studying the past can help them stop any violence from spilling over now."

"I guess." Seraphina abandoned the argument before it got heated. It didn't matter. Angwyndith would never agree with her, anyway.

The button clicked on the next slide and Fairchild gave a quick rundown of yet another senseless war. The MC was a lot more like the humans than they'd like to admit, quick to perceive a slight as a reason to annihilate each other. Maybe that was what Angwyndith referred to in her comment.

"My Host," Angwyndith said, before Seraphina could ask her. *"Angwyndith."*

"I did not end our last conversation in an appropriate manner. I wish to... apologize for that."

Seraphina could feel the struggle in her tone. Angwyndith didn't see the need to say sorry, but was doing it to mollify her. *"It's fine."*

The clock pinged, the movements in the classroom repeating themselves like they did at the end of every class. Fairchild flicked on the light, shouting instructions at them for the next class's reading over the din.

The door behind her opened, and his voice became a megaphone. "Attennnnntion!"

Slap, screech, shuffle. Seraphina stood out of respect, but she wasn't saluting whoever came through that door. She wasn't part of their organization; everyone had made that clear during her first week here.

"Instructor Fairchild, we have incoming. Master Chief Benchley indicated not only would the cadets be useful, but it would be an excellent lesson on field triage." A combat-geared Wielder stood in the doorway, dirt and something that looked suspiciously like blood on his cheek.

Fairchild frowned. "Adept Stanton, we have not trained the cadets yet in that practice. I fear they would only get in the way."

"The Master Chief was clear. All hands needed, regardless of skill set."

"Very well, Adept. Cadets, leave your books here, you can retrieve them later. Pay attention to the tasks at hand and do not question your orders. If they say jump, you jump. Do I make myself clear?"

"Sir, yes, sir." Twenty voices yelled out as one.

Seraphina tried to capture Fairchild's attention but couldn't. *"Does that mean me?"*

"Why would it not, my Host? Besides, this would be good practice for you for the battlefield situations in which you may find yourself."

"I never want to be on a battlefield, Angwyndith."

"No, you do not. But that does not mean you will not find yourself on one. Knowing how to navigate it will be helpful information to have."

Seraphina's stomach rolled over as her classmates filed out in standard formation. She trailed behind them, her feet heavy. As she neared the elevator, Stanton directed her to enter the second car. She squeezed in, ignoring her classmates' frowns and sudden need to shuffle back.

The Adept stood next to her and faced the doors. She did the same as they closed in front of her face.

"Any information you can give us, sir, on what to expect?" Larson said from somewhere in the back, his tone hushed.

"Chaos and blood, cadet. The mission at Eventon did not go as expected and there were heavy casualties." Stanton's jaw clenched as he muttered under his breath, "Mainly us."

Seraphina turned to look at him as the tension mounted, the air thick with the press of bodies. The elevators had always felt spacious before, especially since people either pushed to the far corners away from her or got in the next one. She wished the same thing was happening right now.

Stanton kept his eyes on the doors.

"Look at the Wielder's hands, my Host, but carefully."

Seraphina scratched her nose and used the movement to glance at Stanton's hand fixed firmly on the orb attached to his belt.

"He's really uptight."

"He's ready for battle."

"What?" Seraphina's head came up as she stared at the doors. *"Why do you say that?"*

"He's readying a spell. He does not trust anyone in this contraption, and based on his mumblings, I can guess why."

"Why?"

Larson piped up again, "Adept Stanton, sir, what—"

"You will be briefed, cadet. Save your questions, should you have any, for then," Stanton said, cutting him off as the doors dinged open.

Seraphina stepped out and got mixed up in the exodus of the eight recruits in her elevator, many of them tripping over each other to not bump into her. They joined the formation with the rest of her class.

"Why, Angwyndith?"

"Fall in but keep the walkway clear." The grim faces of the recruits swiveled back to the Adept guiding them through the propped open steel doors protecting the hall.

A shiver raced down Seraphina's spine. They never left those doors open.

Their feet made little noise compared to the shouts and groans coming from the also propped opened doors to the gym.

As she got her first good look at what lay ahead, Seraphina's jaw dropped. *"Oh, my gods."*

6

MANAGED CHAOS

(She Had Nothing to Do)

Seraphina couldn't distinguish between the red of the mat and the people laying on it. Groans and yelled orders mingled to create a cacophony she wanted to drown out by covering her ears, but she couldn't seem to move. Doctors rushed between patients, their green healing aether mingling with the blood spilling out of the wounded, like a Christmas-themed horror film.

Her brain scrambled to find something familiar to cling to. Master Chief Benchley strode to the gym doors, calling out to someone on his left. Her eyes fastened on him like a drowning man clings to a life preserver.

Seraphina clamped her lips shut before any screams could escape. *"What the hell happened?"*

"Nothing good, my Host," Angwyndith said, her tone somber.

"Make a hole," someone shouted down the hall.

Seraphina wrenched her gaze away from Benchley as a stretcher bearing a Wielder emerged from the gym. "Why didn't they protect us?" The injured woman moaned. "Where were they?"

"You're going to be okay, Tina, I promise," said the Wielder doctor striding with her, his fingers clenched around the stretcher. "Just hold it together a little longer."

"Where were they, where were they, where were they, where were they," Tina mumbled, as if the answer to that question would fix everything.

The Wielder's eyes opened, her gaze pinning Seraphina to the wall, their familiar silvery hue filled with pain. Blood and dirt matted her dark hair and red-soaked bandages clung to her torso as her hands cradled her stomach. The Wielder who had been so alive four days ago in this very hall looked like a husk of herself.

Horror filled her, but Seraphina refused to look away, afraid their eye contact was the only thing keeping the Wielder alive. The stretcher zipped past, and the connection between them was severed. A guttural noise brought her head back to the gym.

The Shifter leader from Monday stood transfixed in the doorframe as his teammate disappeared down the hall. In his Warrior form, the bloody bandage wrapped around his upper arm looked like a ribbon. Thin strands held the armor on his left side, as if a giant had swiped at him with razor-sharp claws.

Benchley touched the Shifter's shoulder. When he got no response, he bellowed, "Chief Gabriel."

Gabriel's head turned to address Benchley, his eyes remaining fixed until the last second on the stretcher moving down the hall away from him. Benchley put his mouth near Gabriel's head and spoke. Gabriel nodded curtly and strode down the hall after his teammate.

"I saw them leaving, the Wielder and Shifter who just passed. They were battle-hardened warriors. They seemed invincible."

"No one is invincible. But they are what we fight to protect. This is why the balance is important. Whatever caused this damage should not have been left to continue." Angwyndith's voice sounded fatigued, as if this was something she'd seen many times before. *"I have, my Host. More battlefields and bloody creatures than you can ever imagine."*

"Stop reading my thoughts," Seraphina said, her protest lacking any real strength.

"I am allowed. Is this not a crisis?"

"This is a massacre."

"And massacres are why we Judge. Too many have died in clashes such as this one when there was no need."

"Then why didn't we Judge this?"

"Because the Coda deemed it unnecessary."

A yell from a Shifter sent a Wielder in a blood-smeared white smock running and jumping across the bodies as if at a track and field event. As she arrived at the location to help, a flurry of activity occurred on the floor, bandages and aether flying. A shake of her head at the Shifter's question, and then the Wielder in white sat back on her haunches.

After a moment, the Wielder stood, said a brief prayer, and then strode back to the patient she'd left. The Shifter who had called her over covered the body with a sheet, her head bowed.

Seraphina's chest tightened as her breathing grew shallower. *"The Coda was wrong!"*

A glacial breeze swept up Seraphina's spine.

"My Host—"

"I don't care that you're here or that you're mad. You're wrong. This is wrong!" Her breaths came out in fits and starts and pressure built up like heat across her lungs.

An icy wind flowed across her shoulders and then swirled around her neck like a scarf. The cool feeling eased the tightness held there, and her breathing slowed.

"Oh Gods. I know you're trying to help, but why didn't you stop this?"

The Coda's frigid touch flinched before disappearing altogether. The last of it dissipated near her collarbone, its sadness lingering behind like a melted snowflake.

"I'm sorry, too." She wasn't sure what she was apologizing for. Her anger? Her fear? *"I don't think I can do this, Angwyndith."*

"You can and you will." Steel infused Angwyndith's tone, but it couldn't put any strength into Seraphina's spine as she flinched away from the scene before her.

"I can't. All that blood and oh gods, I think I see bone." Seraphina put her hand to her mouth as bile burnt her throat.

She must have made a noise because the cadet across from her snarled, "Get it together."

She glared back at him; the anger clearing some of the turmoil in her head.

He shook his head. "Useless."

A commanding voice from the gym yelled, "Fall in!" and twenty cadets scrambled to get into a single line along the left side. Seraphina waited for another Wielder to run by with supplies and then slipped across the hall to the back of the line.

Instructor Moynihan barked orders at the first cadet in line, who nodded and then ducked inside. The closer they got, the harder it was for Seraphina to breathe, as more of the chaos in the gym became visible.

Someone called out for help, their hands clutching red-smeared bandages. When no one came, they sank back down, bleating out a need for fresh gauze.

She could do that. She couldn't save any of them, but she could run supplies.

"Good. This will be hard, but you can handle it. You've handled far worse and far more personal than this."

"I don't think so. The people I loved didn't look like they'd been through a woodchipper." She focused on the back of the head of the recruit in front of her to prepare to join in the fray.

Moynihan's instructions could be heard above the din behind him as more of the cadets disappeared inside. "You're on bandages. If we're out, run, don't walk, down to the med bay and get more. They're bringing more up, but they won't bring enough."

"Yes, sir."

"You, stretchers. If they say lift, you lift. If they say move, you move as if your life depended on it, because someone else's does, you got me?" Moynihan barked.

"Yes, sir," Larson yelled back and then ducked inside the doorway.

One by one, the recruits filed in and disappeared into the pandemonium in the gym. Soon it was just her. Moynihan squinted at her and then he turned away.

"Wait, sir, Instructor Moynihan," Seraphina called out.

His shoulders twitched, and he turned around. "We don't have time for you today, Cadet Lastra."

"No, I can help. What can I do?"

"Go to your quarters and stay out of the way."

"What?" Seraphina's mouth dropped open, the words of the combat Wielder who fetched them spilling from her lips. "Master Chief said all were to pitch in, regardless of skill set. I can help."

"Can you heal? Can you lift a stretcher? No. And I don't need any more supply runs, especially from someone who can't carry as much or move as fast as the others. The best thing you can do is get out of the way and let us do our job." She tried to protest, but he lifted his hand. "That is an order, cadet."

Her eyes tracked his back as he stalked away.

"How dare he block you from this experience?" Angwyndith snarled. *"You have just as much right to be here as any of the others."*

"It's not a field trip, Angwyndith." Seraphina slumped against the wall as the adrenaline left her.

"I do not know what you mean by that."

"It's not a fun day out, visiting a museum. People are dying."

"I did not claim it was fun, but you would learn something new."

Seraphina watched Larson lift a stretcher with barely a hitch in his step. Tears filled her eyes when another passed by, one of her classmates' wielding aether to keep a wound closed.

"No, he's right. I'm useless here."

"My Host—"

"No, Angwyndith. I have no magic, no strength, and there isn't someone to Judge. I'm better off out of the way." She turned away from the gym.

"Lastra!" Benchley's voice barked out behind her.

She whipped around, a small ball of hope blossoming in her chest.

"Study the protocols. Learn the procedures. You may not be able to help here, but you can help by not being the problem on the field."

Her jaw clenched, but she nodded.

He stared at her a beat longer, his brow furrowed before something called his attention across the gym.

She took one last look around and then shuffled toward the stairs, pain and death echoing behind her.

She'd not waste an elevator just for her. It was the only thing she could do to help.

7

OVERHEARD & OVERWHELMED

(She Couldn't Study)

The click of the door to the stairs shut out what Seraphina left behind, but her mind wouldn't let it go. Images of Wielders writhing in agony filled her head and their moans echoed around her, as if she were still there in the thick of it.

She needed to focus on something else, something consuming, or she'd start screaming. As her toes breached the top of the stairs, using what she learned in ballet, she forced herself to make the sound of every step as quietly as she could. As if she wasn't there at all.

After seven flights, her thighs burned and her muscle memory took over for her brain, but the images returned. Tears rushed to her eyes, but she clenched her jaw to keep them in. This wasn't helping. But she still could've done more than go to her room.

Hushed voices rose through the stairwell toward her, the thoughts so like her own she stopped with one foot hovering in the air.

"Not everyone's role is on the field, Davies," someone growled. "We all have our roles to play and sometimes that is just keeping out of the way while others do theirs."

The words reverberated off the stone walls, the sound hollow compared to where she had just left. Seraphina crouched down and leaned through the bars to see an older Shifter blocking the door, facing a smaller, bulkier one on the landing below. Something about the smaller Shifter's shoulders seemed familiar. She frowned and inched closer.

"Fine."

"Don't make me make it an order, Guard Davies."

"No need, sir. I just feel that my talents could be better suited elsewhere. I would've shredded that field if I'd have been there. Sir."

"Every Shifter in this building is thinking that right now, Davies, and they're all wrong. Even Chief Gabriel couldn't contain the damage." The older Shifter stepped closer, looming over the guard. "Watch yourself, Davies, or you'll never see your way out of guard duty. Do I make myself clear?"

"Yes, sir." Davies' spine was stiffer than the board on her book rack.

"Good. Now get to your post and stay there until I tell you otherwise." The older Shifter opened the door and held it.

Davies walked through at an even pace, his superior watching him with a sneer on his face. The door shut with a slam, but Seraphina held still until the reverberations ceased, just in case they knew she was there.

"It is possible they could have smelled you, but as you were not a threat, and they were preoccupied, they would not have given you much thought."

"They were pretty aggressive."

"Hmm." Angwyndith kept silent for a moment. *"It is to be expected based on what we have seen this day."*

"What do you mean?"

"There was an incident. It caused a lot of casualties. Everyone, including you, wishes to help."

Seraphina's eyes squinted at the stairs as they hit the floor two up from her room. *"Why do I feel like there's a gigantic piece you aren't saying?"*

"There appears to be a schism between the phyla, even bigger than when I last was present. It is not good and will lead to more hardship, most of all to you."

Seraphina's mouth dropped open. *"What do I have to do with anything?"*

"They cannot protect you if they are only protecting themselves."

The penny dropped as Seraphina hit the last stair. *"You think that's what Benchley meant about not being a problem on the field?"*

"Mayhap. We do not have enough interactions with him to determine that."

Seraphina shuddered as she opened the door to her floor. *"Let's keep it that way."*

"Hmmm."

Angwyndith's warmth swirled out of her throat.

"Leaving already?"

"Not for long. I have something I wish to research."

"Awesome. We'll both be studying then, while people above us die," Seraphina said, bitterness coloring her words with darkness.

"We are doing something worthwhile, my Host. Learning and knowledge will get you further than holding bandages."

"Maybe, but right now, I'd feel more useful if I were holding bandages."

"'It is not for the illusion of a moment to govern the choice of a lifetime,'" Angwyndith said as her warmth withdrew.

Seraphina hated it when Angwyndith did that. The anger chased away a corner of the heaviness Seraphina carried, but she still had problems breathing through the band across her chest. She threw herself on the bed, her knees curled to her chest.

Her laptop chimed, and she dragged it closer to her. She didn't want to talk to Ro right now, but maybe the light chatter would ease the pressure building inside. It wasn't Ro. She frowned and clicked the Facility intranet notification open to read that classes were cancelled for the rest of the week. She flopped on to her back and threw her arm over her face.

Two days without classes would've sounded like heaven an hour ago, before she saw a Wielder edge her way to death. Now it made her feel small and selfish. Benchley's words reverberated in her brain, and she sat up. She could study and make sure never to be the reason for anything like that to happen when she and Angwyndith were on the field.

Her gaze traveled from the trunk to the desk to the bookshelf, getting wider with every second. "You've got to be kidding me." She bounced off the bed, yanked the door open, and raced to the floor with the classrooms. Taking the hallway at a jog, she reached the class and turned the handle on the door.

It didn't budge.

She wiggled it and then swiped her badge. It beeped, the negative sound like a mosquito buzzing near her ear. She pressed her head against the windowpane in the door, the glass cold on her forehead as she peered into the darkened classroom. The maroon backpack hung on the chair where she'd left it, the weight of all her class books dragging it down to touch the floor.

The one thing she was told to do, the one thing she could do, she couldn't.

Seraphina screamed into her arm, the hoodie muffling the sound, and angry tears gathered in her eyes. She pulled on the door, kicking it a few times, but nothing changed.

Maybe she missed something in the notice, something that could free her backpack.

Her hair slapped her face as she whipped around. Seraphina stormed to the stairs, taking them two at a time. She rechecked it twice and slammed her laptop shut.

Her backpack was a prisoner, just like her.

We don't need you.

Moynihan's voice mocked her from inside her skull.

Go study.

The energy boiled inside her as she paced back and forth. The need to do something, anything, other than stay here in this tiny little closet raged through her like a thunderstorm on a hot day. Her breath hitched, the pressure building until she couldn't take it anymore.

She grabbed her purse and ran to the elevators, her fist punching the button multiple times until it arrived. The door swooshed open on the top floor to a pale Wielder holding blood-soaked gauze to their head while being supported by another Wielder.

Tears rushed to her eyes as guilt hit her like a ton of bricks. "Sorry," she said as she scrambled out of their way. Head low, she scurried to the steel doors leading to the lobby, dodging people as she did so.

As she walked through the doors, the brightness of the sun filtering through the windows blinded her, and she squinted through the glare. The chaos in the building had spilled outside.

Transport vehicles backed up to the side gate that led to the back patio and lawn, a thin lane carved out between parked cars shoved out of the way, like a box of Legos spilled over onto the floor.

What if they blocked the Land Rover in?

Panic gripped her, and she wheeled around to the reception desk, tapping her badge on it to get the guard's attention.

The Shifter glanced up at her and then his eyes went back to his screen.

When he didn't look up again, she said in a hushed tone, "I'd like the keys to my car, please."

When she first arrived, the last thing she wanted was to give up her keys, but the guard who took them off her told her it was recommended owners left all keys in the lobby in case of an emergency. She thought they were being paranoid. Now, the cars double-parked to give the transport vehicles room made the reason clear.

The fear that she couldn't leave caused the breath to get caught in her throat, like a moth stuck inside a lampshade, fluttering to break free. The intensity increased, and she knew if she didn't leave soon, the screams in her head would leak out and she wouldn't be able to stop.

She leaned forward and said in a strangled voice, "Now, please."

He sighed, obviously unmoved by her plight, and then said, "Badge."

She pulled it up to eye height and shoved it at him. He scanned it with his handheld unit, punched a button, and then disappeared through the door behind him.

He ambled back and tossed the keys on the counter.

"Where's it parked?"

"Where you left it."

She snatched up her keys and strode to the door, shoving it open and breathing in the fresh air as she forced herself to walk to the Land Rover. She almost hugged it when she found it among the small hatchbacks and sedans.

Sliding behind the wheel, she jammed the clutch in, put the key in the ignition, and held her breath as she turned it. The engine turned over twice. Just as she worried it wouldn't start, it roared to life. She revved the engine a few times and then let it idle. The sharp click of the seatbelt had never sounded so good.

When her phone showed a signal, some of the tension eased away, and she searched for coffee nearby. Down the road a few miles was a little town with a diner, but no coffee shop.

It would do. Anything would be better than here.

A commotion at the door caught Seraphina's eye in the review mirror as she drove toward the gate and freedom. Her hands tightened on the wheel, but she resisted the urge to gun it. She had to clear the guardhouse gate, and then she'd be free.

She peeled out of the Facility's driveway as if being chased by demons. She made it less than a mile down the road before she pulled over and jumped out of the Rover, slamming the door behind her and stalking to the tree line on the other side of it.

Her feet found a rhythm, pacing back and forth while she railed. She felt as helpless as she did when her family had died, when Peter had died. Nothing she could do would change things or bring them back. Nothing she could do would fix the people bleeding on the gym floor. It wasn't fair. None of it was fair, but Moynihan was right.

She was useless.

When no more words bubbled up on her tongue from the dark well inside and her throat hurt, she slumped against the

Rover and slid down to sit on the runner. Tears slipped down her face and she stared at the packed dirt beneath her feet for what felt like hours.

A car driving past brought her back to herself, slowing as they passed. She swiped at her wet cheeks, and then stood and waved them on. Her gaze followed the compact car as it sped up and disappeared around the bend in the road. Just a random human out running an errand on a Thursday. No bloody bodies behind them, no images of dead loved ones in their minds whenever they closed their eyes. She wished she could say the same.

Another wave of sorrow overwhelmed her, but she fought it down. All this crying did nothing to help anyone, not her, not her family, not those poor souls in the gym. Ro was right when she said Seraphina spent too much time in the past. But Benchley was right too. She could make sure she didn't cause needless deaths as the Bodach Host, but also as Seraphina, when on the battlefield.

It was time to look forward, not back.

Feeling lighter than she had in a long time, she wiped her face on the sleeve of her hoodie. A stiff wind whipped up her back, rustling the leaves in the long grass. As the light faded and shadows emerged to snuff it out, she returned to the Rover.

Once on the road again, she gawked at the scenery of rural Virginia. She hadn't paid much attention on the drive to the Facility; her focus narrowed on the directions yelled out at her from her phone, so that she didn't miss the turn on the small side roads leading to it.

Houses dotted the landscape in between the trees, their white or blue siding peeking through the mostly bare branches.

She passed a tractor hugging the edge of the road and a lone car, an old pickup truck with an arm hanging out the window.

She could've been in New Hampshire.

As she pulled on to the main road into town, she slowed down. An orange and red sign, with missing slivers of glass, towered above the gas station and mechanic's bay. Next to the gas station squatted Marion's Diner, the large windows eating up most of the wall space and a large ramp dominating the front. She pulled into the lot and parked next to an old Cadillac with fins. Further down, she saw a small dusty hatchback, a sedan, and a beat-up pickup truck.

The quietness suited her just fine. She flipped the mirror down and checked her face. While her lids were a little puffy, they weren't too bad. No mascara streaking down her cheeks made her decision to stop bothering with makeup after her first week a much better choice than she had thought at the time. She hopped out of the truck and headed inside.

This was much better than being at the Facility.

8

COFFEE, CRUMBLE, & COMFORT

(Catching Up with a Friend)

The smell of coffee and fried onions assailed her as she passed through the vestibule into the main dining area. Booths lined the windows, a narrow path between them and the counter running the length of the diner. Her stomach grumbled. She needed comfort food, and this was the perfect place to get it. Pausing just inside the door, she looked around for someone to direct her to a table.

An older waitress stood behind the counter manned by cracked red vinyl stools fixed to the floor. She refilled the cup of an old guy wearing a flannel shirt and shiny black combat boots while he wolfed down his lunch. The waitress looked up when she came in; her face as fixed as her hair, the long swooping bangs held in place with hairspray and a clip holding the rest. She wore a battered button-down shirt over her jeans, an order pad shoved in the gaping breast pocket.

"Do I sit anywhere?" Seraphina asked, a smile on her face.

"Wherever you want, hon." The woman's smoky voice carried to the door.

Pressing her lips together, Seraphina walked to a booth. Ahead of her in another booth was a girl who looked familiar, a thick coppery braid laying over one shoulder. The girl was consumed by whatever was on the screen in front of her.

"What can I get you?"

"A cup of coffee…" Spying a pie in a glass case on the counter, she said, "What kind of pie is that?"

"Cherry." The woman's mouth opened enough to show the tips of her teeth, but not much more.

"The apple crumble is much better." The girl's voice called out from the other booth. "Seriously, do the crumble. Warm. With ice cream." Her lips twisted into a smile resembling a grimace. "It's that kind of day."

You have no idea.

Seraphina nodded. "I'll have that. Thanks."

A hum vibrated the seat. Seraphina dug around in her bag and pulled her phone out. She'd missed two voicemails and ten texts during the entire time she'd been underground, but none from her Aunt T. She played the voicemails while watching a crow in the tree across the street. It kept calling but received no answering cries.

Much like her and her aunt.

Brushing off the ache of loneliness that swamped her, she deleted the first voicemail as soon as the robotic voice spoke. When she played the second message, Finn's gravelly voice filled her ear, her muscles relaxing more fully than they had in months. She missed chatting with him and not just because he loved books as much, if not more, than her.

"Ms. Covington. I presume you are well, since I received the first shipment of repaired books from you. It confirms my thought that the Celtic Brehon Facility has adequate mailing capacities. I have a book here I would like to send to you, but

I am unsure whether that would be allowed. Please ring me at your earliest convenience so that we may discuss it."

The message ended there. She grinned, remembering the last time they spoke. He'd confessed to using the books she restored for his bookstore to lure her into the shop to talk to her. Maybe this was the same.

The waitress slid a cup of coffee onto the table, its contents sloshing on the saucer. Seraphina murmured a small, "Thanks." She sipped it and sighed. Classic diner coffee left on the burner too long. It tasted bitter and burnt, but so much better than the coffee at the Facility.

She dialed Finn's number before she could talk herself out of it.

"Roget's. How may I assist you?" Over the phone, Finn's voice sounded like rocks being poured out of a bag.

"Hi Finn, it's Seraphina." Silence met her words. "Seraphina Covington? I'm returning your call." Her voice warbled a little, unsure if he remembered her.

"Ms. Covington, I apologize. I put the phone on mute accidentally at this unexpected pleasure. Are you well?"

The last of the tightness in her chest loosened up. "I am. How are you?"

"I, and my store, are well. As always."

She wished she were as confident as him. "I sent *Jane Eyre* a few days ago. Has it arrived yet?"

"No, it has not."

She squinted at the storefront across the road. "You should've gotten it already. Maybe it got hung up somewhere." Or maybe the guard digging through the bins took too long to review it.

"Most likely. If I do not receive it today or tomorrow, I will let you know."

The waitress put the plate of apple crumble in front of her, the ice cream melting in a pool around it.

"I'm sorry for not getting more books to you. You must be wondering what's taking so long."

"I did not expect you to get through the books too quickly, as I assumed you would be busy elsewhere," Finn replied.

"My schedule is full, but not that full. I'll do better."

"Take your time, Ms. Covington. The books are old. There is no rush."

She wished she could be as calm about time, responsibilities, and life as him. "No, but I'm not applying myself as much as I could. So, I'll do better."

"As you wish."

Her lips turned up into a smile. No lecture, no guilt, just acceptance. It was one thing she loved about him. "You mentioned a different book in your message?"

"Yes. It is a present for someone. I could send it to my old restorer, but I fear he may not get to it as quickly as you." He paused, as if choosing his words carefully. "He is retired and has many hobbies. When there is no rush, his forgetting to restore it is not an issue, but here, well, you understand my problem."

For someone made of silica, he had as light a touch as a cat. "Of course. Is it a…" The waitress moved in her peripheral vision. Seraphina hunched over the phone and lowered her voice. "A mundane book or something more unique?"

She'd spent so long at the Facility, she forgot that not everyone was part of the Magical Community. The waitress appeared human and moved like a human, but it wasn't as if the Magical Community all had tattoos in specific spots or a secret handshake.

At least she didn't think they did. She frowned, her thoughts spinning away from the conversation until Finn's voice brought her back with a thump.

"It is quite old, but mundane. There will need to be a replacement of the front flap and end pages, and a few of the pages are damaged, but they all appear to be here."

"Sounds doable." She fiddled with the fork on her plate. "Why would you be concerned about shipping it to me?"

Marbles clicking together in a bag filled the phone as he cleared his throat. "I was not. I simply wished to speak to you."

Her cheeks flushed in pleasure. Dipping her finger into the melted ice cream on her plate, she asked, "How's everything else in Merricott?"

"It is good. Happier than I have seen in a long time. Settled. We shall see what happens in a few weeks, though."

"Oh? What's going on?" She couldn't resist the crumble any longer. Grabbing her spoon, she took a small bite and almost groaned. The crumble achieved perfection, the balance of the sweetness of the topping combined with the tartness of the apples to mingle expertly with the ice cream. She was so intent on enjoying her bite that it took a minute to realize he hadn't responded yet.

She sat up and set the spoon down. "Finn?"

"Your aunt did not share the news?"

"My aunt and I are still navigating the aftermath of... you know."

"Ah. I am sure she will come around with time."

"If she takes any longer, I'll be a corpse."

"Hmm. You have to remember, Ms. Covington, that she is older than you and that time passes... differently for those of us who have been here a while. You just need to be patient."

"That's not one of my strong suits."

"Then it will be good practice to make it one." Amusement lit his voice.

She rolled her eyes. "What's happening in a few weeks?"

"A new... mayor arrives in town."

"A new mayor?" She scrunched up her face. "Oh, you mean a new Hi—, er, mayor, right. That's interesting. I thought it'd go to Mariana or my aunt, since they are the most pow...pular in town."

"That was what I expected as well, but another decision was reached." A muffled chime rang out in the background.

If anyone knew the political ramifications and reasons for the outsider choice for the new High Master of the Cunning Folk to replace Harriman, it was Finn. As she opened her mouth to ask, someone bellowed out his name.

Dammit.

"You have to go," she said reluctantly. "Sounds like Mr. Broadmark needs you again."

"He does indeed, although I suspect he only visits to have company."

"Well, he has good taste." A silence filled the phone, but it felt warm and soothing. "I miss seeing you too, Finn."

He cleared his throat again. "I will send you the book, Ms. Covington. Do let me know if there are any issues with it."

"I will."

"Take care, Ms. Covington."

"You too, Finn."

She set her phone down and dove into her dessert, smearing melting ice cream around the bite before she shoved it in her mouth. "Mmmmm." She smiled at the waitress and waved at the crumble on her plate. "This is fantastic!"

The waitress' glance softened as she straightened. "I'm glad you liked it."

The girl with the laptop paused at the table. "Good, right?"

Seraphina met the girl's amber-flecked brown eyes. "So good. I'll definitely be back for more." They grinned at each other.

"The patty melt is fantastic too." The girl lifted her chin once. "See you around. Bye, Marion." She waved at the waitress and pushed out the door with her back.

Seraphina watched her walk to the hatchback in the parking lot. She walked a lot like Ro—more of a glide than individual steps. She was good, Seraphina would give her that, but Seraphina had spent too much time in the past twelve years with people from the Community trying to pass for human to miss that trick.

Motion behind her brought her attention back into the diner. The counter guy stood and threw down a few bills to the side of his plate.

Marion scooped it up without looking at it and nodded at him as he left, his steps slow but steady. Her gaze caught Seraphina's, who motioned for a refill of coffee. Marion sauntered over with a half-full carafe, filling her cup up and setting the check down on the table. "Let me know if you need anything else, hon."

"Will do, thank you."

Seraphina glanced back out the window and watched the girl drive out of the parking lot, followed by the sedan.

Who was she?

9

ROUTINE QUESTIONS

(THEY WEREN'T IN MERRICOTT ANYMORE)

Five days later, Seraphina lay cocooned in her bed. She didn't want to be late, but she didn't want to get up either. Her resolve to pay attention in class lasted as long as two sessions on the regulations for the movement of goods. Tuesdays were especially brutal. No combat training to mix it up and nothing but codes, codes, codes.

The monotony of her days made it hard to register enthusiasm for anything, except for the diner. She'd been back once but hadn't run into anyone but Marion. She had, however, savored the crumble again. It tasted miles better than anything in the cafeteria, more likely to do with the setting than with the ingredients. Isolation in a restaurant felt more acceptable than isolation in the Facility.

A sharp knock on the door startled her. She shoved the covers off her legs and glanced down, shrugging at her pajamas.

The knock came again, harder. The person must have knuckles of marble to hit that hard. She shoved the tangled mess of her hair behind her ear and cracked the door open to see a Shifter guard. He stepped back as soon as the door opened.

"Seraphina Lastra?"

"Covington."

"Seraphina Lastra Covington?"

The way he said it, stern and precise, made her feel like she just got in trouble for being out too late. "Yes. What's up?"

"You are wanted for questioning."

A knot formed in her stomach. "Why?"

"I am to deliver you to Master Chief Sawyer, ma'am. They do not tell me why."

"Now?"

"Yes, ma'am."

"But I have a class starting in thirty minutes."

He nodded. "Yes, ma'am. Your Instructor will be informed of your delay."

There was no way she was facing questioning in penguin pajama bottoms and an old t-shirt. "Give me five minutes." She didn't wait for an answer and shut the door.

She scrounged up some jeans, a clean t-shirt, and her favorite hoodie and took an additional minute to pull a thick-toothed comb through her hair. She needed to pee. And brush her teeth. But she didn't think Rambo the Rookie would let her.

Rustling through her bag, she found a mint she'd taken from the diner and shoved it in her mouth. It crumbled and melted on her tongue. One problem solved, one left.

Except for the whole questioning thing. Her stomach gurgled, and the knot turned to nausea. She'd done nothing wrong. No one told her she couldn't go to the diner, and no one stopped her. Something tugged at her brain, but she couldn't bring it to the surface, so she pulled the door open and shut it behind her with a snap. The guard gestured down the hall.

"Do I have time to stop in the bathroom?"

He checked his watch. "Negative, ma'am."

"Fine. I hope the questions are short." She flashed a smile at him, but he gestured again down the hall. "Right. Elevator?"

"Yes, ma'am."

All the ma'aming made her feel old. She wiped the crust from her eyes and shuffled down the hall, a wry smile lifting one corner of her lips. *If the shoe fit.* The nausea eased with her internal patter but lingered like the chalky aftertaste of the mint she'd just eaten.

They rode the elevator in silence four floors below hers. The doors slid open, and the guard stepped out, flanking them. She walked forward and stopped, unsure of which direction to go.

When they'd first arrived, Angwyndith had grumbled about their lack of access in the Facility, but Dr. Carruthers, the Site Director who negotiated her contract, wouldn't budge. Seraphina was shocked Angwyndith had even expected them to have access to anything but the main floors, but then Angwyndith didn't seem to get how modern-day military organizations worked. And Angwyndith hadn't been using her time here to figure it out either.

Seraphina frowned. Angwyndith would probably blame that on her, too. Before she could eviscerate herself any further, she asked the guard, "Where are we going?"

"This way, ma'am." He motioned to her left.

They walked down a hallway she wouldn't be able to identify from any other in the building. Shifters in combat gear, or half-dressed in combat gear, walked by. Some of her tension eased as the Shifters barely spared them a glance or looked up from the paperwork in their hands.

Maybe these questions were just part of the process.

Her guide stopped at a door with Master Chief Sawyer on it. He rapped once.

"Come in," a man's voice said.

The guard opened the door and gestured for her to follow.

She stepped in and found herself in an office only a smidge larger than her room. A small Shifter stood up from behind a tidy metal desk, but he filled the room in a way that had nothing to do with his physical form. Her heartbeat quickened. She shifted her gaze away from him and breathed slowly and evenly to calm it down, while she memorized the books on the shelves behind him.

He hadn't moved or spoken, but she could feel the pressure of his gaze. When she couldn't put it off any longer, she flicked a glance at him. He observed her surveying the room as quietly as a cat about to pounce. Angwyndith would have said something about him not shifting to a cat form, but she wasn't here. Maybe she should call her.

No, not yet.

He shifted his eyes to the door. "Dismissed, Guard Samuels."

She glanced behind her as her escort nodded and shut the door. The room shrank, and she suddenly wished he'd remained. Not that the guard would've helped her.

"Ms. Lastra Covington, I am Master Chief Sawyer. Please have a seat." He smiled, but only with his lips, and gestured to a wooden visitor's chair in front of the desk.

She sat, tucking her hands under her thighs to hide their trembling, and met his eyes, remembering at the last minute to look between his eyebrows. His smile widened. "I am responsible for the safety and security of this facility. Part of that requires me to check in from time to time with our visitors."

Her heart thumped harder in her chest.

As if he heard it, he said, "I would like to ask you a few questions. It will be painless, I promise." His voice was softer than she would have expected for his size.

She had a feeling he could sharpen it more finely than any of the scalpels in the lab. "As long as it's less painless than getting poked by Dr. Pianail, we're good," she said with a fake chuckle.

His smile tightened. "The doctor was wise to choose research instead of health care."

She returned his smile, her knee bouncing like it heard a rhythm she didn't. Clearing her throat, she said, "Great. Fire away."

"You arrived at the Facility on June 24th of this year, correct?"

"Yes."

"And your purpose for coming here was?"

She blinked. Angwyndith had been clear on the way to the Facility. Only share necessary information. The less the SF knew, the better for them both. "To receive training."

"And that training consists of?"

"Combat training with Moira. Classes with the other recruits on codes, methods, and etiquette."

"Excellent." He opened the folder, which contained a few pieces of paper she couldn't read, and a notepad and pen. The sharp click of the pen made her jump. He pulled the pad towards him and took a note in neat script. "How else do you spend your time here?"

"I have tests run with Dr. Pianail every other week." She shifted in the chair.

The pen remained suspended over the pad. "Nothing else?"

She frowned. "I eat in the cafeteria. I work out sometimes in the gym, doing ballet to stay flexible."

He scribbled a note and then looked up. His face softened in what she guessed was an attempt to put her at ease. A chill ran down her spine. "Ballet is an underestimated dance. It takes precision to look as graceful as a dancer does."

She nodded.

"Who else have you interacted with?"

"Besides the Instructors and the trainer?"

"Correct." The pen remained poised in mid-air as if time had stopped.

"Um, no one else, really." Seraphina sat back a little, her spine rolling as her hands clenched under her thighs.

"No one?" Sawyer kept his head down, adding a note under the one he just wrote.

She wracked her brain. What did he want to know? "No, no one. Except for Angwyndith."

His pen paused, and he lifted his head. "That is the name of the Bodach, correct?"

"Yes."

His stare intensified. She gritted her teeth and met it head on.

"How much do you talk?"

He'd crossed into the no-fly zone with that question. She sat up and crossed her arms. "Why do you need to know that?"

"I am curious. We haven't had a Bodach and Host in this Facility before." He glanced back down at his notes. "You don't need to answer."

"You've had them in other Facilities then?"

"Yes. The office in London."

Something about the way he said that was wrong. "I wasn't sure there were others around."

"There are. Any other activities besides what you've already told me?"

"No." He was about as forthcoming as Angwyndith on wards. She switched her gaze to the books on the wall behind him while her mind raced. A rip in the spine of a small leather-bound book captured her attention. She could fix that.

"Ms. Lastra?" he prompted.

She ripped her gaze away from the torn book. "Well, there's my job."

"Your job?"

"I restore books. The books I brought with me."

He flipped through the folder near his elbow. "Yes, I see. We delivered a box of fifteen literature books to your room. What do you do with these books?"

"I fix them. The ripped pages, the broken spines."

"That's your job? Fixing books?"

"Yes." Heat crawled up her cheeks.

He made another note, and her fingers curled into fists behind her elbows.

"What do you do with these books when you are finished with them?"

"I ship them to a bookstore in Merricott, my hometown."

"Through the Facility's shipping station?"

"Yes."

"Wouldn't that be another person with whom you've interacted then?" His eyes pinned her in place, and it was all she could do not to squirm in the chair.

"Uh, I guess. So, Ambrosia, the Wielder in the mailroom."

The pen hovered like a bee while he waited for her to finish her sentence.

"Right. Um, there was a security guard in there once, but I didn't catch his name." Just that he was an asshole.

"I will check the records to see who was on duty. What date was that?"

She swallowed while she counted back the days, most of which blurred together. "I'm not sure, but I can send you the date, probably a week ago?"

He put the pen down and stared at his clasped hands. His brow wrinkled for a moment and then, as if he'd made a decision, he picked up his pen. "Please do that. We will implement new process instructions for the mailroom, which will delay the sending of packages by an additional day. Will that be a problem for you?"

One book had already been late, and Finn hadn't minded. "No. There's no deadline for restoring books." Finn's birthday present came to mind. "Except for one."

His stare remained steady while he waited.

"It's a birthday present, but it hasn't arrived yet." She frowned. It should've come already.

"Of course." He still hadn't blinked.

His hands hadn't moved either, not even a twitch. Angwyndith would've been disappointed; she took great pride in noticing hand movements. He pulled the notes off the pad and slipped them into the folder. "Thank you for your time and cooperation, Ms. Lastra Covington." His tone dismissive, he stood.

Relief rushed through her. She stood so quickly the chair almost fell over. As she reached to steady it, she saw Sawyer twitch behind the desk. Flustered, she muttered, "You're welcome," and fled for the door.

Just as she put her hand on the knob, he said, "If you talk to anyone else at any point during your stay here, anyone at all, please let me know through the Facility's message board. And send me those dates when you get a chance."

She nodded. Her hand tightened on the metal as she twisted it, a smidgen of panic bursting through her when it didn't turn all the way. The door slammed into the toe of her sneaker and the sound reverberated around the small room. Wincing, she stepped out of the way and glanced back at him.

A frown marred his face, but it smoothed out as if by magic when he caught her staring at him.

"Have a good day, Ms. Lastra Covington. You can leave the door open."

"Will do."

Guard Samuels stood on the opposite wall, his hands behind his back. He straightened even taller, like a rubber band about to snap, and then nodded in the direction from which they came earlier. The pressure on her bladder came back with a vengeance, but she wasn't asking him to stop. She wanted to get off this floor and away from Sawyer as soon as possible.

When they reached the elevator, she jabbed the up button. As the doors opened, her guard reached around, swiped his badge, and pressed her floor.

"Have a good day, ma'am."

"Thanks. You, too."

The doors slid closed, and her shoulders slumped.

What was that about?

10

DISTRACTIONS, DISTRACTIONS

(It Wasn't Working)

The clank of weights didn't disturb Seraphina as she stretched over the bar attached to the wall. Breathing deep, she stretched further, feeling the constriction in her muscle before it relaxed. She stood up straight and lifted her foot off, toes pointed, muscles quaking.

Glancing around, she found a patch of floor not covered by the mat and sat down to put on her sneakers. As she tightened the laces, the tightness in her stomach returned. The SF had put the gym back together since the triage, but she still couldn't look at it without seeing people writhing in agony. In her last session with Moira, she had spent more time circling Moira than fighting her to not touch the blood-colored mat. It hadn't gone down well, and Moira had dismissed her early because of it.

She bowed her head and took a deep breath. She wasn't going to cry in the gym where people could see her. Being here was hard enough; she didn't need to make the space more uncomfortable.

Head down, she walked swiftly toward the door, desperate to get away. She'd thought working out would be a great way to relieve the stress of her earlier interrogation with Sawyer and keep the nightmares at bay, but she may have made it worse.

A shadow crossed her path, and she careened into the person it belonged to before she could stop herself. "Oof," she said, as she bounced off him.

"Whoa there." The Shifter reached out to steady her before she fell over the bench behind her, his hand withdrawing after the initial touch.

She'd seen him somewhere before, but she couldn't place him. "Sorry about that. I wasn't looking where I was going."

"That's alright. You okay?" His voice was gentle, as if she were a wounded animal.

Maybe she was.

"I'm fine. Just tired from working out."

He held the door open for her. "After you."

Her hands clenched. Now she'd have to make small talk.

A small laugh huffed out of her. She would've killed to chat with someone before and yet here she was, begging to get away.

The guy trailed her to the elevator, his clothing making a small squeak every time he took a step, like a mouse whose tail got stepped on.

Praying it would arrive soon, she jabbed the elevator call button.

He came to a rumbling stop next to her. "How long have you been dancing?"

"Since I was thirteen. I'm not particularly good at it."

"I don't know about that. You seemed graceful enough to me. And wow, are you flexible."

She flicked him a glance from the side, her brow furrowing.

He laughed self-consciously. "Sorry. That came out wrong. I'm not flexible, like at all, so it's... never mind." He shook his head, his voice trailing off.

The tension coiling in her chest eased. "I'm not flexible compared to people who are proper dancers. And I have to dance at least six days a week, otherwise I lose it little by little."

"Yeah, I hear that. If I don't work out every day, I... uh..." He frowned, as if what he wanted to say wouldn't come to mind. "... wouldn't be as buff as I am in my hu—, er, other form."

A small smile hovered on her lips. "So, your human form is your weakest, then?"

"Uh, no, no. It's just not my best form." He cleared his throat and jabbed the elevator button. "For the quiet time, it sure is taking its sweet time in coming."

She laughed, and her shoulders stopped hovering near her ears. "It's fine. My parents were Shifters. I get that the non-warrior form is the weakest, even if you could still almost bench press a car. You haven't offended me."

He sighed in relief. "Right, right. I've heard of you. The human born to Shifters. How did that happen?"

Of course, he asked the impossible to answer question, the one that had haunted her since childhood. Humans came from humans, not Shifters. Angwyndith, who should have known, had been no help at all.

"No idea. It's not exactly textbook stuff. And I look a lot like my dad, so it's not like my mom got it on with a human." The blood rushed to her face, and she snapped her head to face the elevator.

"Yeah, well, it's not supposed to be possible. There's a reason phyla don't mix, besides the obvious ones. The pictures they show in phylum biology when they do are enough to turn you a eunuch for life." He barked out a laugh.

The earlier conversation with Angwyndith came back, hitting her like a small gut punch. "I didn't have those classes. I wasn't in the same schools."

"Oh, right. Because of the whole human thing. Gotcha." He fell silent, his cheeks puffing up as he blew out a breath.

"Yep."

He shifted his weight to the other foot, tapping his badge against his leg. The icon reminded her of something. Slándála. Security. The cafeteria. The pieces clicked together.

"You were right about the fried chicken, by the way."

His eyes widened. "Good. I hate fake food. If the Coda wanted us to eat chemicals invented by other phyla, it wouldn't have given us fruit."

"You may have a point, although fake lemon juice has its place. Like when you don't have any fresh lemons."

"Then don't make lemon chicken. It's not that hard. You either have the right ingredients for the dish or you don't." He shrugged, taking the bite out of his words.

"I get that." Not clear why they were arguing about fruit, Seraphina pressed her lips together. And then it hit her like a bolt and the question tumbled out before she could stop it. "Why are you talking to me?"

He raised his eyebrows and the small tufts merged to look like thick spider legs instead of fur.

"I mean, I'm sure you know who I am. Most people can't stand being within six feet of me and yet here you are, arguing over fake food." She gestured to the space between them.

"You mean that whole Host Bodach thing?"

She nodded, curious about what he'd say.

"Eh, I see it like this. Right now, you're just a girl, standing in front of an elevator that's never coming, waiting for it to open."

A smile slid across her face as she recognized the line from *Notting Hill*. "That's true. It's seriously slow."

"I mean, sure, I heard about you, and I don't think I want to meet the Bodach any time soon. Ha ha, not like I would need to or anything. Ha ha ha. I haven't done anything wrong except in line with my job." His laugh boomed out, a jittery edge to it. It faded into silence, which he broke by clearing his throat. "But you seem normal enough to me. You're not glowing, your feet remain firmly on the ground. So, I figure, what's the big deal?"

"Exactly. There is no big deal unless Angwyndith is around and angry. I wish more people understood that."

"Angwyndith is the, uh, Bodach?"

"Yep." Seraphina stepped in to the elevator, swiped her badge, and pushed the button for her floor, stepping back to give him room.

He did the same, picking a floor two levels down.

The silence stretched between them as they rode to her floor. "Well, it's been nice chatting with you. I'm Seraphina, by the way." She looked down, shaking her head. "Which you probably already know."

He nodded at her. "Ted, but most people call me Teddy. Nice to meet you, Seraphina."

The door bumped her in the back. "Right. I'll let you go. Have a good night." She smiled again and waved, before wandering toward her room, the doors swooshing closed behind her.

She flopped on her bed, the smile lingering on her face. It felt good to be treated like a normal person again.

11

POKED & PRODDED

(Something Wasn't Right)

Dread crawled up her back as Seraphina peered into the glass panel that ran the length of the door to the lab. The dim interior made it hard to see if Dr. Pianail waited for her like a dragon guarding a gate. Seraphina wasn't late, but it was close.

She swiped her badge and stepped into the antechamber for the lab. While she washed her hands, she glanced over her shoulder at the glass-encased closet on the back wall. Some of her tension drained away at the sight of cleaning supplies and other mundane items filling the shelves in neat lines.

One less thing for the doctor to yell about.

Stepping away from the sinks, she patted her arms off with the provided towels, the rough fabric feeling like sandpaper. The scanner light next to the steel door between the antechamber and the lab was green. Taking a deep breath, she pushed through, the smell of sage and alcohol overpowering her as soon as she stepped into the sterile environment.

She weaved her way through the grid of tables to Dr. Pianail's test bench, careful to avoid the stone basins with flickering orange fire or ward circles cast on the floor. Too soon, she reached the safe zone outside of Dr. Pianail's workstation, marked by the tape on the floor.

Seraphina peered over at the potions, test tubes and sterilized needles laid out on the table. A full complement of tests awaited her today. Swallowing the lump in her throat, she cast around for something to distract her.

Four holding cells spanned the back wall of the lab. The cells had floor to ceiling glass panels and reinforced glass doors with steel beams and cross bars ornamented each one. She traced the line of the steel beams, her thoughts spinning on what they used them for. Were they prison or containment cells?

Movement flashed in the one farthest to the left, and her pulse raced. They'd always been empty, but not today. Tucked into the corner with his face turned away stood a Shifter. At least he looked like a Shifter.

She drifted to the glass, stopping mere inches away from the ward on the floor. Leaning over to get a better view of the symbols, she hoped they'd tell her if it was containment or prison. She wanted it to be containment.

As if sensing Seraphina was out of her depth, Angwyndith's warmth ignited from her inner core, sliding up her torso with comfortable familiarity. Since the Eventon incident, Angwyndith only surfaced to see what Seraphina studied. But never to help understand it.

Irritation spiked through her. *"Good afternoon, Angwyndith."*

"My Host. That is another ward you should avoid at all costs. It would do more than just throw you against the wall. You should study it and see what you can learn."

Seraphina sighed. *"I can barely understand the one from the hall and you want me to study this one? Not gonna happen. I have too much going on with catching up on classwork as it is."*

"Hmph. I will capture it and we can study it together later."

"Fine."

The word dropped between them like a pebble in a still lake. Seraphina waited to see what ripples Angwyndith would ride. Teacher or observer?

"I see you are at the lab again," Angwyndith said after a beat.

Observer then. Seraphina understood so many more nuances in Angwyndith's tone now versus when they first began talking to each other over the summer. The last statement was neutral, but the slight edge of judgment carried through it, regardless. *"Yep. Same schedule, different day."*

"More tests? There seems to be an unusual amount. What else could they be looking for?"

"Your guess is as good as mine. Probably better."

The Shifter in the cell turned to face her. She froze as she met his glowing white eyes. He stood in Warrior mode, his body covered in fur, his long fingers capped by lethal claws. In Warrior mode, Shifters' arms and legs were similar in length, allowing them to walk on two legs and still use their hands to open things.

But not this Shifter. His body had transformed wrong, like a mix of his human form with his Warrior one. His arms were too short, his muzzle a combination of human teeth and canine snout. For a moment, she thought she saw a flash of fear before the muscles in his jaw bunched.

Seraphina tilted her head, her brow furrowed. *"What's wrong with him?"*

"I do not know. A Shapechanger with human features. Why would they do that?" Angwyndith said, a weird note in her voice Seraphina hadn't heard before.

Horror rose as she remembered the conversation she'd had with Teddy. "*Unless he's the child of a human and a Shifter. And it all went wrong.*" Goosebumps fanned out over Seraphina's arms. "*Could this happen to me?*"

"*No. Children born of that mix do not live past their first few hours. There is too much difference between them. Besides, your parents were both Shapechangers.*"

"*And yet, here I am. For all intents and purposes, a human.*"

"*You are different.*" Angwyndith stuttered on the last word, as if she couldn't say, "you're a freakshow," in proper terms. "*Your humanness… is a puzzle I fear you will never unravel. Your parentage should not have been of Shapechangers.*"

Seraphina hated her humanness, especially at the Facility.

"*No, my Host. Do not hate that which you are. That way leads to bitterness and heartache.*"

"Ms. Lastra. I am busy with other research today. Dr. Myers will attend to your tests." Dr. Pianail's voice cut through the quiet of the lab like a hacksaw, cutting off their conversation.

It was probably for the best. It would've only gone downhill from there.

Seraphina glanced over her shoulder to locate the Wielder who'd stick her with needles today. A short woman, her brown hair pulled back tightly into a bun, motioned her over. Seraphina turned back to the glass. The Shifter tilted his head as if puzzled.

Exactly like she'd viewed him.

Sadness rushed through her, and she raised a hand to wave at him, her fingers curling before the wave even got started. At least her tests were just that: blood draws and spells thrown at her while she stood in a warding circle. He had it so much worse than her.

He blinked back at her.

She dropped her hand and mouthed, "I'm sorry," before heading to the workstation.

"Have a seat, Ms. Lastra," Dr. Myers said, gesturing to the stool near her bench. Standard test tubes lined the table, waiting for yet more of her blood.

Seraphina sat facing the cells and caught the Shifter still watching her, his nose testing the air. Could he smell her from there?

Dr. Myers pulled her arm over the bench and rubbed alcohol on the bend in her elbow.

"What's wrong with him? Why is he caged up?" Seraphina asked.

Dr. Myers glanced at Dr. Pianail and then at the Shifter now watching their every move. "He's a danger to everyone in this lab."

"Yeah, but his eyes are white. He's not in fight mode."

The knot of the tourniquet snapped against Seraphina's skin like a rebuke. "Ten minutes ago, before you arrived, he was howling at the glass and attempting to break the ward. Looks can be deceiving. Especially with Shifters," she muttered under her breath.

Seraphina glowered at her. "What does that mean?"

"Make a fist with your hand." Dr. Myers tapped her skin and slid the needle in. She pushed a tube on the end and said, "Let it go."

Seraphina took a deep breath, still not comfortable with needles, no matter how many times they pricked her, and met the Shifter's eyes again.

"He looks sad." She knew how he felt.

The doctor replaced the current tube with another. "Gabriel's fine."

Recognition clicked into place, the last memory she had of him striding down the hall after the dying Wielder helping her put the pieces together. The color left Seraphina's cheeks. "That's Chief Gabriel? What did you do to him?"

"Nothing he didn't know when he signed up for it."

Her detached tone bothered Seraphina, refueling the irritation from before. "Whether he volunteered, your *experiment* obviously went wrong," Seraphina snapped.

"Be careful, my Host. There is more going on here than a simple test gone wrong."

"What are you talking about?"

"Nuances and splinters," Angwyndith muttered.

"What?"

"I was not talking to you. I was a making a note for myself to investigate later."

"So sorry for interrupting," Seraphina said, her eyes rolling.

A sour smile twitched on Dr. Myer's lips. "Gabriel knew the risks. His training prepared him for this eventuality."

"I doubt he knew he'd get twisted into whatever form he is now."

"He had both the foresight to know what he was doing and the experience to know it could go wrong, all that is required for a proper decision to be made." Dr. Myers jammed another test tube into the end of the needle, pushing hard, and Seraphina winced.

Seraphina hated these tests, and she hated this lab. She should have paid more attention to the contract she signed.

A deep thump boomed from the back of the room, followed by the staccato beat of the Shifter's fist against the glass. His eyes warmed to a deep red, and the rhythm increased. Aggressive mode.

"*That is not good, my Host. He has little, if any, control. What have they done to him?*"

"*I don't know, but I don't like it. At all.*" Seraphina's eyebrows drew together as she met Gabriel's gaze. The color leeched out of Gabriel's eyes like a draining pool of water, and the drumming stopped.

"What did you just do?" Dr. Myers asked as she removed the needle from Seraphina's arm.

Anger sliced through Seraphina as the items on Dr. Pianail's bench made more sense. "I showed compassion. You should try it sometime."

"You have no idea what you're talking about." Dr. Myers pressed a cotton ball to the puncture site and made a note on the checklist next to her. "You're done, but you'll need to be back here on Monday. Dr. Pianail has scheduled a few test potions for you, if we get them completed on time."

Seraphina didn't agree to any of this, and she'd be damned if they used her for tests on him. "*Angwyndith, did the contract we signed say anything about testing?*"

"*Did you not read it?*" Angwyndith's warm sigh tickled Seraphina's throat. "*I am not here to fill in the lack of knowledge you have access to by other means. I am not an encyclopedia to be used whenever you are too lazy to do the work.*"

"*I am doing the work, Angwyndith.*"

"*Yes, now. That does not make up for the work you did not do before.*"

Seraphina bit back the reply on her tongue at Angwyndith's condescending tone. As tempting as it was to blast her,

Angwyndith was right. *"Please, just answer the question. I don't have the contract with me."*

Another flutter filled Seraphina's stomach.

"No, it did not." Angwyndith bit the words out.

Dr. Myers cleared her throat, bringing Seraphina's attention back to her.

Angwyndith's ire could've been aimed at Seraphina, the contract, or the Facility. Most likely all three. Seraphina would deal with it later. "Sorry, but I think I'll pass."

"That is not the agreement." Dr. Myers' nostrils flared.

"There is no agreement for testing. I sure as hell didn't agree to it." Seraphina crossed her arms, the tape over the injection site pulling at her skin.

The doctor flicked her eyes over to Dr. Pianail's station. After a moment, she said, "Very well." She moved back to her bench, already moving on to the next thing on her list. "You can go now."

"Fine." Seraphina pivoted on her heel and headed for the door.

Relief at being done with the tests warred with what the Facility had done to Gabriel. She stopped when she reached the threshold and looked at him once more. He faced the corner of his cell, his clawed hands clenching and unclenching.

Like a jigsaw puzzle where the pieces were thrown in the air and left to lay where they fell, she and Gabriel were held together by a thin thread of who they once thought they were. Except his pieces were on the outside and hers were on the inside.

Tears rushed to her eyes. He hadn't asked for any of this and neither had she. What was she doing here?

12

ODD QUESTIONS

(SHE MADE A FRIEND)

The chime jangled over Seraphina's head as the smell of burned coffee assailed her nose. Some of her ever-present restlessness seeped out into the linoleum at her feet. A couple sat at the end booth, tension evident in the shoulders of the woman whose back was to her. On the other side of the diner, the flame-haired girl from before bent over her laptop, hot pink headphones in place.

The pink headband sparked a memory of someone sitting alone, like her, in the Facility cafeteria. "It's that kind of day"—that was what the girl had said the first time they'd interacted, the day of the Eventon incident. Seraphina took two steps in the girl's direction but stopped, crippling indecision holding her in place.

Marion raised her eyebrows and said, "Anywhere you want, hon," in the same tone she had the first time Seraphina had come in.

Heat crept up Seraphina's cheeks, and she nodded, her eyes downcast as she walked toward the couple instead and slid into a booth. The girl had given her a food recommendation; that didn't make them friends. Besides, if she was from the Facility, she probably already knew who and what Seraphina was.

Marion stopped by and shifted to one hip, a coffee carafe in her hand.

"Hi, coffee please, and do you have any of the apple crumble today?"

"Nope. We got cranberry though."

"Oh, nice! I'll have that and ice cream on the side then."

"Suit yourself." Marion flipped the cup on the table over and filled it before wandering off to the awkward couple at the end.

Seraphina took her phone out and checked her messages. A few texts from Ro about some trip she was taking and an email from her aunt checking in. That was the total of her news. She put the phone down when Marion slid the plate in front of her.

When she was halfway through the dessert, the flame-haired girl stopped by the booth, her coffee cup in one hand and her laptop in the other. "Is the cranberry good? I couldn't decide."

Seraphina looked up, her mouth full, and mumbled, "It is." The redhead stood by the table, her laptop tapping her thigh. Seraphina gulped down the food and took the plunge. "Do you want to join me?"

An enormous grin broke out on the redhead's face, "I kinda do," and she slid into the booth on the other side. "I'm Sorcha, by the way."

"Seraphina."

"I know. I've seen you in the cafeteria, and as the new human, word gets around," Sorcha said just as Marion stopped by to top up their cups.

Seraphina froze, her eyes widening as the woman at the end booth rubbed her chin on her shoulder, a move Ro used to do when checking someone out behind her.

"With all the coders I work with, I didn't think any normal humans existed anymore," Sorcha said casually, while waiting for Marion to finish. "I'll try the cranberry as well, please, Marion."

"Ice cream?"

The conversation faded into the background as Seraphina's pulse pounded in her ears.

"Have you not served me two days a week for months?"

Marion flipped her notebook closed, walked back to the counter, and served up the pie. Plate in hand, she disappeared into the back, the flap of the swinging doors mesmerizing Seraphina. A laugh erupted from the end table, and Seraphina snapped her gaze to the couple. The woman reached across to tug on her boyfriend's cap, and he smacked her hand away, a playful smile on his face.

Sorcha tapped the table. Seraphina wrenched her gaze away from the couple and fastened it on Sorcha, who tilted her head, her lips twitching into a nervous smile.

Seraphina's eyes widened as her brain scrambled to remember what Sorcha had just said. "Yeah, well, um, I'm as human as it gets. I can't even configure my email." She sipped her coffee, using the movement to calm her racing heart.

The air rushed out of Sorcha's lungs, and she slumped against the booth. "They don't make it easy at the company, do they?" She winked.

"No, they really don't." Seraphina was relieved she didn't have to navigate the minefield of what to call the Facility. "So, is that what you do for them? Coding?"

"Yeah. Nothing overly exciting. My job focuses on the mainframe and the major programs everyone uses to communicate with each other."

"So, you're IT?"

Sorcha's face froze, her expression unreadable. After a moment, she said, "Not really. I mean, sort of, but I don't deal with problems. I deal with solutions. What do they have you doing?"

Biting her lip, Seraphina glanced around the diner.

The guy faced her, a few days' scruff on his chin and a baseball cap covering the rest of his face. His girlfriend said something he didn't like, and his lips thinned, his eyes flicking to Seraphina's and then out the window again.

Afraid they might be listening, she kept it vague. "Training. Lots and lots of training."

"They have you taking the starter pack, then."

"Yeah."

"It's been a while since I took them, but I do recall they were incredibly boring, yet stressful at the same time." Sorcha rolled her eyes.

"Exactly. Too many regulations that all sound very much alike."

"Yes, but all are very useful. I'd pay attention to those if I were you."

What did *that* mean?

Seraphina frowned. The lingering effects of Sawyer's interrogation had her seeing enemies everywhere. Sorcha was being nice, just like Teddy.

Marion set Sorcha's pie down without stopping, her other hand pulling out a check from her back pocket as she passed. She dropped it on the table between the couple, but they both were too engaged in watching the passing cars to acknowledge it. Marion shrugged and gathered up the plates between them.

The ping of an incoming message pulled Seraphina back to their table.

Sorcha pulled out her phone from her top pocket. "No way!" She popped open her laptop. "Cadwally just started streaming and I am dying to see him defeat MikeStriker."

"Uh, say what?"

The girl threw her head back and laughed, while her fingers flew across the keys of her laptop. "Ugh. That's me, always ahead of myself. They're gamers. I'm a gamer. Cadwally is awesome at this game, a giant in the field, who rarely streams. He's online now and I can't miss it."

"Right." All Seraphina knew about games was the solitaire she played when she was really bored. She'd rather be reading.

"Whoa! That was insane." Sorcha looked up over the top of her screen, saying, "You have to see this. Seriously, it's so cool."

Seraphina switched sides of the booth, sliding in next to Sorcha. On the screen was some sort of moon buggy thing bouncing over bleak terrain. Staticky voices echoed through the headphones Sorcha had around her neck. The buggy door opened, and the camera shifted to characters in helmets and spacesuits, heavy duty guns in the view as they ran for the cover near the buggy.

"Go get 'em, Cadwally!"

"Uh, yeah, go get them, whoever you are," Seraphina said, trying to sound enthusiastic, but it was a buggy on a fake planet.

Sorcha must have caught her tone, because she said, "Okay, so this warehouse has a bunch of stuff in it. Supplies are limited in this game. Cadwally," a green tipped fingernail tapped the screen, "just dropped the hammer on MikeStriker." She pointed to red dots on a circular map in the upper right corner. "MikeStriker thought he could just waltz in and steal it, but Cadwally must have people in high places. He always knows where the game hides the good stuff. He just rocked up and now they're going to fight for it."

It took a moment, but if she peered closer, Seraphina could see beyond the splashes of color and numbers scrolling up the page to the action happening around them.

"Okay, that might be cool." She'd still rather be reading.

Sorcha kept up a running stream of the action on the screen, including mumbles of what MikeStriker did wrong. The headphones slung around her neck squawked in sync with her comments. After a while, Seraphina found herself just as hooked, cheering when Cadwally won.

"High five!" Sorcha said, her eyes bright. She leaned away so they could slap hands. "That was amazing. I'm so glad I didn't miss it!"

Craning her neck to smile at Sorcha, the awkwardness of being on the same side of the booth with someone she'd just met hit Seraphina like a Mack truck. She went back to her side of the booth, cradling her now cold coffee mug.

Sorcha didn't seem to care as the words gushed out of her about how epic it all was. Most of it went right over Seraphina's head, but it wasn't codes or ward puzzles, which made a pleasant change.

Marion dropped their checks on the table and topped up their coffee mugs. "It's just after five, hon."

Sorcha whipped her head to the clock above the swinging kitchen door. "Crap. I can talk all day, but I need to head back. My shift starts in twenty."

"Oh, okay. Thanks for sharing that with me," Seraphina said, her stomach sinking at the thought of being alone again.

"Hey, would you be interested in learning how to play that game?"

"Um."

"Forget it." Sorcha slid out of the booth. "I forget that not everyone I meet is a gamer."

Seraphina hesitated. This could be her one chance to make a friend. What would learning a game hurt? She'd still have time to read and stare at the paint on the walls.

"No, I'd like to learn. Where do I start?"

"Do you have a laptop?" At Seraphina's nod, Sorcha continued, "All you have to do is search for the game's name, *The Last Centauri*. Set up an account, download it, and then meet me in the cafeteria tonight on my break at 10 pm and I'll show you how to get started."

"Tonight?"

Sorcha slapped her forehead again. "Sorry. You've probably got better things to do at 10 pm than watch me eat dinner on my break and play video games."

"Hardly. New human, remember?" Seraphina said, pointing to herself. "I can absolutely break from studying to meet you then."

"Awesomesauce. I'll see you then." Sorcha sauntered away from the table and yelled goodbye to Marion on the way out.

Seraphina took a sip of coffee and grinned. She felt like an eleven-year-old girl invited to her first slumber party. Eager to get back and download the game, she threw some dollar bills on the table and waved to Marion on her way out.

As she crossed the lot, a guy came out of the mechanic's bay, wiping his hands on a red towel smeared with oil stains. He lifted his chin at her.

She threw him a nervous smile and hurried to the truck; her keys out and ready. She jammed the key in the lock and had just opened the door when a voice behind her said, "Nice ride."

Startled, she swung around. "Thanks."

It was the guy from the diner. His girlfriend shrunk behind him, wearing a similar ball cap, and playing with the straps of her purse. "If you're selling, I'm buying," he said.

"What?" Seraphina flicked a glance at the three people watching her. The mechanic on her right and the couple on her left hemmed her in. The tension from earlier unfurled in her stomach, and she clenched her fingers around her keys.

"If you're looking to sell, I'm looking to buy."

She tilted her head, her brow furrowed. "The truck?"

Baseball cap shrugged and said, "Sure."

"Sorry, but no."

"I'd pay you what it's worth." His eyes were unreadable under his cap.

The need to get in the Rover and get away was so strong it almost choked her. "Doesn't matter. I'm not selling."

He squinted at her, his tongue sliding out to wet his lips. "Alright. If you change your mind, Jack here knows where to find me." He waved at the mechanic.

"I won't." She forced the words through tight lips.

"You never know which way the wind will blow."

"I know this wind and it's not for me." She had no clue what she was saying.

Baseball cap nodded, said, "Have a nice day, ma'am," and ambled away, his girlfriend trailing him.

She scrambled into the cab and slammed the door, locking it behind her. The rumbling of the engine as she cranked it up never sounded so good. She shoved the gearstick into reverse, backed up and peeled out of the lot as if her pants were on fire.

As she cruised out of town, she glanced back in her rearview mirror to see the mechanic still staring after her, his hand on his hip, the red towel a stain on an otherwise dark and grim image. Small-town people were weird.

Looking to shake the fear racing through her, she reached over to turn on the radio. Demi appeared in the passenger seat and growled. Her hand hit the horn and her foot slipped off the gas, the Rover losing its momentum.

"Jeezus crackers, Demi. You scared the crap out of me!" Her heart pounding so hard it hurt, she guided the Rover to the side of the road and put her head back against the seat, taking deep breaths.

Demi chuckled and flapped his tongue at her.

"It's not funny." The naked little Elf waggled his head at her, the spikes on his head clacking together. "Fine, fine. It's good to see you, but what are you doing here? How'd you even get here?" She gestured to the surrounding woods. The last time she'd seen him was in New Hampshire.

He launched into a long tail of hitching rides on trucks and hunting through the woods until he saw her outside one day. By the time he was done, Seraphina's heart rate slowed. But something he said at the end picked it back up again.

She faced him. "Demi, you weren't on Facility grounds, were you? They have wards and loads of security you can't see."

He shook his head, muttering their wards were easily breakable.

"No, they aren't. Don't test them."

He shrugged and blew out a huff of breath, his head rolling.

She didn't think he could roll his eyes, but that movement seemed to be what he was doing. "Right. You wouldn't be that stupid," Seraphina said wryly.

His clawed hand touched her shoulder, and he leaned in, his eyes large and drooping. He told her in a cloud of noxious air what he knew about the Facility and an Elf who reigned supreme there.

"Wait, what Elf? There are no Elves reigning anywhere. Well, not that I've seen. Do you mean the little Brownie who cleans the upper floors?"

He shook his head and said more garbled words she couldn't understand. For a moment, she felt like she was back in the diner, listening to Sorcha talk about the video game.

"I'm not following you."

He sighed dramatically and scratched his stomach, his tongue lolling in the air while he thought. She watched him, a bemused smile on her face. She'd missed him, even if he drove her crazy.

After a beat, he shrugged and said a lesser being like her wouldn't understand.

Her smile faded. She sighed and started the Rover, trying not to let a silly Elf get to her. A dark gray sedan appeared on the horizon behind her, but she had plenty of time to pull out. Demi's squawk brought her attention back to him. She glanced over to see his spiked covered back and naked butt mooning her, his face smashed against the passenger window.

"Demi!" She couldn't help but laugh, some of the tension easing. He really was a silly Elf. "Do you want to go, then?"

He nodded.

She wound the window down and he hopped up on the door frame, waved his spear, and said he'd see her around. Before she could blink, he was gone.

"Bye," she yelled as she rolled the window back up. The sedan had made little progress in catching up, so she pulled onto the road and headed toward the Facility.

She made a friend and caught up with another, so it wasn't a total loss. For once.

13

GAMES, GRUB, & GOSSIP

(They Were Just Like Everyone Else)

Seraphina's fingers raced across the keyboard as she mashed the left button on her mouse. The shot hit dead center and the sound of a ship disintegrating into a million pieces filled her headphones.

The rush of winning her first space battle flowed through her and Seraphina lifted her arms in the air and yelled, "Yes! Suck it, EvoNarc24!"

Across the table, Sorcha's tinkling laugh ended with a snort, which set Seraphina off. Tears slid down her cheeks as she gasped for air. "Oh, my gods, that was hilarious."

Sorcha's normally icy white cheeks were bright red. "No, that was embarrassing." She arched her back and stretched out her arms, yawning. "I take it you won then?"

"Yes. It was close, though. I almost thrust myself into a nearby asteroid, but course-corrected in time. Flying in this game is hard."

This was the fourth time they'd hung out in the past week and a half, meeting either at the diner for pie or in the cafeteria to play *The Last Centauri*. It felt good. Normal. And it made all the frustrations and stress she carried lighter.

"Forget all those space movies you've watched. The developers really took the time to create the mechanics to mimic actual space flight. Not that we'll ever get to experience it, though," Sorcha said.

"Is that what you want to do, go to space?"

Sorcha squinted over Seraphina's head. "Don't you?"

"I've never really thought about it. Maybe. The journey's long, so I'd probably run out of books."

"They have these things, called eBooks, that you can load on a device."

Seraphina threw a balled-up napkin at her, missing by a mile. "I know about eBooks. I'm not a complete dork." She sat back in her chair. "I'd miss the physical copies: the way they smell, the way they feel in my hands. It's why I do what I do."

Murmurs and clinking silverware filled the space between them as Sorcha finished typing something on her laptop. A wave of peace washed over Seraphina as she took it all in.

"What's that?" Sorcha finally asked. "I thought you just trained all the time."

"I do, but in my copious free time, I restore old books and get them as good as new as possible, without destroying the look and feel of the original."

"Really? Wow. Sounds..."

"Dull." Seraphina laughed. "I know, but I really like the intensity, the detail and delicacy of it."

"I get it, I think. I spend my days creating sequences of letters and numbers in a language universal to computer geeks. Creating a program to close a door to malware or to improve the way something functions is a little like that. Manaan help you if you miss a loop or a trick and something gets in." Sorcha's face clouded over, the playful smile draining from it as she stared off at the wall behind Seraphina's head.

A quiet pall cast over the table and Seraphina crossed her leg, waiting for Sorcha to come back to their conversation. She knew not to ask what had captured Sorcha's attention; the few times she'd tried before were rebuffed. To be fair, it wasn't like Seraphina was spilling her guts, either. Any time they got too near her family, she skittered away and asked about the game.

Sorcha's use of "Manaan" gave Seraphina the last clue she needed to determine what phylum Sorcha came from. She could usually tell, either by size or the way they carried themselves and she'd already crossed off Shifter. The Shifters at the Facility didn't wear their human forms and Sorcha never seemed to take hers off.

The Motion phylum made sense. Sorcha was a lot like Ro, shifting in and out of emotions with a lift of a hand or a shake of the head. And in many ways, she wasn't. The more time Seraphina spent with Sorcha, the clearer it became of how much Ro chose what she said and how she said it. Sorcha let it hang out all the time; Ro only did so when she was drunk. Even then, Ro was a surgeon with her words, never sloppy. It made her question how well she knew Ro, even after all these years.

Sadness crept over Seraphina like a heavy cloak, removing the glow of the win and the laugh. Everywhere she turned, she found she knew less than she thought.

Sorcha shook her head, like a dog shaking water off its coat, and asked, "Do you miss it being here?"

The question caught Seraphina off guard. She bit her lip and concentrated on docking her ship while she tried to remember what they'd been talking about.

The tap of a finger on the table brought Seraphina back to the hanging question.

"One sec." Seraphina opened the hatch door on her ship and headed inside the terminal, missing almost being blasted by a space pirate. She looked over her laptop at Sorcha while her character took the elevator down to the ground floor. "Book restoring? No. I'm still doing it. I brought a box of books with me."

"Wow. That's dedication."

"It's my job," Seraphina said, shrugging. "I have a client back home, although I think he's just doing me a favor."

"Sounds like a good client."

A picture of the solid bulk of Finn sitting behind his counter, reading a book, flashed in her mind and a warm smile crossed Seraphina's face. "He is. What about you? Do you like what you do?"

"I love it. I wouldn't do anything else. Well, maybe I'd code a game, but that's not in the cards right now."

"What kind of game would you code?"

Sorcha blinked at her.

"Right. Space."

"Duh," Sorcha grinned. "What other kind is there?"

"I have no idea." Seraphina picked up her cup, her lips sliding to one side when only a smear appeared at the bottom. "I need more coffee. And maybe snacks. Definitely chocolate." She stood. "Do you want anything?"

"No more coffee for me. But can you grab me some of that trail mix?"

Seraphina pulled a face. "You're so healthy."

"You would be too if you burned energy as fast as I do."

"I don't know. I burn a lot of energy and still eat a lot of junk food. It just burns off naturally." Seraphina walked away but still caught Sorcha's muttered, "Then you're lucky."

The cafeteria had emptied while they'd been playing, but there were still a few people around, including the Shifter filling up a massive sixty-four-ounce travel mug with coffee. After waiting long enough to find out it was the Mary Poppins of cups, Seraphina veered off and filled two bowls with trail mix and chocolate-covered raisins.

A tray slamming into the metal carts near the trash made her jump. Teddy stood in the path to the door, having a conversation with another familiar-looking guard. Whatever was said caused them to turn and glare in one direction. She followed it to the table where Sorcha sat.

Wandering back, Seraphina frowned at Teddy and his friend as she placed the snacks between them.

Sorcha glanced up to say thanks and caught her frown, turning to see where it was aimed. "Don't mind them." Her teeth crunched down on a pretzel hard enough for the pieces to spray the table.

"What's their problem?"

"They're Shifters."

Seraphina rested her chin on the top of her laptop. "So?"

"So, they're a bunch of speciest jerks who don't like me because I'm not one of them."

"One of them is pretty friendly to me, and that's saying something."

"Ha." Sorcha rolled her eyes. "He probably wants something from you."

Seraphina squinted at Teddy, confusion swirling in her stomach. "I don't think so. I have nothing *to* want. Is that really what you think they're like?"

"Yes. Where have you been living?"

Derision twisted the simple question into an insult, and Seraphina stiffened. "New York City."

Sorcha laughed, the sound harder than the coating of the candy in the trail mix. "That explains it then."

"Explains what?"

"Never mind. Forget I said anything."

"Too late." Sorcha didn't look up from her keyboard, so Seraphina pushed Sorcha's laptop cover down. "What does that explain? That my friends are more inclusive?"

"Are your *friends* all from the same phylum?"

Seraphina stared at the ceiling as she went through the ranks of people surrounding Ro. She slumped. "Yes."

"There you have it. Every phylum sticks to their own. That's all I meant."

Seraphina raised her eyebrows, thinking about the conversations with her aunt. "Ok. I've sort of seen that. But I thought since everyone works together, it wasn't as big a thing here."

"Not from what I've seen. You must not have gotten to the part in the history class where they talk about why the SF was formed."

"We've talked about the wars and issues with... my kind encroaching on everybody." Seraphina squirmed at talking about her phylum like they were the problem.

"No. There's a specific section you should pay attention to. It'll explain a lot."

A chair screeched nearby, putting a noise to Seraphina's irritation as once again she was in the dark. "Give me the highlights."

Sorcha fiddled with the cord on her computer. "Short version, the phyla kill each other for power, land, and resources, and they're good at it."

"Sounds just like human world history. All the wars fought for oil, gold, and religion."

"Except you can at least make more of you quickly. It doesn't work that way for us. You kill one pup and you've set the phylum back years, if not decades."

Seraphina took a sip of coffee while the thoughts raged in her brain. Her mother pushed the boundaries of her body to have another child. All that resulted was a messed-up mom and a human child. It also put her Wielder aunt and Shifter Uncle marrying out of their phylum into perspective. Both her aunt and uncle had denied their phyla a child when they got together. "I never really thought about it that way."

"Why would you? It's not a problem you have."

"That's not fair. There are plenty of people who want kids and can't have them."

Sorcha sighed. "And yet, there is an abundance of kids without parents, starving to death, living on the streets, etc. It's not the same magnitude of the problem, Seraphina."

Her patronizing tone grated. "Right. Everything's more special when you're in the MC." Seraphina rolled her eyes. "I know. I get it."

"No, you don't."

"You have no idea what I get or don't get."

The light fixture over their table flickered, throwing it into shadow as a fluorescent tube went out.

"No, but I know more about this place than you." Sorcha leaned forward over the lid of her laptop, the whites of her teeth glowing despite the darkness. "Did you know they have a whole lab section devoted to improving birth rates for the phyla?"

Seraphina got whiplash from trying to keep up with Sorcha's mood changes. "No."

"Or that they have another division working on eradicating illnesses that can wipe out an entire family? They are on the cusp of innovation for our kind in so many areas, improving our lives."

She'd really drunk the Kool-aid. From what Seraphina had seen, this place was not the be all, end all. "You sound like a recruiting commercial."

"So what? While the SF may be harsh and have crazy rules, they do good things here, Seraphina." Sorcha sat back into a patch of light, munching on a handful of trail mix. "You don't see it because you don't need to."

If one more person told Seraphina what she didn't know, while refusing to fill her in, she was going to scream. "They're not all sunshine and rainbows here, Sorcha. Do *you* know they have a division devoted to testing? Because I do and I've seen their work. It sucks."

"There'll be setbacks, there always are."

Seraphina's anger boiled over at Sorcha's casual tone. "I wouldn't call what they did to Gabriel a setback," she shot back.

Sorcha frowned. "What are you talking about?"

A surge of triumph filled Seraphina. Finally, she knew something Sorcha didn't. "The Shifter with the half human face in the lab on level twelve? That guy? That guy didn't get what he paid for. And he didn't help anyone in the process."

Sorcha glanced around and leaned forward. "Stop talking. Right now. I don't want to know, and I don't need to know."

"Why, because it's a Shifter?"

"No, because it's a security clearance thing," Sorcha hissed. "You'll get me in trouble, and I'm already... just shut up about it."

"Fine."

"You don't understand. I need this job. I can't afford to lose it."

"I've not said another word. You're safe from the great SF." Seraphina crossed her arms.

Sorcha shut her laptop and unplugged it from the wall. "It's easy for you. You don't have to worry about backlash."

"Yeah, being the freaking Host is a cakewalk. Everybody wants to be me. Too human to fit in and too scary to talk to."

"It's not the same thing."

"Feels that way to me," Seraphina snapped. "You realize you're one of *two* people who aren't instructors who talk to me here, right? And even then, the instructors only do so when necessary." Churning underneath all the sarcasm was a growing pit of despair. The one new friendship she'd made was sinking faster than the Titanic.

Sorcha flinched. She finished wrapping her cord around the power block, her face concentrating on it as if it were a bomb she was defusing. She set it on top of her computer and looked up, her jaw clenched. "Look, I'm sorry."

Seraphina braced herself, forcing her face into a neutral, even though her lips were tighter than a rubber band stretched past its limit.

"I have some stuff going on in my family and you just touched a nerve." Sorcha sighed and grabbed another handful of trail mix, decimating the contents of the bowl. She threw a few pieces into her mouth and chewed, her expression smoothing out. "What do you say we go back to playing games and talking about bad TV the next time we hang out?"

"Um, what?"

"Tuesday, diner, pie?"

Feeling like her car had slipped on an icy road and spun around a few times before settling back in the direction it had been originally facing, Seraphina asked in disbelief, "You still want to hang out?"

"Yes. Of course." Sorcha froze in mid-movement. "You don't?"

Guilt over telling Sorcha something she shouldn't have crept up Seraphina's spine. "Yes. I mean, I want to hang out. And I'm sorry too. I don't know what I can and can't talk about—no one told me. I assumed since you can visit floors I can't," she waved at the six additional colored boxes on the bottom of Sorcha's badge, "that you knew about everything."

"They didn't give you the list in orientation?"

Seraphina's mouth formed an "O" as she recalled a table of the different meanings for the colors on the badge.

Sorcha laughed, the mood lightening a little between them. "The SF is massive. I can only see a tiny corner of it, and even that corner is tightly controlled." She glanced at the clock and shifted again. "So, we good?"

"Yes. We're good. We can just avoid that topic we were just talking about. Just like politics at Thanksgiving. Or religion."

Sorcha grinned. "Exactly. See you at the diner, then?"

Seraphina matched her smile and replied, "Absolutely."

As Sorcha walked away, Seraphina's smile slid off her face. There was so much she'd missed, both in classes and in her conversation with Sorcha and Angwyndith. She needed to go back and review it all again. Wards, history, politics. The list kept growing, especially if she included the regulations and combat strategies Moynihan and Fairchild drilled into them.

She groaned. Being here was worse than grad school. It was enough to give her a headache, and she hadn't even really started studying yet.

14

THE MONSTERS IN THE DARK

(She Met the Most Interesting People)

Seraphina closed the book with a thump and added it to the pile on her right. The wall of useful books had steadily shrunk while the wall of useless books grew like fungus in a dank bathroom. She was no closer to figuring out wards than she had been when she started.

She fiddled with the spiraled edge of her notebook. Maybe she wasn't as smart as she thought she was. Maybe she should just focus on her business. Why did she need to know this stuff, anyway? She was the passenger, not the driver, and it gave Angwyndith something to focus on, pointing out what Seraphina didn't know.

A blaring whistle shrilled above her head and then zeroed in on her ears like a hungry mosquito at two am. Grimacing, she slapped her hands on her ears, which took the decibels down a notch. After an interminable minute, the whistle stopped, but continued to ring in her ears.

"The Facility is on lockdown. I repeat, the Facility is on lockdown. All nonessential personnel remain in your positions," a woman's voice bleated out.

The silence was as deafening as the empty chairs and tables around her. The library doors clicked shut with a finality that struck Seraphina in the chest. Across her stomach, Angwyndith's warmth swirled to life, intermingling with a chill Seraphina hadn't felt since the incident in the gym.

Oh gods, no.

She picked up the pen, but couldn't concentrate, her foot twitching against the chair. The jiggling turned into a bouncing knee as the dread slipped up her spine in pace with the cold of the Coda. No Bell had rung. She couldn't have missed that even with the shrieking because the last time it had rung, it vibrated hard enough to set her teeth chattering. So why was the Coda here?

Angwyndith stretched inside her, and Seraphina pounced as soon as it was done. *"They've locked down the room. What's going on?"*

"I do not know."

"Shouldn't you?"

"Should I not what? Know what is happening outside of my Host in this large stone Facility?"

"The Coda is here. The Facility is in lockdown. Do the math."

"There is no 'math' to be done. One and one do not always make two. Surely you would have heard the Bell Toll if we are to Judge. Did you hear a Bell, my Host?" Angwyndith said, her irritation presenting in the simplicity of her statement.

It set Seraphina's teeth on edge. *"No, I heard a scream, though."*

"A scream is not our problem. You do remember my teachings from before, correct?"

Seraphina closed her eyes and took a deep breath, the urge to yell getting stronger. *"I am aware of the process. The Bell rings, we move to Judge, the Inquisition of Hearts begins, yada yada yada. Someone dies."*

"That is correct, although I do not recall ya-da ya-da ya-da being said nor conveyed."

"You know what I mean."

"That is not relevant. Communication is the core to our understanding. Without it being done properly, we cannot rise and meet the needs of our duties."

Angwyndith's tone dipped into her teaching mode, which Seraphina did not want to hear. *"It's just the last time I felt the Coda this intensely, we were outside Harriman's house."*

"That is true, but that was a Judgment. The intensity, as you call it, was normal. This feels less so."

It was like Angwyndith enjoyed torturing her with practicality and proper sentence construction. *"Can you ask it what it wants?"*

"No. " Angwyndith bit the word out.

"Oh-kay then. Just asking. I thought you had a thing with the Coda." Seraphina tried to ignore the swirling arctic air circling up her arms by opening the next book on the pile. It was like ignoring an itch from a rash: the intensity increased the longer she pretended it wasn't there. Her knee bounced faster.

"The Coda has its own aims and goals," Angwyndith said, her words stiffer than the wood of the table.

Did Angwyndith just admit she didn't know something? *"Ah. Okay. I get it. It's you and you're me when the Coda is involved."*

"The Coda is not involved. I am not following."

"Doesn't matter," Seraphina said, her pen now tapping in rhythm with her knee. *"I wonder what the lockdown is about, then."*

"You will be safe here."

Seraphina sighed. "*I don't really have a choice. I just wish someone else was here with me who knew what was going on.*"

"*I am here, my Host.*"

"*Yep, and you just said you didn't know what was going on.*"

Seraphina could feel Angwyndith gathering for a strike. "*Why would anyone else visit this room? These texts are too simple for anyone to learn anything from.*"

Seraphina's knee stopped jiggling as the words sunk in, echoing her earlier thoughts. Angwyndith had gone for blood and found it.

Angwyndith stopped moving around inside. A sure sign she was thinking. And then Seraphina's scalp tingled.

"*My Host, I see you have been working on the ward. Any progress made?*"

Avoidance, Angwyndith's second favorite tactic. "*Nope. I'm too simple to get it.*"

"*You take things too quickly to heart. It is not always about you, the things I say.*"

Before Seraphina could spill the angry words on the tip of her tongue, the shrill whistle screamed again. The pen clattered to the desk as she covered her ears. "*Seriously, what is going on? And can they not with the screaming?*"

"*You have to give them credit for using what is at hand. I have not heard a Banshee call in some time, but it is most effective in getting our attention.*"

"*Yeah, that and splitting my eardrums. Is that really what they sound like?*" The icy wave surged up her shoulder blades, circling toward her neck. Her fingers curled into a fist.

"*Yes, my Host. It is not as alluring as the mythology would lead you to believe. And yet, highly effective.*"

"*If you want me to run away.*"

"Right into their waiting arms. They can project the sound in a way that disorients the average human."

Before she could respond, the glacial mass moved up her neck and into her head. A headache spread across her forehead, like when she'd eaten her frozen yogurt too fast. *"Angwyndith? What's happening?"*

"It appears the Coda has something to show us."

"You don't know?"

"It does not always reveal itself to me, Child," Angwyndith snapped.

Seraphina suppressed a smile at her frustration, but the humor in her situation dissipated. The lockdown and the Coda happening at the same time were not a coincidence, no matter what Angwyndith said.

A commotion in the hall outside bled into the library. Boots ran by the doors as voices called out, "Clear."

From what Seraphina remembered from Moynihan's class, they were sweeping the floor. She hoped this was a drill or that they were just being careful. Otherwise, she'd need to find a weapon fast.

She eyed a thick tome on the bottom of her pile. That might be it. She could use the chair in a pinch, but it was heavy, and Moira already showed her how it could be used against her when fighting someone stronger than her. Something everyone in this facility had—more strength.

The chill intensified.

"Angwyndith..."

The wall in front of her split into tiny pinholes of darkness and she could see everything the wall was made of, down to the smallest atom. The darkness grew blacker than the blackest of night as the pinholes swallowed everything in their path as if the wall no longer existed.

Oh my gods.

The nothingness coalesced directly in front of her, terror holding her frozen in place.

"*Fascinating,*" Angwyndith whispered in awe.

"*Fascinating as in cool, look at that, or fascinating as in I'm about to be sucked in?*"

"*Technically, the Void could swallow you, but I do not think that is its intent.*"

Seraphina's mouth dropped open. "*The Void? As in, this is something from the Void phylum, who isn't supposed to be on this planet? That Void?*" Her voice got squeakier with every word, like a Saturday morning cartoon character.

"*Yes, my Host.*"

The Void were mythical beings made of darkness and the gaps between, or at least according to the Grimms' *Compendium of Creatures* Seraphina had read yesterday. It had shocked her when she found out Grimm's fairytales were based on actual events. She had spent one semester in college studying them and hadn't seen it.

The more she studied the Grimm fairytales and interacted with the Magical Community, though, the more she could see the real beings behind the folklore. She just didn't know enough about any of them to recognize which stories they each featured in.

The darkness shifted before her into a large moving mass, somewhat in a shape like hers.

"*Is it trying to be me?*" she whispered, her heart thumping harder than a racehorse running the Kentucky Derby.

"No, my Host. I believe it is mimicking your shape to make you feel more comfortable."

"Uh, not helping."

"I have never met a Void. They do not appear on this world, at least not to my knowledge. All I know is what scant information I have read over the centuries. I do not have a reference point for them in a way that would be helpful."

"Later, when this is over and I'm not dead by black hole, I'm going to crow about that. But that's not what I meant. I meant the Void is seriously freaking me out."

Before she could say more, Seraphina's eyes stretched as if they were trying to eat her face. The Coda's polar energy rushed to them. Images too fast to capture streamed through her brain. Darkness. Starlight. Swarms. Something thrummed in her chest, like the clicks and squeals of dolphins, but different, multi-layered with echoes of deeper noises. They drilled into her worse than the Banshee's scream.

The Void's mass gestured, distorting the bookshelves behind it. Seraphina's brain hurt. The cold bit deep into her bones, and her chest ached. Bombarded from all sides and at all levels, her fingers dug into the seat of her chair as if grounding her to her reality.

Just when she thought her body would implode, a final image appeared of a row of marching creatures with weird masks covering their faces. The masks looked human, but the skin was stretched taut over them, like a thin film from a horror movie.

A deep scream erupted from her. "What the fuck was that?" Her words came out like she was talking through molasses.

The Void shrank back from her.

"Oh gods. I'm sorry. I didn't mean to scare you," she said and then giggled in slow motion. Why was she trying to soothe something that could absorb her in an instant?

It stopped moving and leaned closer. She felt like it was looking right through her, inspecting every atom of her being, digging through her pores down to the cellular level. She stopped breathing, afraid to move.

It stood.

Her legs pushed her off the chair as she stood to face it. But her body wasn't under her control. "Who did that?" she whispered.

The Void swirled around, bowed, and then the ceiling disappeared into darkness and seeped back into being as the Void faded away. The Coda left with it, her face tingling in its wake.

A rush of adrenaline surged through her, leaving her lightheaded. It was almost like the time she took Valium before getting her wisdom teeth removed, but the intensity had been increased to one thousand.

The clamor outside the door heightened.

A voice with a clipped Irish accent behind her said, "That is not something you see every century."

Her head bobbled around to see someone near the back wall. He took a step back when he glimpsed her face.

"Where did you come from?" Seraphina slurred as all hell broke loose behind her.

15

THE CHESS MATCH

(A Game Was Afoot)

Angwyndith cursed as the Void emptied itself into the ceiling of the library. She had asked no questions and hadn't interacted with it at all. The tedium of this time and space challenged her ability to be interested and present in everyday life. Gone were the days of a long ride to their next location, storytelling over the fire, or submersing themselves in a library full of exceptional books.

The Coda lit up the Deep Space Between, the twinkling lights merging until they were all-consuming.

Why did one from The Void visit?

The cold intensified as the lights dimmed.

That is not my mission?

The sparkling around her increased.

I do not understand. If the Void is not the mission, what was the purpose of its visit?

A previous Host's memory book floated down from the shelf and flipped to an image on the last page. The chill nipped at her warmth.

Ah, this is our quarry?

The lights at the top of the ladder winked.

The gollums pictured were relics of the past. But they were not the issue; finding the one who raised them was. Gone were the days indeed. No longer could she rely on the gossip of a messenger in a tavern. How were they to achieve this task when the Child was challenged by a simple ward?

Angwyndith sighed.

The arctic cold snapped at her; the lights shrinking back and then brightening.

I understand. I will find a way.

When the voice spoke from the back of the external space, Angwyndith cursed some more. She failed to note anyone else in the library and it could have cost her Host her life. A Higher Elf leaned against the shelves, their ankles and arms crossed. When the Child faced them, they turned their face away.

Angwyndith chuckled at his fear. The Child still carried the visage from the Coda.

The doors to the library slammed open and boots streamed in.

The Child's head wobbled back around, and she gasped.

That is not normal behavior, even for someone as young as this.

Angwyndith did a fast scan of the Child's body and mind. It was as if the Child had fallen into a vat of mead and drank it until she burst and then tried to navigate a simple dining area. The Void had scrambled her ability to think and reason.

She had no idea why the Child felt the way she did. The Coda communicated directly with the Void; the Child should have been separated from it. But she was not. Angwyndith prepared to take over the Child's body, even though her own stores of energy were fast depleting.

The Child said, "No," her hand flapping in the air around her.

"My Host, you appear to be altered from your interaction with the Void. I suggest you allow me to interact with those in the external space."

"I don't need you," the Child said out loud.

The Shapechanger leading the charge into the library paused and flicked his head. The team behind him fanned out into the room. They now faced six hostile Shapechangers from all sides except one. The one where the Elf stood.

"My Host, please. This is not an ideal situation."

"Duh." The Child squinted at the Shapechangers. "What do you want?"

"It appears something startled them, which led them to break into my library with the finesse of the Dun cow." The High Elf appeared next to the Child.

"Whoa. You're, like, all sparkly. How are you doing that?" The Child's head wobbled forward as she looked closer at the chest of the Elf before her.

The Elf's mouth curved up into a smile.

"Where is it?" A deep male voice demanded somewhere to their left.

"My Host, please. Let me handle this." Angwyndith's warmth slid up the Child's chest and neck.

"No. I got this Angwyndith," the Child slurred as she turned toward the noise. "Where is what? We got a lot of books, and you need to be more spefif... speffific."

The Elf chuckled.

The Child teetered back in his direction, before slopping her head around to face the imminent threat.

"Following a pattern of ward failures, we last had contact with this room at 13:01 hours. It came back online at 13:03 hours. What happened and where is it?"

"Was only a minute? It felt so… long time." The Child stumbled. "Imma need to sit down." She fumbled for the chair and plopped into it, her legs splayed out weirdly.

"My Host, if you will not let me speak for us, then please do NOT tell them something they do not need to know." Angwyndith grew more frantic as she watched the Child sift through memories and comments before pointing at the Shapechanger. *"No, my Host. Do not say that to him."*

"Why not?"

"Speak here, in the Space Between, first. And second, that would cause offense, the likes of which we would not recover from."

"Oh. That wouldn't be good. Everybody already hates me."

Angwyndith's warmth moved into position. The only safe action was to take over the Child and face the consequences later. Her duty demanded it, especially if they wanted to live through this encounter.

"I am sorry, my Host. You leave me with no other option." Her warmth spread out, sinking deep into the Child's physical form, and pushing aside the Child's aethereal body. The Child slapped at her arms.

"Stop it. We didn't agree."

Angwyndith slipped fully into her Host and picked up her head. It wobbled still, which could not be helped. It was not as regal as she would like to appear to the High Elf, but that also could not be helped.

"You will relax your posture and approach us in a more affable manner. There is no danger here." Her voice did not have its usual power due to her depleted energy stores and the Child's distressed body.

"Well, well. What have we here?" The Elf whispered next to them.

Priorities, priorities.

Angwyndith focused on the Shapechanger who spoke last. It killed her to ignore the bigger threat in the room, but the Elf merely observed them.

"Why is he so red?"

"I will answer your questions later, my Host. For now, please just stay quiet."

"Hmph. That's my body. Mine. I'll not stay quiet ever."

Angwyndith bit back her irritation and threw the weight of her anger at the Shapechanger. His aetherial aura turned a deeper shade of red. His control slipped further; she needed to do something drastic, something she did not like to do.

"Archibald Orion Hoyer. You will cease your intimidation practice at once or face the consequences."

"Oooooh, Angwyndith. Hammer down."

Concern rushed through her. It made no sense that the Child's thinking remained tainted by the Void. When Angwyndith assumed control, her symptoms should have cleared.

Angwyndith shifted the Child's body into a position that she could use to drop to the floor and avoid the Shapechanger's inevitable charge. She understood now why there were no stories of the Void on this world; they scrambled the inhabits too greatly.

"Stay," Angwyndith commanded as the Shapechanger shifted his weight to his back foot.

"Uh oh, you shouldn't have said that, Angry Death. They don't like dogs. Being dogs. You know what I mean."

"He is contemplating charging you, which would cause imminent harm and potentially involve the High Elf next to us. It would make a complicated situation infinitely worse. This body is not obeying my commands as it should and so insults are required." Angwyndith

cut her words off, her cadence too like the Child when she babbled.

Coda be damned if she picked up that habit.

"Its 'cause you dint ask permission."

"No, Child, it is because you are afflicted by the Void."

"Oh no. Really? How we fix it?"

"You will do as you are told or I will turn you inside out," the Elf said. "There will be no mauling of anyone in *my* library unless I wish it to be done. Do I make myself clear?"

Angwyndith glanced at the Elf beside them. What was one of his ilk doing here?

The Shapechanger glared, but shifted his stance to standing tall, his arms tucked behind his back. "At ease," he growled at the other Shapechangers. As one, they mimicked his stance.

"That is certainly a more pleasing sight to behold." Irritation crossed the Elf's face. "If I am not mistaken, you have never visited my library, or you would know the rules." He leaned forward. "Explain yourselves."

"He's scary, Ang."

"He is a High Elf, Child. They contain a lot of power. I thought they were all away, in Summerland."

"You thought wrong," the Child said, giggling.

The reason they did not have access to a better class of books became clear. Elves were not known for sharing and their rules for doing so complicated and inane. The Wielder Director of this Facility could not grant her and the Child access to something the Wielder did not herself control.

This would be much harder than she expected, but at least they no longer needed the Wielder to get to the better class of books. One simple being removed, one much more challenging remained.

A spurt of energy infused Angwyndith at the thrill of the chase.

The Shapechanger flinched but held his ground. "I do not report to you, Elf."

"I presume the wards set up in this room, which are quite formidable, alerted you to an issue. Am I correct?" Angwyndith asked to ease the tension.

The foolish Shapechanger's red glowing eyes turned in their direction.

"Control yourself, pup, or I will do it for you," the Elf said, his tone tight enough to cut.

The Shapechanger snarled, his lip twitching upward to show a canine. Rapid footfalls approached the library.

"*Ooooooooooo—they're in trouble now. Big guns is coming.*"

"*How do you know that? You can see who's coming?*"

"*No. I can hear her. Only one person walks like that. Dr. Carruthers.*"

The Wielder walked into the room and paused at the threshold. "What exactly is going on here, Warrant Hoyer?"

"*Told you.*"

The High Elf assumed his previous casual position, but the dark blue-tinged tips of his pointy ears told another tale. He did not like the Wielder either.

Angwyndith could use that.

"Ma'am. At approximately thirteen hundred hours, the wards in the upper part of the building flickered. The threat moved down each of the floors, ending here. At 13:02 the wards in this section of the building ceased to exist, coming back online at 13:03. I assembled my team, and we breached the doors two minutes later. At that point in time, she," his rigid claw pointed at the Child, "eyes as black as pitch and almost as large as her face. I demanded to know what had happened."

"That's what it felt like. My eyes were eating my face," the Child said.

Angwyndith stifled the smile that attempted to escape. *"Hardly, my Host. But they did increase in size."*

"I am aware of the reason for the lockdown, Warrant, as I was the one who ordered it."

"Ma'am, yes, ma'am," Hoyer said as he pulled his arm behind his back again. But the red in his aura increased. The Wielder was unpopular with the Shifter as well.

Interesting.

"And you, Ms. Covington?" The Wielder's hard stare shifted to them.

Angwyndith blinked. How should she handle this?

"Ms. Covington is otherwise indisposed." The aether around the Wielder contracted, and Angwyndith smothered the self-satisfied smile threatening to erupt. "A medical evaluation is recommended when we are finished."

"Angwyndith, I believe you wish to be called?"

"That is correct." Insolent creature. The Wielder knew perfectly well what to call her.

"Ah. Is there a threat needing to be addressed?"

"If there were, I would handle it and you would not be needed at all."

The Elf choked out a laugh.

"And yet, here you are, in my Facility, looking to me for help," the Wielder said.

Angwyndith clenched her Host's teeth. "I merely seek combat training for my Host and knowledge," she dipped her head at the Elf, "for myself. If you choose to call that looking to you for help, you are free to do so."

The Wielder's lips tightened. She had enough intelligence to hear the underlying message: the help being proffered was a pittance.

Pleased with how well she handled the Wielder, Angwyndith faced the Elf. "As you are here, I wish to parlay with you regarding the sections of the library you deny us."

"I did not deny you anything, Bodach. I merely did not give you everything you asked for."

"That may be, but we were promised access to this library."

He waved his hand around. "And you have it."

It was always a game with them. "I do not call the considerably basic information present in these shelves access to the library. I already know most of them and the ones I do not know hold little value."

The Elf raised an eyebrow, the sharp point pulling his rounded eye into a tear shape. "Then you are not looking hard enough. 'How characteristic of your perverse heart that longs only for what happens to be out of reach.'"

The game begins.

"Choderlos de Laclos. I do not need to look hard to see the obvious. 'That reading good books is like engaging in conversation with the most cultivated minds of past centuries who had composed them.' And these are not the finest of books."

"Wait, are you telling me I'm reading bad books?"

Only a potential insult could stir the Child from her stupor.

"No, Child. I am telling him *you are reading bad books. The devil is in the details. We are playing a game for access, and I wish to win."*

"Descartes." He yawned. "Too easy by far. "'Classic'—a book which people praise and don't read.' This portion of the library features the foundation of knowledge, something I fear you lack."

"*Oooo, burn.*" The Child's words came out clearer than before, as if she were more alert.

"Mark Twain. Do try harder to challenge me," Angwyndith said drily.

"*Get him, Angwyndith.*"

"*Hush, Child.*" Angwyndith could feel her warmth sapping. She could not keep this game up much longer and be alert to ensure the Child's safety. "'All our knowledge begins with the senses, proceeds then to the understanding, and ends with reason. There is nothing higher than reason.' Something I fear you lack. Or have you ignored the centuries of knowledge I have attained through experience and not just words? If you reason it through, you will see why I wish to see the books not on display here."

"While this is a fascinating discussion, I have other priorities. If you wish your host to receive medicinal attention, we must see to it now." The Wielder's smooth voice broke into the intimate setting they had created. "I would also like a report on what exactly happened in this library."

Angwyndith and the Elf turned their heads simultaneously, causing at least one of the Shapechangers to step back. "We do not report to you. If there was something you needed to know, we would inform you of such," Angwyndith said, a bite in her tone.

"*Hey, I already said that!*" the Child yelled. "*Whoa. Ang, I'm not feeling great. What's happening?*"

"*You'll soon receive attention to address that, my Host. Give me but one moment to make my point.*"

"Your points usually take at least five minutes of exposition first, so you might want to take a leaf out of my book." The Child chuckled. *"You have all my books. And all my leafs."*

Ignoring the hysterical laughter echoing in the Space Between, Angwyndith focused her gaze on the Wielder.

"And yet, the Facility is under my purview, and something occurred to threaten its safety. I wish to know what it is. Immediately."

The Elf cleared his throat. "Technically, that is not true, Dr. Carruthers. The library is under my purview. I merely allow you access to it. The incident happened in my territory; thus, it is my information to know and to share."

Though not entirely unheard of, Angwyndith had come across an agreement like this before. However, it was unique that an Elf would share its territory with the external world of the Security Forces. What was his game?

Aether gathered around the Wielder like metal to magnets, interrupting Angwyndith's musings about the Elf. Keeping the Child's expression as neutral as her slippery facial features allowed, Angwyndith pushed the Child's body out of the chair into a defensive stance. She'd made a mistake underestimating the Wielder's power. The Wielder had not gained her current position without having significant power.

The Elf shifted to stand more balanced on his feet. His hands hung loosely by his side, not immune to the challenge the Wielder faced either.

When the aether stopped converging, Angwyndith sagged the Child's body against the table behind them. The interactions sapped her waning energy and weakened her ability to remain focused for too long.

"Very well. If you deem it appropriate to share, I would very much like to know the details of what transpired here. Now. I have other places to be. Ms. Covington can make her own way to the med unit down the hall when you are ready to do so." The Wielder pivoted on her heel and clicked out of the library as serenely as she came in. Only the wave of aether hurtling after her gave away her emotions.

The Shifters followed her out in a single line.

Angwyndith shifted her gaze back to the Elf. "Do we have an agreement, then?"

"Immanuel Kant, and yes. I will give you time to explore the library at your leisure. However, in return, you must tell me the story of what occurred here today."

"Do we want to do that? I don't think we want to do that. Do we?" the Child prattled.

"It is the best deal we can make at the present time, my Host. I do not know enough about him to bargain successfully. While I could exchange literary quotes for days, your body is taxed." The Child did not need to know of Angwyndith's fatigue; the Child was distressed enough. Angwyndith flicked a glance at the Elf. "Very well. My Host will provide that information to you verbally once she is fully herself. Shall we say in seven days hence?"

"Done."

"Excellent."

He smiled, displaying a full row of sharp, luminescent teeth.

"I will be returning control back to you, my Host. Do not speak out of turn. Do not mention what occurred here, and do not let your guard down."

The Child tittered.

Coda save us.

The fatigue swamped her waning energy as Angwyndith pulled herself out of the Child's physical form but remained connected to her senses. She may not stop the Child's blathering, but hopefully she could stop her from spilling all their secrets.

Who was she kidding? This was doomed to be a disaster.

16

HEALING, HARMONY, & HEADACHES

(She'd Never Drink Again)

Seraphina oozed back into her body. The room spun, the books blurring together into a patchwork quilt. She stared at the end of her nose, hoping the trick she learned in ballet would work its magic. The dizziness increased.

She switched her focus to the Space Between. Angwyndith still hung around, but she had less warmth than normal. "Are you alright?"

The librarian sent her a quizzical look.

"My Host. For the love of the Coda, please speak to me in the Space Between."

"Sorry."

"You should see the medicinal circle to ensure there is no permanent damage."

Alarmed, Seraphina sat up. She set her elbows on the table and one slipped off the edge. *"Whoops. Permanent damage?"*

"You are not yourself. It is... concerning."

"How long will it last?"

Angwyndith sighed. *"I do not know."*

"Seriously?"

Angwyndith said nothing.

"Seriously. 'kay."

If Angwyndith was at a loss, things were bad.

"Not bad, my Host. Unknown."

Seraphina pushed herself up. Her legs wobbled and then locked into place like a newborn deer.

More of Angwyndith's warmth seeped away.

The Elf straightened and then rapped out, "Caide."

When the little Brownie she met in the cafeteria appeared on the table before her, she gasped and then grinned at him. "Hey there."

The Elf frowned, and the Brownie shrank back.

"Oh no. I didn't mean to scare you. I'm a little punch drunk."

The Brownie sidled away from her.

"I'm sorry." She blinked. "Wait, is Caide your name? Awesome."

"Are you finished?" The Elf asked.

She stared at him, wide eyed. "Are you talking to me?"

"Who else?"

"Did I do something wrong?" She scrunched up her brow. Something squiggled in her memory, something to do with etiquette and rules. Before she could pounce on it, it dissolved into the mist in her brain.

He raised an eyebrow.

Uncertainty held her in place, and she waited for Angwyndith to jump in. When the silence continued, Seraphina said, "I'm finished."

She stumbled to the door and winced when she bounced off the door frame. Keeping her hand on the wall to stay upright, she slid down the hallway to the medicinal unit. As soon as she entered, someone took her elbow and helped her to a table. A familiar-looking Wielder studied her from all angles and then shoved something under her nose.

Seraphina gagged and pushed it away. "I'm not faint, just a little drunk."

"Have you had any alcohol today?" The Wielder asked, her tone drier than Seraphina's mouth.

"No. They don't serve it here." Seraphina frowned, thinking of all the times she could've used a drink since she'd arrived. The room swayed around her. Now was not that time.

The Wielder stepped back to the table. "Then allow me to continue my examination."

"Fine." The cool minty feeling of the Wielder's aether swept over Seraphina's brow.

Angwyndith's warmth swum back to the surface like water spilled on a boat, pooling in one spot, and then oozing away into another as if she was as wobbly as Seraphina. *"My Child, they are examining your aethereal field."*

"Mmmmhmmm. That's what they do."

"What?" The Wielder asked, her head tilted.

"Space Between!" Angwyndith snapped.

Seraphina waved her hand, and the Wielder moved away to a table filled with jarred herbs. *"Sorry. It's how they do it. I think. I sort of remember my aunt doing something like this when Demi poisoned me."* A yawn nearly split her jaw open. *"Don't you know this already?"*

"I do, but I do not know what they will find after the Void's visit."

"You mentioned permanent damage."

"It is a possibility."

Angwyndith's tentative response wasn't comforting, but then neither would it be when Seraphina told her about the Elf. *"Did you catch the whole time I was in the library?"*

"I believe so." Angwyndith's warmth stilled. *"Why do you ask?"*

"I... may have pissed off an Elf." She cringed, waiting for the inevitable explosion.

"What did you do?"

"Wow, that was really clipped. Good diction."

"What. Did. You. Do?"

"I said hello to the Brownie the Elf called. He got mad."

The silence stretched between them. Just as Seraphina was going to ask if she was still there, Angwyndith spoke.

"You interrupted a High Elf when he was speaking to one of his subjects."

"Is that bad?"

Angwyndith sighed. *"It is not good, but not damaging. Did you say anything else?"*

"I don't think so. I thought a few things, but I'm positive I didn't say them out loud."

"My Host, you will be the death of me." Pages fanned in her ribcage as Angwyndith caught up. *"You said nothing out loud that would harm my ability to see what the Elf is hiding. But never interrupt an Elf when they are speaking to someone lesser than them. It is a sign of disrespect."*

"Okay." Seraphina grumbled as the Wielder handed her a cup, the overpowering smell of rotten lemons wafting out of the steam rising off the top of it. *"What's this?"*

"Out there, Child."

"Sorry. What's this?"

"Feverfew tea. It will help with your head. As far as I can tell, there is no permanent damage, but if you could tell me what occurred, it will help me determine that for sure."

"No, Child."

"I know, Angwyndith." She winced at Angwyndith's whispered expletive and the Wielder's flinch. "Sorry, too many conversations going on right now. If you can't see damage, then no damage. I'll just drink this and go get lunch. Second lunch. I'm starving."

The Wielder gave her a hard stare. "We can't be sure without more information, Ms. Lastra. I'd like to run more tests."

Visions of the research lab and Gabriel swished through Seraphina's brain. "No more tests." She gulped down the tea, grimacing when it burned her mouth. "There. Done. I'm good, right?"

"Very well. Keep your secrets, but no one will help you unravel them if you do."

Seraphina had nothing to say to that. No one wanted to help her, anyway.

The Wielder squinted at her for a moment and then shook her head. "You will most likely crash soon. I recommend you don't linger in the cafeteria."

"I never linger in the cafeteria. All those people staring and whispering ruins my appetite." Seraphina sat up, happy the room only smeared in her vision.

The Wielder's eyebrows drew together and then she bowed her head and the memory clicked into place.

Seraphina licked her lips and asked, "Did Tina make it?"

"Tina?"

"The Wielder, Evoker, injured at Eventon. The last time I saw her, she was on a stretcher, and it was not... good."

"I am not at liberty to discuss another patient." The Wielder's jaw clenched. She stepped away to put away the herbs scattered on the counter nearby.

Hope flickered to life. "If she's still a patient, that means she's still alive, right?"

Shoulders stiff, the Wielder nodded once.

"Good. Thanks."

"I'm just doing my job."

Exhaustion crept over Seraphina like a wave on the shore, lapping at whatever energy she had left as she slid to the floor.

As she reached the door, the Wielder put a hand on her arm and then snatched it away as if burned, her brow furrowed. "Just because my initial scan didn't show any damage doesn't mean there isn't any. If your headache increases or your equilibrium remains off, please come see me immediately. "

Seraphina nodded, the room shaking only a little. "Will do. Thanks again."

The Wielder examined her as if she were trying to peer into Seraphina's brain, reminiscent of how Seraphina's aunt used to look at her.

Sadness merged with Seraphina's fatigue. She wanted to talk to her Aunt T, tell her what happened, ask about the healing scan and what it could and couldn't see. But her aunt wouldn't pick up the phone.

She and her secrets were on her own.

***

Seraphina stumbled into the half-empty cafeteria, ignoring the silence and subsequent rush of speaking as she headed to the buffet line. She veered off to get some pizza and then double-backed to get fries and a burger. The tray felt heavier than her trunk as she shuffled to the closest table and flopped into a chair. She shoved food into her mouth as soon as possible.

The call of her room and her bed grew louder than the growling of her stomach, but she kept eating. She rested her head on her free hand to keep it propped up.

Chairs screeched in the quiet cafeteria as the last of the crowds vacated it. She glanced at the clock, catching Teddy's eye as he chatted with another guard near the door.

Teddy caught her eyes and lifted his chin at her. The guard he was talking to said something else and hit him on his arm. Teddy shrugged and ambled over to her table, hitching his belt up as he did. "Hey there. Are you alright?"

She glanced at her plate and shoved the last fry in her mouth, her head bobbing off her hand and almost onto the table. "I'm good." She pushed the chair back with her knees. Grabbing the tray, she wobbled, righted herself, and wandered to the dirty dish bins and trash.

Teddy followed at a slight distance, making no move to touch her even when she stumbled. "I heard you encountered something in the library."

"Yep." She kept moving one foot in front of the other until she stood in front of the cart.

He leaned in. "Everyone's saying it took out all the wards. Is that true?"

She cleared the tray, the dishes crashing into the bin with a clatter that made the throbbing in her head worse. "I have no idea."

He held his hands up. "Just asking. There're all sorts of stories rumbling around the halls today."

A pang of guilt pierced the fog of pain and fatigue. "Sorry. I'm a bit short-tempered right now. I have no idea what happened in the library, or with the librarian."

His eyes widened. "He showed up?"

"Yes. Is that weird?"

"Well, he rarely shows his face, so I'd say yes."

"Huh." Weariness swamped her. She put a hand on the cart to steady herself, the cold metal biting into her skin. "Right. I need to sleep."

"Need some help to get to your room?"

Her first instinct was to say no.

"No, Child. He asks too many questions."

A spike of rebellion rolled through Seraphina. "If you could walk me there so I don't fall over and make an ass of myself, that'd be awesome."

His face lit up. "After you."

"Thanks."

"No problem. What are friends for?"

A group of Wielders walked off the elevator, giving them a wide berth.

"Assholes," Teddy mumbled.

"Don't worry. I'm used to it," Seraphina said as she shuffled inside.

A frown flashed on his face.

She waved her badge at the screen. The doors closed, but the elevator didn't move. "Dammit."

Teddy held out his hand. "Want me to do it?"

"No, I got this, thanks." She waved it slower this time, and the screen lit up. She punched her floor and sagged against the wall.

"Wow. You're really beat, huh?"

"Yeah. I'll be fine tomorrow."

I hope.

"So that thing in the library caused this, then?"

Seraphina closed her eyes. "Something like that."

"What was it?" He whispered the question.

"I don't know," Seraphina said, her tone sharper than her senses.

"Forget I asked. Geez."

"I really don't want to talk about it. My head hurts and I'm exhausted."

"Oh, I get it. I'm just a security guard. Running lockdown drills and checking people in. Why would you tell me?" he said, an old bitterness tainting his tone.

Seraphina sighed and opened her eyes. She really didn't want to deal with this right now. "It's not that."

Mercifully, the doors dinged on her floor. She wandered out and used the wall to keep her upright, conscious of Teddy following her, his anger leaking out with every squeak of his uniform.

Everybody wanted a piece of her today and she had nothing left to give.

At her door, she waved her badge and blocked the keypad with her body as she punched in the code.

"Do you need me to walk you in?"

"Nope. I've got it from here. Thanks for walking me this far." Her lips tugged into a half-smile, but she used her body to block access to her room. "Seriously, thanks. I totally appreciate it."

He grunted. "No problem. Catch you later, dance girl."

She nodded and shut the door on his face. She flopped on the bed and pulled the covers over her as the fatigue overwhelmed her.

This day could not have been weirder.

17

TRAINING MONTAGE

(COMBAT INSTRUCTORS WERE DEMONS)

Seraphina dragged her feet to the gym, a light coating of dread making it harder to get there than normal. She missed all her classes on Friday, including Combat Training. Brutal wouldn't cover whatever torture awaited her within.

She pushed through the doors and halted. Moira grappled with a large Shifter, both slick with sweat. It was like watching a honey badger attacking a bear. Moira flowed and danced around him, moving in to strike and dancing away before he could hammer her with his meaty fist. She squirmed out of a hold that should have held her, wrapped her legs around his ankle, and tripped him. Quicker than Seraphina could see, Moira crawled on top of him and had him in a headlock with her arms and her legs. After he attempted to throw her off, he tapped the mat.

Seraphina clapped; she couldn't help it. "Wow, Moira, that was impressive."

Moira glanced her way, helped her buddy up, and then wiped her face with a towel.

Seraphina's smile faded as the silence grew between them. She swallowed the lump in her throat as she moved closer.

Moira chewed on a protein bar and chugged water. The Shifter she fought stood nearby, wiping his face down with a towel, his posture relaxed but attentive.

"Hey Moira. Sorry about missing Friday's session. I crashed hard after the library incident and woke up three hours past our normal time."

Moira scrutinized her. "You slept past 1400 hours?"

"Yeah. I dragged myself to the cafeteria for food, but otherwise stayed in my room to recover."

"We have a procedure for what to do when you miss a class. You didn't follow it. When I hadn't heard from you, I assumed you were MIA or decided you no longer needed to train." Moira's face remained neutral; her tone wooden.

The air whisked out of her lungs. Seraphina hadn't bothered to check what to do if she couldn't make a class. "No. I still want to train. I still need to train. I can't even take down a fawn at this point."

Moira didn't even glance at her.

The light dread turned to a heavy weight in her stomach. How did she fix this?

Wracking her brain, she recalled a passage in one book about culpability. The exact words slipped from her grasp, but she hoped the gist was enough. "I apologize for failing to follow protocol and informing you I missed class because of an illness. It won't happen again."

Moira tilted her head, her lips tight. "No?"

"No."

"Why are you apologizing for it?"

Half-forgotten lines from the orientation clawed their way to her brain. "Without order, there'd be chaos. Without procedures, nothing would be accomplished. I broke procedure."

"And yet you told the Site Director you didn't need to follow procedures or report to anyone," Moira said.

The other Shifter hadn't moved since they started talking, but the weight of his gaze pressed down on Seraphina.

Resentment buzzed through her. Angwyndith had decided not to share the library incident with anyone, but once again, Seraphina took the hit for it. "I can't tell Dr. Carruthers what she wants to know. I report to someone higher than her."

The other Shifter threw his towel on the bench, disgust plain on his face.

Seraphina's stomach sank. How did she follow the rules while not following the rules? An idea popped into her head. "The Elf made it clear it was his knowledge to know and share, even if I wanted to report it to Dr. Carruthers."

"Eoghan was in the room?" Moira and the Shifter exchanged a glance, their postures suddenly wary.

"Is that his name?" At Moira's nod, Seraphina said, "Yep. I'm pretty fuzzy on when he arrived, though. I wasn't paying attention."

"Rookie mistake," Moira said.

A small spark of hope fired to life. That sounded more like the Moira from before. "Exactly why I need to train."

"So, something happened in the library," the big guy said, ignoring their exchange.

"Yes. And, no, I'm not telling you what."

A small smile crinkled his lips and then he nodded at Moira, "Thanks for the session, Moira. I'll catch you later. I'm going for a run."

"Later, Smalls."

His long strides ate up the distance to the door leading to the patio.

"Smalls?"

"That's his name." Moira shrugged. "You okay to work out?"

"I think so. No ill effects besides a headache and exhaustion."

"Willow, Dr. Liesl, said in her report that you would be, but then she was working on limited data." There was a glint in Moira's eye.

Seraphina grimaced. She hadn't even asked for the name of the Wielder who had healed her on Thursday. "Are we training, Moira?"

"You bet your ass we are. Go get warmed up but make it short. We have to make up for lost time."

Seraphina nodded, grateful one bridge hadn't burned on the pyre of her silence.

***

Exactly an hour and fifteen minutes later, Seraphina jogged on shaky legs to the elevator. Her gratitude for Moira died in the first fifteen minutes of the session, followed by loathing and then raw persistence to survive.

As she cleared the steel doors, voices echoed down the hallway.

"Any word on how the data left the Facility?"

"No. Sawyer's pissed. He's tearing everyone a new one."

The pit in her stomach cramped at the mention of the Master Chief's name.

The elevator dinged. "They better figure it out soon then."

Seraphina picked up her pace. Between the longer training session and stretching, she had no time to shower before class. She thrust out a hand in between the doors to stop them from closing and stepped in. The two guards inched away from her, one of them sneering. She ignored them.

After a quick dash to her classroom, she squeaked into her seat as the clock ticked over the last minute. Some recruits glared over their shoulders at her, but she stared straight ahead. She had every right to be here until they told her otherwise.

The knot in her stomach grew when the person just below her answered a question from Instructor Moynihan. Rather than a random call out, Moynihan had a boulder rolling approach. Every class, he moved through the rows of recruits with his questions. He made it clear that they needed to be prepared for their turn or it will be their turn for the rest of the semester.

She didn't think he was joking.

It was nowhere near her turn last Wednesday. She flipped through the book, desperate to find the code they were talking about. Did she read the wrong one or did they skip around on the day she was out?

Her mouth dry and her palms sweaty, she met Moynihan's gaze.

He opened his mouth.

The room shrunk down to the two of them, and she held her breath.

His gaze flicked to the first row. "Cadet Lunds."

Angwyndith's warmth spread over her stomach and up her chest, warring with the churning of her stomach. Moynihan was a stickler for the rules. He also had sent her away from the gym triage. Had he dismissed her for good?

With a shaky hand, Seraphina wrote down the code section Moynihan asked Lunds about. While she'd made progress with Moira, she didn't have the same relationship with any of the other instructors. If they used her procedural fail to get rid of her once and for all, she'd be on her own.

"*No, you are not, my Host.*"

"*You don't even know what I'm thinking about.*"

"*That is true. I do not know what you think when I am not here. But I can tell you are upset, and that usually equates to you beating yourself up for something outside of your control.*"

Seraphina sighed. She didn't need the armchair therapist Angwyndith was turning out to be. "*This was inside my control. I could have followed procedure and told my instructors I was out sick. I didn't follow them after the library incident, either.*"

"*You are not here to give them information.*"

"*Then why am I here?*"

"*I thought it was self-evident.*"

Seraphina rolled her eyes. Angwyndith could be a pain in the ass. "*Enlighten me anyway.*"

"*I am not the only thing that is a pain.*"

"*Stop reading my thoughts and you won't hear the insults I throw at you.*"

"*Stop throwing insults my way and mayhap I will stay to train you rather than let you muddle about on your own,*" Angwyndith replied, her words as brusque as the threat in them.

"*I think I already am.*" Seraphina glanced at Moynihan.

Angwyndith scoffed. "*They can teach you the basics. I can teach you to master it.*"

"*Then teach away. It's obvious I'm failing everywhere.*"

"*You are not failing at learning, but you are failing to apply yourself properly to the task at hand. You already had the proper information to manage your interaction with the Elf, but you did not recall it and thus almost caused irreparable damage,*" Angwyndith said, exasperation leaking into her tone. "*If you approached your training in the way you approached restoring a book, you would go further with less time."*

Seraphina rubbed her face. Everyone expected her to know what was the most important bit out of the hundreds of information they taught her. It was like a pile of sand; for every shovel she shifted, more came to take its place. *"Restoration uses my hands, not my brain. I think I'm only good at the one thing."*

"How did you learn to restore the books? One step at a time. These creatures can teach you the first step or two. I will teach you the rest. But you must pay attention to what they teach and apply it in your daily life. Practice is the only way to take something foreign and make it your own."

"I know that," Seraphina said, frustration tightening the words into a bite.

"Then apply it."

"It isn't that simple."

"No?"

The word hung in the stillness of the Space Between. It took Seraphina years of practice, study, and memorization to know the materials best for fixing the many issues in the books she restored. And a lot of the hours and classes had been tedious. She had almost quit the program in her second semester, but Ro spurred her on by pointing out how happy Seraphina was when she'd restored her first book.

She sighed. Angwyndith was right. If she'd focused on her studies, she would've known the code Moynihan discussed, even with a missed class. Something she'd already thought about weeks ago and then promptly stopped doing when she got bored.

Moynihan dimmed the lights and discussed a combat approach theory with a real-life event to illustrate it.

"Right then. Stop talking so that I can focus."

Angwyndith's warmth slipped away to pool in her stomach, her satisfaction evident in its quickness.

She couldn't control anyone else's behavior, but she could control her own. And it was time to start doing so.

18

SPIRIT WAS NOT ENOUGH

(She Lost this Round)

Angwyndith awoke in the Deep Space Between, the lights entwined around the ladder winking at her. Any battle worth winning required strategy and preparation. The Elf was a formidable opponent. She had no doubt he would increase their game play and dole out fewer hours in the locked section of the library.

She called the infinite bookshelf to her. Something about his comment on what the library books contained clued her in that he would go after the knowledge he felt she had forgotten. Angwyndith had the knowledge, of course, but studying it would bring it quicker to her fingertips.

She took a moment to revel in her certain success and the deliciousness of reading something with depth and intricate details, before bending her thoughts to the task. She reviewed as many of the early study tomes as she could, mindful the clock was ticking. It would not do to get too absorbed.

Before too long, the lights on the ladder near her blazed. She rose swifter than before up the ladder to the Child, and the Child pounced on her before she'd finished connecting.

"Angwyndith? Good. I need to talk to you."

"Is there an urgent matter I should know about?" Not likely. What the Child considered urgent, Angwyndith did not. How the Child would handle a genuine emergency worried Angwyndith, but they would face that when the time came.

"Yes. No. Sort of."

A rustle of cloth and a squeak gave her the clues Angwyndith needed to connect to the Child's vision. She stepped down a rung and took in the view.

Books and notes littered the bed. Colorful squares stuck to the walls like moss on a tree, random notes scrawled across each one.

"You have *been busy."*

The Child paused and surveyed the room. *"Busy getting nowhere, but yeah."*

Angwyndith could feel the anxiety running through the Child's frame. *"What concerns you, my Host? It has been seven Earth days since our last conversation with the Elf. We are due at the library and should not dally."*

"Yeah, I know. I just finished reading an etiquette book. Elves are seriously uptight about punctuality."

Angwyndith bit back the comment about yet another book on etiquette. At least the Child had increased her education. *"When you can move faster than most eyes can see, you would be as well. Now, what is the issue you wish to discuss?"*

"I've been thinking about my last chat with Demi and the one with Eoghan about to happen. Demi was freaking out about an Elf nearby. At the time, I thought he meant Caide, but now I know he meant the librarian."

Angwyndith doubted the Boobrach's fear was for anything other than his next meal, but knowing the librarian's name could be a boon. *"You think he knows something about the High Elf we can use?"*

"Honestly, no."

At least the Child caught that much about her little friend. *"But?"*

Anxiety regarding their potential tardiness flickered through Angwyndith, the lights on the ladder blinking in a fast-swirling pattern around her.

"Whenever I tell anyone here that I met Eoghan, they freak out. It's unusual that he showed himself. Add to that Demi's concern, and well..."

"You fear there is more to this than appears."

"Yes." The Child's breath rushed out of her, her body sagging with the weight of it.

"I will check to see if the Boobrach had anything of value to say, my Host. One moment." Angwyndith called up the memory, pausing on the specific moments where the Boobrach spoke the Elf's name. It was as she suspected. *"There is no cause for alarm, my Host. All the Boobrach's concerns, as well as everyone else's, are based on the unknown."*

"What do you mean?"

"The Elf is a secretive, yet powerful creature. His domain is the place of knowledge, the heart of the Facility, but they cannot call him when they wish to or know his motives. Secrecy breeds distrust."

"All you do is keep secrets," the Child said, her tone insolent. *"Maybe you should take your own advice."*

"This is not about that." Angwyndith reined her anger in before it got out of hand. The Child lacked the mental capacity for strategy, preferring instead to rush around in a panic, bouncing from topic to topic. This shortcoming, however, was Angwyndith's strength.

"No?" The Child left the words hanging, much like Angwyndith had done in their last conversation.

Most vexing that the Child had learned what Angwyndith had rather she did not. Her temper almost slipped, but she stopped it in time. Speaking of time… *"My Host, proceed to the library. We can continue our conversation along the way."*

"What about Demi? He knows Eoghan." The Child scooped up her ribboned necklace and notebook and walked at a snail's pace toward their destination.

Angwyndith wished to urge her to move faster but refrained. *"I have reviewed the Boobrach's rambling. From the parts that made sense, none of what he mentioned was anything other than typical High Elf behavior. The Boobrach did not give tangible and concrete information. I wonder that you put so much stock in it."*

"I put stock into it because he knows him, Angwyndith. You are so quick to dismiss information that comes from people you deem beneath you. It's freakin' annoying."

"The Boobrach is not beneath me, Child. I view his information from the perception of his hierarchy. He has little if any power within the phylum of The Thought. Thus, any action the High Elf takes would be perceived by the Boobrach as bigger and harsher than any taken by one such as he."

"So, it's Demi's fault the High Elf is a dick?"

"It is the Boobrach's perception of such behavior, not the actual behavior itself." Angwyndith could feel this conversation getting out of hand. The Child needed to understand that not everything was about victims and wrongdoers. Power, ability, and skill went much further than being in this or that group. *"Let me attempt to phrase it another way."*

"Right, because I'm too stupid to understand it in the way you've expressed it."

Angwyndith seethed. *"You prove my point. That is your perception of my words, not my actual words or my intent. The way you perceive the world has added emotional meaning to something that was not meant in that manner."* Anwyndith paused for emphasis. *"I did not call you stupid, nor did I infer it. You did that yourself."*

A heavy silence invaded the Space Between. The Child would try the patience of a tortoise.

The lights on the ladder blazed in a warning flare.

"Let me try again, my Host. What I meant by my statement is this: Eoghan may be cruel, unfair or problematic, or he might act in a way that someone of his station and power acts. It does not make him cruel or unfair, merely a High Elf. The Boobrach could view his actions from a skewed mindset because of the distance between them in rank and power."

"We aren't going to agree on this. An asshole is an asshole, no matter the power dynamics between the two people impacted."

Angwyndith held the comment she wanted to make; it would serve no one, least of all her.

"But I take your point that perception is everything and my perception might be a... tad off," the Child said, picking through her words with care.

"A measure of a person's worth is not by his words alone, my Host. You are so much more than you give yourself credit for."

Angwyndith could feel the Child mulling over her statement; she only hoped the Child heard it as she meant it.

"Thank you for that. I think you're wrong, but it was nice of you to say."

"I do not lie, my Host, nor do I embellish the truth." She also did not tell the Child everything. There was no need to overwhelm her when a simple ward could easily do so.

"Hmmm. Okay." The Child reached the library and wandered through the main doors. *"We're here. Now what?"*

"Now, we negotiate."

The Child stood in the library, shifting her weight from one foot to the other. *"Negotiate what?"*

"More time in the library, my Host. He agreed to a minimal amount of time."

The Elf made no appearance. Angwyndith reconfirmed the terms she and the Elf had discussed and settled to wait. He would appear and they would continue their game.

Angwyndith filled the time by reading from her shelf. The Child wandered over to the books on Elven custom, pulled one down and read. The ticking of the clock echoed in the empty room.

"I don't think he's showing, Angwyndith. Isn't he late?"

"In his eyes, no. He will show," Angwyndith muttered, keeping her thoughts to herself as to what would happen if he did not.

Angwyndith had flipped through three books before the Elf made an appearance. He smiled at them and sauntered to the table where they sat. "I see you have made yourself comfortable." He lifted the book up to see the cover on the front. "Quite comfortable."

The laughter in his voice grated.

"Everyone's gotta start somewhere," the Child said.

The Elf raised an eyebrow.

Angwyndith growled and said, *"Tell him we wish to see the rest of the library."*

"So, I think we had an agreement to see the rest of the library." The Child's heart picked up its pace.

"There was no think, my Host. He agreed."

"Did we? I distinctly recall giving you access to the library. This," he spread his arms wide, "is the library."

"I already had access to this part."

"Yes, I know. And you've put it to such good use, Child."

His condescending tone sent Angwyndith over the deep end. *"Insufferable ego. I am taking control, my Host. I need to speak with him."*

Angwyndith's warmth slipped over the Child's form, but the Child pushed back.

"Why? Because he called me the same thing you did? No. There's no real danger in place, no Bodach duties necessary here."

The warmth pushed further, but the Child's will held it in place. *"You cannot engage with him. He will make a mockery of you. Be reasonable."*

"I am being reasonable. You're annoyed and likely to piss him off. I need this library; you don't. Besides, we had a deal."

The lights on the ladder flared, and an icy breeze ruffled Angwyndith's warmth. The Coda once again interfered with her duties. Angwyndith sighed and withdrew the building warmth. *"Very well. But you must speak to him as I would. I will tell you what to say."*

"Oh-kay."

"Now. I believe we had a deal. Exploration of the library for a tale of a something that should not have been here." Eoghan settled back against the table, a thin veneer of calm settling over his features. And yet, his extremities were tense.

He was more eager for the knowledge than he wanted it to appear. Angwyndith could use that. *"Stick to the deal. He agreed to access to the library you have not yet seen."*

"The deal focused on the part of the library I haven't yet seen," the Child said.

"Did it?" A smile slid across his face but did not reach his eyes. "Tell me the tale and I will show you what you have yet to see."

"What do you want me to say? Or rather, not say."

The Child's tone held a peculiar note Angwyndith had not heard before. She would ferret it out later. *"A bit of something to whet his appetite should do. Tell him you were in the library studying and the lights flickered. That was your only warning."*

"That's not what we agreed. If we want to see the other books, we need to give him what he wants."

"We can interpret our agreement as loosely as he. Tell him only what I said." Angwyndith could feel the Child balking in her thoughts. *"I know what I am about, my Host. Please do as I say."*

The Child cleared her throat. "I was studying during the building lockdown. The lights flickered, the siren wailed, and they locked down the doors. I could hear them clearing the hall."

Eoghan leaned forward. "And then what?"

"And then I saw you and the doors burst open."

"I know. I was there. What I wish to know is what happened in between."

"In between what?" The Child's hands curled into fists, her unease showing.

"Your response was perfect. Stay calm. He cannot harm you."

"You keep saying that, but I don't think that's accurate."

He put his hands on the desk and captured the Child's gaze. "Do not play games with me, Child. You will not like the result."

The Child's heart raced in a frantic rhythm. "I'm not. For one, I'm not good at them. And for another, I imagine you've had a lot more practice."

Pride assailed Angwyndith at her Host's verbal assault of the Elf. *"Good, my Host. Do not let him see your fear."*

His eyelids narrowed to slits. "We had an agreement."

"Tell him we are keeping to the spirit of it. Be clear, my Host. Say 'spirit.'"

"We did. And we are keeping to the spirit of it."

He pulled back as if slapped.

"I don't think he liked that, Angwyndith."

"It matters not what he likes. A bargain is a bargain. Hold firm."

"If that is the way you wish to play it, so be it. You are no longer given access to the part of the library you have explored."

The Child gasped. "You can't do that!"

"Oh, but I can."

The lights twinkled in an accelerating pattern, mimicking the thoughts rushing through Angwyndith. If she were not careful, they would lose all access to the library. *"Use the agreement with this Facility."*

"I have a deal with Dr. Carruthers that includes the library."

"And yet you told her the last time you spoke you do not report to her. Those words would nullify any agreement between you."

The Coda be damned.

He boxed them in tighter than the plot of a Grimm fairytale. It had been longer than she cared to admit when she had last tussled with a High Elf. Mayhap she had overestimated her abilities.

"Angwyndith? Is he correct about that?"

"Mayhap," Angwyndith bit out, ignoring her Host's panic.

"Mayhap? Mayhap I just lost access to the one room that filled in years of training because you went toe to toe with him?"

Positive this was the first round and more games would follow, Angwyndith said, *"Hush, Child. Let him win this round."*

"There won't be any other rounds. He owns the library," the Child wailed as her brain spun into high gear, fear of not learning what she needed to swamping her thoughts..

"This is a game we play, the High Elf and I. We will gain back access to the library in our next conversation."

"I can't wait that long, Angry Death."

Angwyndith's irritation at losing this round to the Elf and that horrid nickname increased tenfold. Before she could respond, a glacial wind knocked her down the ladder. She fought the Coda as she crawled back up, clinging to its rungs with all her might. Orbs of light dove toward her, like sparrows protecting their nest.

Her behavior had not warranted such an assault. Anger swirled from the darkness within her, giving her the strength to remain connected. Through the howling wind, she heard the Child speak.

"The agreement we reached was written, not verbal. According to Code section 4214.f of *The Policies for Polite Interaction*, 'it is binding even if a verbal amendment occurs at a later date. The verbal agreement must be amended in writing in order to be binding.'"

However did the Child get from spinning in place to this? It was almost masterful. The wind stopped and Angwyndith hung from the ladder, her warmth all but spent. The lights settled back into their normal rhythm as the cold departed as fast as it had arrived.

The Elf remained as still as a statue, and then a smile curled the corner of his lip. "Bravo, human. For that argument, you win access to the most basic, I believe that was the word the Bodach used, of books in this library. Pay close attention." He waved his hand. The shelves glowed a light purple, the spines on the books lighting up as each one was touched. "You can only access the books you just saw. Any other attempt to touch books not from that selection will result in a very painful experience."

The Child stared at the shelves, attempting to memorize each one.

"I will have it in my memory books, my Host. There is no need to fret," Angwyndith said, fatigue slowing her words. The books he chose were even more basic than what the Child had been studying previously.

"Says the one who doesn't need the books on the other shelves."

"Is that clear?" the Elf asked.

Angwyndith felt the anger licking along the Child's veins. *"Do not give in to your anger. You'll put us in a worse position."*

"Worse than the one you've put us in?" Sarcasm dripped from the Child's tone.

Angwyndith bit back the statement on the tip of her consciousness. She wanted to eviscerate them both, but it would get her nowhere.

"Crystal. You've made your position so clear, I'd have to be an idiot to miss it."

How dare the Child intimate such a thing! A Bodach was no idiot.

"Excellent. Enjoy your studying."

"I will." The Child grinned at him with all her teeth, much like a snarling dog.

Angwyndith railed in the Space Between.

The arctic air returned, circling around Angwyndith's form, pressing closer and closer, until it almost smothered her. A book flew from the infinite shelf and opened before her. Her words to the Child sparkled from the page.

I understand. I am not perceiving this correctly.

The cold blanket squeezed for a moment and then sighed away as if it had never been.

Much like her victory this day.

19

RESULTS & REVERBERATIONS

(SHE WAS ON HER OWN)

The scratch of a pen on paper filled the otherwise silent library, the noise fueling the anxiety riding Seraphina like a half-swollen tick. Without the books, she'd be lost. She had a tenth of the knowledge everyone else had. The books doubled that, and Angwyndith had just thrown them away as if they were nothing.

Seraphina's mind spiraled on the disaster they'd made of their time at the SF. Dr. Carruthers had wiped her hands of them, the instructors didn't care if she even showed up, and now they couldn't access the books in the library she needed. Add to that the snickers and hostility from everyone else, and they were totally screwed.

She bent over the table and wrote faster.

"We are not in the position in which you place us. We still have the upper hand, my Host. I have already captured the books you have access to in my memory. There is no need to capture them on paper as well."

If Angwyndith had lips, she'd be sticking the bottom one out. Seraphina shook the cramp out of her hand as she scanned the still glowing books. *"What happens when you're not around?*

What happens when what I need to do doesn't suit your wishes? This list is for both times." Seraphina frowned at the paper. It was as if Eoghan knew what books she needed and chose the ones right next to them.

"Yes, my Host. That is exactly what he did," Angwyndith said, her tone taut. *"And I will share my memories with you whenever you need them."*

"And yet, Angwyndith, you never do."

"That is incorrect, my Host."

"Fine. You've given me insights on what different Elves are named or how certain powers work, but the actual knowledge needed to interact with them? Nada. You always say knowledge is power and today proved that to me. And yet you hoard it like a bee hoards pollen."

"You have had no need for all the information I hold," Angwyndith snapped.

"I need to understand wards. I need to understand how the phyla are connected and the proper etiquette when talking to them. Gods, I need to understand why the Magical Community is separate and divided. There are so many things I never learned that I took for granted." Seraphina scooped up her notes and headed back to her room. *"I'm not doing that anymore."*

"I have already said I will provide you with the knowledge you lack."

"Great, because there are books in my room that may or may not need to be sent back to the library without me touching them. And I need to know if that's the case and how to accomplish that without telling anyone what happened." Seraphina's anxiety swept out of her, leaving her as deflated as a balloon after a party.

Angwyndith only sighed in response.

"I'll take that as a yes," Seraphina said as she walked up the stairs to her floor.

Once in her room, she scanned the books on the bed. None of them glowed, but neither did any of the books in the library anymore, so what did that prove? *"Angwyndith, can I touch these books?"*

Warm tingles swam up her neck to her head and face, pooling behind her eyes. The dust motes floating in the air sparkled as everything came alive. Seraphina focused her gaze first on the stack of books on her desk. The bottommost book about Elf origins and customs glowed.

"Strike one. What an ass."

Angwyndith said nothing. Seraphina turned her gaze to the books scattered on her bed. The book on basic Ward magic also glowed.

"Dammit."

"You have completed your study of that book, my Host. And I can explain the concepts you failed to capture."

"Right. So how do I get it off my bed without touching it?" Once again, silence met her question. *"Angwyndith, stop pouting and help me."*

"This is a logistical problem that will encourage a deeper under-standing of puzzles. I will not give you the answer."

She walked right into that one. Too exhausted to spar with Angwyndith, Seraphina said, *"Fine. I'll figure it out myself later. If that's all you got, you can go do whatever it is you normally do when you're not here hovering."* That may have been too close to a go away, which she was trying not to say to Angry Death. *"I'm going to study for tomorrow's class and work on another book for Finn, so nothing exciting for you to pay attention to if you had better things to do."*

"Very well, my Host. I have a few things I need to research."
"Awesome."

Angwyndith's warmth oozed away, like a sad kid crawling into bed and huddling under a blanket.

Seraphina sat down at the desk, determined to cram more of the code section into her brain. At least she learned something: don't negotiate with Elves.

***

In the cafeteria a few hours later, her stomach as full as her brain, Seraphina cleared away the mess from dinner and headed over to fill her mug with coffee and grab a candy bar. Studying was as appealing as the dried-out apple slices near the trail mix, but she'd still not caught up to the others in her class. Between her and the doors, Caide wiped up a large puddle of spilled soda.

Indecision warred within. The last time she spoke to him, he didn't seem to like it. Her toe tapped the floor. But he did like to clean.

She crouched down next to him and almost lost her balance, dropping her candy bar and spilling coffee on her hand. Caide lifted his head, his eyes wide. His gaze shifted to her hand.

"Hi, Caide." She sucked the coffee from her hand and then wiped it on her sweatpants. His eyes followed every move. "Wow, if I studied half as hard as you cleaned, I'd be much further along."

He glanced at her from the corner of her eye.

"I hope you didn't get into any trouble with Eoghan because of me."

He shook his head, his mop once again eradicating the stain.

"Good." Envy at his dedication swirled through her like a fall wind. "You must be why this place is so clean. It looks great."

He blinked at her.

"When my friend Demi does that, I assume that's a yes." His brow furrowed. "Sorry. My friend Demi is a Boobrach. I grew up with him, or rather I grew up and he remained the same."

Caide's mouth dropped open. He chittered at her hesitantly. It took Seraphina a moment to decipher it, his accent having more of a twang than Demi's.

"Yes, he's my friend. He comes in and out whenever he feels like it, but he always cheers me up and he has helped me in the past."

Caide stood with his hand on his mop.

She couldn't tell from his face what he was thinking. "Caide, are you able to return a few books for me to the library?"

He shrugged.

"I have some books in my room that I... uh, can't return. If I point them out to you, could you take them back?"

He blinked again.

"Right. I'm taking that as a yes. I'll meet you in my room whenever you're ready, okay?" She smiled at him as gently as possible. He seemed a lot more skittish than Demi, but then Demi believed reckless bravery was a positive trait.

The mop moved around the floor in the rhythmic pattern once again; if he hadn't nodded, Seraphina wouldn't have known he had heard her.

"Good. I am most appreciative of your assistance." From the books she read, saying thank you to an Elf had more connotations than a nod in a silent monk's sanctuary. And she was not looking to be beholden to an Elf, even if he was harmless.

One problem solved, so many to go. She grabbed the candy bar as she stood and turned to leave, but Teddy blocked the way.

"Hey!" she said.

He grunted.

She shifted to one hip and took a sip of coffee, weighing his mood.

He leaned to the left and looked at Caide for a moment. The expression on his face reminded her of her uncle's when they had to have a serious talk about Shifters. He motioned her away from the mess.

She followed him, her eyebrows scrunched. "Is something wrong, Teddy?"

"You've been spending time with that wisp," he said, the muscles in his jaw twitching.

"Wisp?" That word rang a bell, and not a good one.

"The Sylph."

Seraphina glared at him. "You're going to have to be more explicit."

"Red-haired chick. Human form."

"Sorcha? She's a Sylph?" Her glare morphed into a grin. "How cool is that? I never thought I'd meet a Sylph." Sylphs were of The Motion but were air-based instead of water-based. Having never met one the whole time she'd hung out with Ro, she'd assumed they kept themselves separate from everyone. Her smile faded as the pressure from his gaze grew heavier. "What's the problem?"

"You already pissed off a bunch of people you shouldn't have. Messing around with her won't fix that."

Stung, Seraphina snapped back, "I'm aware of my situation."

He leaned forward. "Are you?"

As the pressure from his stare eased, irritation spiked within her and she shifted her gaze to his forehead. "What's your deal with Sorcha?"

"She's trouble. You don't want to get mixed up in it."

"Mixed up in what? What are you talking about?"

"She's not as innocent as she looks. For your own good, keep your distance." He tapped the Slándála patch on his arm. "I know things you don't."

She frowned. "Like what?"

"Nothing I can share. She's just not someone you want to know in this place."

Sorcha couldn't settle long enough to hide anything and, besides, Seraphina enjoyed hanging with Sorcha. "Uh, okay," Seraphina said as she rolled her eyes.

Teddy's shoulders got wider—a clear sign of Shifter aggression. "You calling me a liar?"

Seraphina took a step back, fear warring with anger. "No."

"Good, because I ain't one."

"I never said you were, Teddy," she said, keeping her voice low and even. When his posture didn't change, she added, "I'll keep your warning in mind."

"I'm just trying to look out for you, you know. That's what friends do, right?"

"Right." Except friends didn't intimidate each other.

He blinked, and the weight of his gaze eased. His shoulders, however, remained where they were. "You can't be too careful around here."

She took a sip of coffee to wet her now dry mouth and forced herself to smile. "I know. Thanks for the heads up. I'll be careful."

He shook his head and ambled off.

Sorcha was a walking, talking brochure for the SF, completely harmless except for her swinging moods. His paranoia had twisted her into something she wasn't. Unless... She squinted at his back, her brain in overdrive. His slip of calling Sorcha a wisp and Sorcha's comments about separate phyla suddenly made more sense.

Or did it? Was he being a speciest? Or was there more to his warning?

20

POLITICS & POWER

(SHE HATED FABLES)

The hall lights flickered to life in front of her as Seraphina traversed the empty corridor, her reflection smeared in the darkened room doors as she passed. Her backpack thumped her butt in rhythm with her steps, but no song accompanied the beat. She'd stuffed her brain full of lists, codes, and history yesterday, as part of the new topic schedule she'd crafted, and it hadn't come back online yet.

After a long argument with Angwyndith as to which books on Eoghan's allowed list were worth Seraphina's time, they'd carved out a small selection of history, philosophy, and essential aethereal mechanics books. What Angwyndith didn't know was that Seraphina planned to read all the books on Eoghan's list. She'd only debated about it with Angwyndith to pull Angwyndith out of her sulky funk.

The Mythology of Origins was the book on her study schedule for today. According to Angwyndith, the book was supposed to be the Magical Community's equivalent of the Big Bang theory and the Bible, all rolled into one. If Seraphina knew how the phyla came to be, and what their philosophical differences were, maybe it would shine a light on whatever was going on in this Facility.

A door creaked behind her and the hairs on the back of her neck stood up. Her heart in her throat, Seraphina whipped around. "Who's there?" Her words reverberated down the hall and met only the whispers of a sound.

She leaned forward, her breath caught in her throat. The gleam of the stairwell door caught her eye, and she glimpsed the furry foot of a Shifter disappearing into the stairs before the door clicked shut. She closed her eyes to slow her breathing. Just a Shifter going about their business.

She hated Sundays at the Facility. Too much silence and not enough people. It was as if they all had some place better to be. She wished she could say the same. She'd rather be anywhere else but the library again.

Duty called, though. The book she needed was in there, among a few others. She'd been surprised at the variety of books she had access to. Maybe Eoghan wasn't as evil as Angwyndith thought. Or maybe he wanted her to think that.

She shook her head and finished walking to the library. Paranoia was Teddy's gig, not hers.

While the visual effects of Eoghan's magic no longer lingered on the two sets of bookshelves he'd marked, her memory supplied it for her. She set the backpack on the chair and ambled over to it. Her finger slid down the spines of the first set, feeling the ridges of the old leather as she moved from book to book.

As she brushed by a shelf, icy fingers slithered up her spine and down her arm. A book near her hip vibrated, rocking from side to side. Heart thumping, she leaped toward the wiggling book and pulled it off the shelf. She wrapped her arms around it and backpedaled until she hit the nearest table, her eyes glued to the books.

When the cold evaporated as if it had never existed, her shoulders slouched. Two book muggings in her life were enough; she didn't need another one, especially not here. Why was it *always* the library? It was as if the Coda didn't want her to like books. Or libraries.

With a quick glance around, she set the trembling book on the table. She placed her body in front of it, her hand near the cover so that it looked like she turned the pages. She had no idea if people knew about this part of being a Host: that books yearned to share their knowledge with her so much, they opened themselves up to her.

She rolled her eyes. If she only relied on Angwyndith for knowledge, who had tighter lips than a mob boss, Seraphina wouldn't know anything. Maybe that was why the Coda showed up.

The pages slowed and rocked to a halt. She scanned the title of the chapter and groaned. Of course, it was a fable. The memory of the last fable she'd studied burned, and she squirmed to get away from it. The book, however, wiggled closer.

Resigned, she plopped in a chair and pulled the book toward her. After reading it twice, she sat back. Why was the Coda showing her *The Hunter and the Hart*? She wasn't a deer, and she wasn't vain. Most days, she avoided looking in the mirror, let alone admiring herself in it. Besides, would the Coda even care about her vanity?

She wrote a few words in her notebook and then pushed the text away, disgusted by how little she got from it. What else could it mean, though?

When nothing more came to mind, she slammed the book shut, marched over to the bookshelf, and shoved it back in its original slot. Right next to it was the book she was looking for. Groaning, she slid it out.

She examined the *Mythology's* cover. Its soft leather showed years of handling in the few places where the outer layer had worn off near the spine, but the cover still felt smooth to the touch. She opened it up and flipped through the initial pages, her eyes skimming past the staining around the edges of the paper.

The first entry was the simple, yet elegant, origin of the world mythos based on the Mother of them all, the Creator, and her spawning all twelve phyla from her own light. Based on the almost page-long footnotes attached to the story, scholars of all ages had fought over whether it was real, just like humans did about religion, the moon landing, whether the Earth was round, and anything else the brain could say was false. Humans were simple, but then so was the MC, if this origin story was anything to go by.

She turned the page and came upon the details about the phyla, their myths, and quirks. Bending her head down, she began to read.

***

Two hours later, Seraphina's notebook was stuffed with notes, arrows, and scribbles, and she'd barely scratched the surface. All the little comments she'd heard in Merricott, from Ro, and from within the Facility made sense. It was as if she found the code she needed to make the connections between the phyla light up like a Christmas tree.

Or, in their case, strings of dynamite.

The phyla made US and world politics look like child's play, and that included the top four who weren't even players on the board. Or at least one of them wasn't until a few days ago when the darkness that was the Void ate the world in front of her.

Before it could take root, Seraphina shoved the memory away from her like a bad dream. Maybe the Void did her a favor by showing her there were uglier things out there than the Guide who killed her family. Or maybe her brain would crack open like an egg from all the terrifying things she would see. Being the Host of the Bodach didn't just give her an annoying companion, it also opened her up to facing down all the things that went bump in the night. Had she known then what she knew now, she would've left the Big Top Tent and never returned.

No Angwyndith, no Judging, no Coda. She imagined her life, free of all responsibilities besides work, dating, and what to wear to the bar on Friday night. The visual died like a broken movie projector, fading from view before it even got started. Seraphina couldn't have escaped Angwyndith, even if she'd run to the other side of the planet.

At least now, she could learn as much as she could about the Community she was born into like any other member. Unless Angry Death played yet another game with the Elf and lost. Distaste curled her lips.

Games. It was all games to them. Including the Guides.

Her hand clenched around her pen as she thought about the Guide trapped in her grandfather's ring. She'd wished she'd never met him. She wished her grandfather hadn't either but wishes changed nothing. They'd still be dead, no matter what she did. Sean Harriman proved that. All his efforts to save the Wielders would've doomed them instead.

The clock's ticking broke through her miasma of darkness. Piling her notebook on top of the *Mythology* book, she slung her backpack over her shoulder and strode out. She had just enough time to get a daily mission done before she met Sorcha in the cafeteria for another gaming session. She couldn't get behind on something Sorcha counted on her doing, not after their last interaction. Seraphina didn't want to give Sorcha any other reason to torch their budding friendship.

Gods knew Seraphina could do that on her own.

21

MOOD SHIFTS & MINDGAMES

(They Always Blamed Her)

The acrid smell of fried fish turned Seraphina's stomach as she scanned the faces of the people who had just entered the cafeteria. Their muffled laughter told her what she needed to know. She checked the time again and refreshed the intranet messaging system for the third time since she sat down.

Nothing.

Her chest tightened, and she clenched her teeth to keep the anxiety from showing. Maybe someone told Sorcha to stay away from her as well. It *had* been a few days since Seraphina's conversation with Teddy, and she and Sorcha hadn't spoken since. But then that was the norm for them. Set a time, meet up, set a new time.

Except for today.

Seraphina looked around the cafeteria again. A Shifter at a nearby table glanced her way, his expression hard to pin down. She dropped her gaze, the pain in her chest twisting. Something was wrong.

She scrolled through the news and tips on the intranet, but nothing popped up. A quick check of the MC news sites told her the same thing: a plea from a Wielder whose daughter was missing, an accident at a lab, and a minor cave-in near a Dwarf settlement splashed along the tabloid-like headlines that fooled the most clueless of humans.

It had fooled her too until Ro had said they were genuine stories hidden in plain sight. But then it didn't take much to fool Seraphina; all her interactions in the Facility proved that. She'd give Sorcha ten more minutes. Seraphina didn't feel so exposed when it was the two of them sitting together.

Fifteen minutes later, she slammed her laptop closed, feeling like a third grader at a birthday party where no one showed up and everyone else noticed. The chair screeched across the floor as she stood, and heads whipped around to stare at her. Heat rushed up her neck, and she muttered, "Sorry," as she walked out of the cafeteria with quick steps.

With her head down, she almost bumped into Sorcha in the hall, but Sorcha put her hands up at the last minute.

Seraphina rocked back on the heels of her Converse. Some of the tightness eased. "Hey! I thought we said five."

Strands of Sorcha's normally perfect hair stuck out of her braid in all directions. Her face was paler than normal, and her eyes were the fiery blue of blown glass.

Seraphina's smile slid off her face like a cooked egg in a non-stick pan. "What's up?"

People walked past and glared at them.

Sorcha flinched, her fingers fiddling with the edge of her sleeve. "Do you want to go to the diner?" she mumbled.

Seraphina kept her face as neutral as possible, instantly back to when she was nine and standing in front of her grandfather's desk, waiting for the blow to fall. "Sure. I just need to grab my purse."

"Can you drive us both? The car I normally use isn't mine, and she..." Sorcha stumbled to a halt, tightening her lips. "I don't have a car today."

"Of course. My room is down a level."

"Can we take the stairs?"

Alarm bells shrieked out a warning as Seraphina half-jogged to the stairs. This was more than just a few words from Teddy. She unlocked her door and hunted around for her car keys. Sorcha leaned against the open door, her silence spurring Seraphina on.

"Keys, keys. Where are my keys?"

"They're not at the front desk?"

"Nope." As she swished the blanket out of the way, one of the sticky notes with a rune on it fluttered to the floor. Seraphina picked it up, her lips pursed, and then stuck it back to where it belonged.

Sorcha made a strangled noise.

Seraphina's forehead scrunched up. "What? Leaving my keys was optional and I opted not to give them back. I like have control over my things."

"Sure." Sorcha's gaze skidded away from Seraphina's and bounced around the room, finally settling on the book rack. "Is that your work, then?"

"Yeah. This one's almost ready to be shipped out." Seraphina rifled through the debris on her desk for her car keys. The sooner she found them, the sooner they could leave.

"Why's it in that contraption?"

"It needed a new spine, so I've clamped it in position so that it curves the right way. The glue's almost dry. I'll mail it off tomorrow."

"Who do you mail it to?"

"I told you, my client. He owns the bookstore in my hometown. Aha!" Seraphina held her keys up.

"You ready to go?" Sorcha nodded. "Let's hit it then."

Sorcha turned as if made of wood and stumbled out of the way.

Seraphina hoped she'd tell her what was wrong on the way to the diner. Otherwise, the day was going to be long and torturous as Seraphina danced and sang to keep the conversation rolling. She shut the door and set the lock. It beeped three times.

Sorcha started, her eyes wide.

"One sec," Seraphina said. "I've got to reset the password again. I swear, it feels like an everyday occurrence around here."

Sorcha kept her distance, but Seraphina could feel her watching. Feeling weird, she angled her body to block her fingers as she keyed in the new lock code. When she'd first arrived, her escort had explained the additional key code was to give the inhabitants their privacy and to enter the room if a power failure occurred. He'd said that the SF would never enter their rooms without their consent.

Seraphina had snorted at that. She had no doubt her room had been entered at least once while she was away by the way her things had been moved around. Unless it was Caide, just cleaning, but she doubted he'd move her stuff around.

She frowned at the turn of her thoughts as she set the lock. Sorcha's mood, Teddy's warning, and the looks they were getting were rubbing off on her. After the three beeps repeated itself, Seraphina peeped at Sorcha and her stomach tightened. Sorcha studied her like Ro had, that one time in high school when Ro thought Seraphina had stolen her paper and claimed it as her own. "Are you okay, Sorcha?"

"Fine. Can we go?"

"Sure."

Feeling an urgency she didn't understand, Seraphina strode to the elevator, punching the button several times.

Sorcha trailed behind her like a sad puppy, her head down.

When the elevator arrived and was empty, Seraphina sighed in relief. They rode in silence to the lobby, which followed like a bad stain out to the parking lot.

"This is me." Seraphina indicated the Rover with her hand. She unlocked the door and leaned over to unlock the passenger side.

Sorcha climbed in and buckled her seat belt, her eyes roaming across the dashboard and ancient radio with its push button channels. "I wish I owned a car."

"I don't own it. My aunt lent it to me to drive down here because... well, reasons." Seraphina started the Rover and jammed it in reverse. She really didn't want to get into her family drama right now. Once on the open road, she glanced over at Sorcha and asked, "Are you okay?"

Sorcha rolled the window down and let the wind rush over her face. The cold seeped into Seraphina's jeans, her hair tickling her nose in the breeze. A pregnant silence filled the car, the only sound the rush of wind through the window, smelling of old dirt and the change to fall.

"Could you stop?" Sorcha said, the urgency in her voice making Seraphina jump.

"What?"

"The car. Stop here please."

Seraphina pulled over. Sorcha jumped out of the truck, slammed the door behind her and ran into the woods.

Seraphina drummed her fingers on the steering wheel. Was she screaming? Did she need time alone? Distinctly remembering her own pacing back and forth after Eventon, she sat back and waited. When twenty minutes had passed and Sorcha had not returned, Seraphina got out to see what was going on.

Leaves crunched under her feet as she wove her way into the forest. She found Sorcha sitting on a tree stump, her hair standing on end, the energy in her eyes almost electric. "What's wrong, Sorcha?"

Sorcha jumped up and paced in the clearing. "What's wrong? They interrogated me. For hours. Me! That's what's wrong."

"What? Who interrogated you?"

"Sawbones Sawyer. The Director of Security," Sorcha spit out.

Visions of the friendly 'chat' she had had with him flashed across Seraphina's mind. "Why?"

"Because they think I'm behind the leaks. Because they think I'm betraying the Community." Blue-tinged tears leaked down Sorcha's face and she wiped them away with her wrist.

The whispers and snatches of conversation clicked into place. "Oh. That's what everyone had been whispering about."

"What did you think they were talking about?"

Seraphina bit her lip. "Me and the library."

"Gods, it's not all about you, Seraphina. Real lives are on the line here."

A pinch of pain hit Seraphina just below her ribcage. "I didn't know my life wasn't real."

"That's... Fuck." Sorcha turned her face up to the darkening sky. "That's not what I meant. I meant the leaks are endangering real people. Community people."

"Obviously." Seraphina wrangled with her temper. This wasn't about her. Or humans. Who weren't real. "Okay, so why do they think you're involved?"

"I'm not one of them."

Seraphina tilted her head, frowning. "One of who?"

"A Shifter."

"That can't be the only reason. I'm not one of them and they aren't looking at me."

Sorcha's gaze veered away to the trees before settling on the dead leaves near her foot, which she stirred with her toe.

The anger turned to dread. "Sorcha?"

"I have access to the information that has been leaked." Sorcha bit her lip. "It's not me. I wouldn't do that. I would never do that. But I have access. And I leave campus. Just to go to the diner, but it's enough. And then..." Her voice trailed off.

"And then what?"

Sorcha sucked in her cheeks and held Seraphina's gaze.

The penny dropped, along with Seraphina's stomach. Sawyer had pulled her in for an informational interview after she'd left the Facility for the first time. She winced, remembering his words to tell him when she interacted with someone new. Which she hadn't done. "You've been talking to me. At the diner."

"Yes," Sorcha whispered.

The glares and the whispers that followed Seraphina down the hall, the guards that always seemed to lurk nearby, made sense now. Not to mention that weird couple at the diner.

"He didn't mean the truck," Seraphina whispered. "He meant information. Well, fuck a duck."

"What?"

A rush of fear smothered the air coming to Seraphina's lungs. "Nothing. Nuances and splinters." Sorcha's brow furrowed and Seraphina waved it away, understanding Angwyndith more than she ever had. "A conversation I had with... it doesn't matter. I had nothing to do with it. I don't even know what *it* is. But of course, they're focused on me. The one time I'd rather it not be about me..." Her voice trailed off as the leaves stirred in the wind.

A bitter chuckle escaped from Sorcha, and she shook her head. "Sorry. It's not funny."

"It kind of is." Except for the part where the SF thought she had something to do with whatever "it" was. She needed to talk to Angwyndith ASAP. And she needed to update Sawyer on the people she'd been talking to.

Was Teddy a part of it, too? No. He warned her about Sorcha, not the other way around. She groaned. Every interaction she'd ever had after talking to Sawyer took on a new darkness. Was it all to catch her doing something she wasn't doing?

"Angwyndith!" she yelled into the Space Between.

The seed of doubt started by Teddy in the cafeteria blossomed into a small plant, and Seraphina kept her eyes peeled on Sorcha's face. "If going to the diner with me is a problem, why did you suggest it after they just finished questioning you?"

"I needed to get out. I needed to leave. They hear everything there." Sorcha's face fell, and she pressed her fingers into her forehead. "Manaan! What did I just do? I didn't think. I'm sorry. Fuck, this is bad. This is really bad."

Seraphina studied her expression. It seemed real, but then what did she know about Sorcha? Nothing. A chilly breeze ruffled Seraphina's hair, and she shivered. "Yeah, it is. For both of us."

Where the hell was Angwyndith? She was always around when Seraphina didn't need her and wasn't present when she did.

"No. You don't get it. I like what I do, but it's more than that. I need this job. *My family* needs this job, Seraphina. They all rely on me. I don't have aunts who have cars to lend me, even if they're ancient as Rome."

"Have some respect," Seraphina snapped. "That truck was my uncle's. My aunt only lent it to me because she couldn't face sitting in it after he died."

"At least you have that much. Do you know what I got from grandmother, who used to be a pillar in the Community? Nothing. They took everything from us based on a rumor. A rumor someone else started. And now here I am, repeating history because of *you*."

Anger licked along Seraphina's veins, almost smothering the fear. "So let me get this straight. It's *my* fault you have nothing? It's *my* fault they pulled you in for questioning? Because I just met you. And I'm beginning to wish I hadn't."

"That's not what I meant. Stop taking everything so literally!"

"Stop being such a bitch and maybe I will," Seraphina yelled back.

"Gods!" Sorcha screamed, the sound echoing off the trees. "Everything's such a mess." Her face crumpled, and she covered it with her hands, her shoulders heaving with her sobs.

Emotions stretched and twisted between them, pulling Seraphina down in their spiral. She sat on the tree stump and put her head in her hand. Sorcha's sobs died out in hiccups and stalls, much like their friendship just did.

"I'm sorry," Sorcha said from behind her hands. "They woke me from a deep sleep and dragged me to a holding cell where they grilled me for hours. It freaked me out, and I took it out on you." She dropped her hands and stared at Seraphina across the space between them.

What seemed like a small clearing suddenly felt like the Grand Canyon, so deep was the trench. Seraphina had no idea how to move forward. "I'd say it's okay, but it's really not."

"It's not?" Sorcha wiped her face with her sleeve.

"No. But does it matter?" Seraphina sighed. "They could be waiting to drag me back to the Facility as we speak."

"I'm sure they'll just want to talk to you. Be honest. Tell them what you know."

"It'll be a quick conversation, because I know nothing. About anything." Seraphina shook her head. "Your family isn't the only one tarred with a dark brush. We may have money, but we don't have much else. And any time there's something bad going down, all eyes look to the Lastras. Even here I can't escape my family name. Maybe we really are cursed."

"What do we do now?"

"Well, we can't go to the diner anymore, can we?" Her one escape, now barred to her.

Sorcha winced but didn't disagree.

"So, I guess I take you back to the Facility and wait for them to come for me. Or go to them." Seraphina shook her head again, her mouth tight. "Angwyndith's going to love this."

"Angwyndith? The..."

"Bodach. Yeah. Her. Yes, we talk. No, I'm not going to tell you what we talk about because I can't and because I don't want to. She was right. About all of it." Seraphina kicked a clump of dirt. "Dammit. I think that's the worst part."

A little brown paw landed on Seraphina's leg, and Sorcha screamed.

22

FRENEMIES

(It Was Never How It Looked)

A hiss and a rattling of spikes erupted next to Seraphina as Demi went into full warrior mode. She jumped up and stepped in front of him, her heart pounding as she faced six feet of seething Sorcha hovering over the ground.

"Stop. He's a friend. He's harmless." Seraphina put her hands out in front of her without thinking. Swearing, she dropped into the defense posture Moira taught her. "While I can't take you on, I'll give it my best shot. You do not get to attack him."

"What is that?" Sorcha bit out from between white lips.

"*Who*. He's not a what. And he is Demi."

Demi hissed again, yelling at Seraphina to get out of the way.

"No, Demi. She is, was, a friend. You just freaked her out."

Sorcha cackled and sank to the ground. "Seriously? I don't think I can take anymore."

Demi let loose a stream of curses and insults, poking Seraphina in the back of the leg with his spear.

"Ouch. Dammit, Demi, I'm trying to protect you. Stop poking me." She rubbed the spot he hit and moved to the side to avoid any more.

He cursed her out and showed all his teeth, comparing her to the rabbits he ate for breakfast.

"Right. That's enough!"

He snapped his mouth shut and stood tall, his eyes blinking at her.

"You just called me a rabbit, Demi. I am not a rabbit." Seraphina sunk back down on the log; her legs shaky. "I'm officially over this day."

Sorcha laughed, a wild note whipping around at the end. "Of course, you're friends with an Elf." Her breath caught as her mouth shaped the perfect O. "An Elf outside the system."

"What?" Seraphina's head snapped up.

"You have someone on the outside. Does Sawyer know about him?"

"No. And he's not going to know."

Sorcha took a step back, her hand near her throat.

"Sorry, that came out more threatening than I meant it to. He's a friend. Who hunts moles and rabbits. He's harmless. They don't need to know about him. Especially not if it'll alert Eoghan to his presence."

Demi launched into a full tirade about how he wasn't harmless since he could break their wards.

"Demi, shut up. You've not done any of that."

He hissed at her, the outrage clear on his face.

"Okay, okay. You have broken wards in the past, but you haven't broken these wards."

Sorcha sucked in a deep breath. "I thought I was wrong... He can break wards? And he knows who's inside? Oh my gods. You *are* involved." She turned and bolted through the trees, moving faster than Seraphina could track her.

"No. Sorcha!" Seraphina yelled, the full impact of what just happened hitting her harder than a Mack truck. "Fuck," Seraphina screamed before she ran toward the Rover. She needed to get back to the Facility and stop Sorcha from telling them about Demi.

Angwyndith's warmth slipped up her stomach and pooled in her throat. Demi kept pace, blinking in and out of existence.

"Where have you been?" Seraphina asked.

"You appear distressed, my Host."

"Too much. Check the book." Seraphina vaulted over fallen logs, her muscles burning. The whipping of pages mirrored her labored breathing.

"This is not good."

"You think?" Seraphina made it to the Rover and scrambled to get inside.

Demi flashed in on the passenger seat beside her, pointing his spear at the Facility.

"No, Demi. You can't come. It's already messed up. She'll tell them about you and they'll hunt you down. You need to go as far away as possible."

He growled and stamped his spear.

"He appears quite firm in coming with you."

"They'll capture him and torture him. Or worse—give him to Eoghan."

Angwyndith hummed a little.

"You are not seriously suggesting what I think you're suggesting."

"The Boobrach hinders you with his brash behavior. Mayhap it would be good were he to be otherwise occupied."

Anger unfurled inside her. "He. Is. My. Friend. Unlike you or Sorcha, I don't abandon my friends."

"I do not have friends to abandon, so that is a moot point. Besides, the friends you claim to have are not as much your friends as you think."

"What are you talking about?" Seraphina was sick of everyone telling her what she didn't know and yet accusing her of things she did know, which she legitimately didn't know. Her head hurt.

Angwyndith hummed again.

"I don't have time for this right now," she snarled at Angwyndith before focusing back on Demi and the one thing she did know. "We can't risk you running into Eoghan. Go home, Demi. Now."

Demi blinked at her and then his spikes drooped.

"I'm sorry, but this adventure is mine alone to walk. You understand, don't you?"

He nodded and her heart dropped.

Demi's spear disappeared, and he hopped up on the window ledge Sorcha left open. "I'll see you soon. Maybe tomorrow?" Her voice broke a little on the last word.

He wagged his tongue at her and hopped down. She waved at him, tears prickling the back of her eyes.

Seraphina started the Rover and swung a U-turn, heading back to the Facility. She had an urge to put her foot down and drive past it, never to return. But pretty much everything she owned was in that building, including Finn's books. She shook her head and slowed to turn into the gate. Sawyer was a smart guy; maybe Sorcha was wrong.

She swiped her badge, but the gate remained down. The guard facing her stared hard in her direction and then picked up a phone. A trickle of dread slipped into her stomach. Could Sorcha have made it back already?

"You cannot ignore this conversation, my Host."

"I'm not."

"Your actions would say otherwise."

Seraphina checked her rearview mirror. The second guard stepped out of the guardhouse and stood in front of the barrier to leave the Facility.

"Not everything is about you, Angwyndith. Something's up."

Angwyndith's warmth swirled up her neck. *"What do you mean?"*

"My badge normally opens the gate, no drama. This time, it took a call and the guard to open it. And then one of them left their little hut and blocked the exit."

"They are on high alert due to the security breach. I am sure it is nothing. The Sylph could not have made it back this quickly."

The guard at the gate waved Seraphina through and she drove forward. Ahead, from the front of the building, three security guards stepped down the stairs, moving methodically toward the parking lot. Her heart hammered in her chest and the urge to throw the truck into reverse and squeal out of here grew.

Everything was replaceable.

"No, my Host. That will only convince them they were right."

Her hands clenched on the steering wheel, but she pulled into her usual spot and reached over to roll up the passenger side window. When she sat up, she faced the guards. One of them stood in front of the car and the other behind, effectively blocking her in. The other peered at her through the driver's side window.

"Think it's nothing now?"

Seraphina's hand remained on the steering wheel as she faced down the guard at the front. He had a scar that ran across his cheek into his hairline. It looked nasty and had to have been caused by something that even their Shifter metabolism or a Wielder couldn't heal. The knock on her window made her jump.

"Seraphina Lastra?" The guard's voice carried through the glass.

"Covington," she replied automatically. Swallowing hard, she turned to face him.

"Can you step out of the car and come with us, please?"

She licked her lips. "What's going on?"

"Step out of the car, ma'am."

Scar guy hulked up.

She glanced in the rearview mirror and saw the rear guard do the same.

Shit.

They saw her as a threat. If they'd only stop to listen, they'd see she feared them.

"That is why they are afraid, my Host. Creatures who react from places of fear are unpredictable. With me here as well, they do not know what they face."

"I have to get out, don't I?"

"I will be here and will ensure your safety."

Some of her fear eased. Seraphina had a master negotiator with her, after all. The fear rushed back as she thought of the time with Eoghan.

"This will be different, my Host. They are not ancient, they are not wise, and they do not know with whom they engage." Angwyndith's voice increased in severity with every word.

"I'm going to grab my bag and step out of the truck, okay?" Seraphina said to the guard nearest her.

"Hand me your keys first."

Oh gods, no.

"No. I'm keeping my keys." They locked gazes. At the last moment, Seraphina shifted her glance to between his eyebrows. She could feel the compulsion stare hitting her face, like bits of gravel sprayed from the road.

"You are doing fine. Stay courteous."

Seraphina took the keys out and held them up. He nodded curtly. She reached behind her for her bag and slipped the keys inside. As soon as she pushed the door open and slid to the ground, the emptiness of keeping the keys hit her. Her one act of rebellion to the rules was meaningless. If they wanted her keys, they would've just taken them.

Angwyndith's warmth covered Seraphina's head like a soft blanket. *"Stay calm, my Host."*

Seraphina slipped her bag over her shoulder and the guard nearest her stepped back when she exited. He gestured toward the Facility.

She walked forward, suddenly grateful for all the moments she'd had to ignore stares in the building, because she needed that superpower now. Anyone walking past stopped, moved to the side, and ogled her.

Breathing through her nose to stay calm, she sailed through the lobby to the elevator. The doors opened before they arrived. She gripped her bag strap a little tighter and stepped inside, her heart hammering inside her chest.

Standing at the back with one guard next to her and the other two standing sideways, their eyes on her, she had a panicked thought. They could kill her and no one would know. Ro would eventually notice, as would Finn, but what could either of them do about it?

"They will not kill you. Stay focused on your breathing."

"They could, though, Angwyndith. No Judgment glory to stop them."

"I would stop them." Angwyndith's voice boomed in her head. The guards' eyes shifted toward her.

"I think they heard that."

"No, they did not. They may have felt it, though."

"You sound pissed, Angwyndith." Seraphina pushed her hair behind her ear. The guard next to her twitched in response.

"I am not. I am merely aggrieved in the manner in which we are being treated."

The elevator doors swooshed open. They had not stopped on any other floors like they normally would have. She swallowed, Sorcha's freakout making a lot more sense. "Where are we going?"

Scar guard gestured to his right. They walked down a similar hall to the other floors, except no scientists wandered the halls. Guards appeared everywhere, some in full battle gear, others in half. They were all Shifters, who paused and watched them walk by. She only recognized one, Smalls, the guy who fought Moira.

He glanced at her and then back down at the paperwork in his hands, his muscles bunching in his jaw. Her fear overwhelmed her faster than Angwyndith's warmth, and she found it hard to breathe.

"Deep breathe in, deep breathe out," Angwyndith coached.

"I'm scared."

"I know. But this is just a conversation, nothing more."

The pressure built up in her chest, and she couldn't contain it any longer. She blew out a deep breath before it suffocated her, even if it gave away her anxiety.

Window guard glanced at her but said nothing.

"You guys must practice being intimidating," she said, trying to lighten her mood. No one said a word. "Uh, you're doing a great job at it."

"In here, please, Ms. Lastra," the window guard said, gesturing to a bare room with a table and three chairs.

"Covington," she said.

"Have a seat and put your bag on the table."

"What's this about?"

"Have a seat and put your bag on the table, please."

She sat in the single seat and lifted her bag over her head. After she placed it on the table, Scar guard took a position in the corner and the others filed out.

An omnipresent silence filled the room and Seraphina's knee bounced a staccato rhythm on the floor.

Oh gods.

23

THE INTERROGATION

(It Wasn't Her)

The longer Seraphina sat still, the quicker her pulse raced. She tried to distract herself by studying the room, but it was a gray concrete box. No sounds beyond her own broke the silence; not even the overhead lights hummed.

"How do we handle this?"

"You answer their questions but divulge nothing. If they ask you what you had for breakfast, you say what you ate and stop there. No conversation about how good the food was or how you could use a cup of coffee right now."

"You make me sound like a blathering idiot." Her hands cold, Seraphina slid them under her thighs.

"No, my Host, but you babble when nervous."

"You know that's pretty much the definition of blathering idiot, right?"

"Technically no, but mayhap my words were ill chosen."

Sawyer stepped in, wearing a simple black shirt and cargo shorts. He sat opposite her and set the folder and the tablet he carried down, each one square with the table's edge.

She met his eyes, remembering at the last minute to look between his eyebrows.

"Ms. Lastra, I would like to ask you a few questions." His voice was neutral, like a doctor to a patient.

"Do not correct him, my Host. He will use it against you."

She tried to smile, but it came out as a grimace. "Fire away."

"You arrived at the Facility on June twenty-fourth of this year, correct?"

"Yes."

"And your purpose for coming here was?"

She blinked. "To receive training from the SF so that we may collaborate in the future. We've been through this before."

"You have spoken with him before?" Angwyndith asked.

"Yes." The fluttering of fanning pages tickled her diaphragm.

"You should have mentioned that, Child," Angwyndith said, her voice tight with irritation.

"It was a nothing conversation. Besides, you should've paid more attention."

"Hmph."

The fanning continued. *"What are you looking for?"*

"Everything that has happened before we arrived at this room."

"It'll be a short read then."

"I am aware," Sawyer said, "but I want to be sure nothing has changed. And that training consisted of?"

"Combat training. Classes with the other recruits on codes, etiquette and history."

"Excellent." He opened the folder, which contained a few pieces of paper she couldn't read and a notepad and pen. "What else have you done during your visit?"

"Dr. Pianail did some testing on me. It hurt." She waited to see if he responded to that like he did from their first conversation. He didn't. Her stomach clenched tighter.

"How else did you spend your time?"

Seraphina frowned. "I ate in the cafeteria. I used the gym a few times outside of combat training for ballet."

"Anything else?"

"*What is he looking for?*"

"*Something specific. We do not know what it is.*" Angwyndith sounded perplexed.

Glad she wasn't the only one confused, Seraphina asked, "Like what?"

"Any other activities besides what you've already told me?"

"I studied in the library." The knot writhed in her stomach. "I went into town."

"You've left the Facility then?" At her nod, he continued, "When was the first time?"

She braced herself, her fingers curling into fists. "Before we last spoke."

"And what did you do in town?"

"I went to the diner and had pie and ice cream."

Sawyer scanned his notes and then flicked his eyes at her, his expression indiscernible.

"*He already knew that.*"

"*He did indeed.*"

The dread returned, heavier than before, and the increased tempo of her bouncing leg shook the table. Seraphina placed a hand on her knee, and it stilled.

Sawyer's lips twitched. "What else do you do?"

"I don't know. I spend a lot of time in my room."

"What do you do in your room?"

"Read, chat with a friend, play video games, restore books."

He raised an eyebrow. "What games do you play?"

"Only one. *The Last Centauri.* It's a space game."

"And what friend do you chat with?"

"Roslynn Griffiths."

Scar guy stiffened.

"That got a reaction."

"I told you, my Host. The Griffiths are more than they appear to you."

"And the books you restore?"

"What about them?" she said, exasperated.

He waved his hand. "What exactly do you do to restore them?"

"I take old books, fix the broken pages, give them new spines if I can't save the old ones, clean up the covers, reattach pages to spines, etc. I gave you this information during our first interview."

He pretended not to hear her, his head down as he wrote a few more notes.

"He is testing you. Stay calm and just answer his questions."

Frustrated, Seraphina ignored Angwyndith's advice. "But you knew I'd be doing that. Not only because it's in my agreement, but because you inspected the books when they arrived."

"We only inspected them. At no point was it mentioned you'd be restoring them until our last conversation." He shuffled the paper in the folder and then pinned her with his gaze. "What happens to the books you restore?"

"I send them to my customer, who may or may not send a few new ones to me to restore."

"And this customer is?"

There was no way she would give up Finn. She'd already gotten him in hot water once. "What difference does it make?"

"My Host."

"I am merely looking to get the complete picture. It doesn't matter. I can check with the mailroom."

Seraphina slumped in defeat. "Finn Hanes, owner of Roget's bookstore in Merricott."

"The Magical Community in New Hampshire?"

"Yes."

His pen tapped a list in front of him, the sound echoing like a shot with each one. "We have here that you've shipped out seven books since you have arrived. Is that correct?"

She mentally counted the books she'd finished. "Yes."

"Excellent." He consulted his notes again. "During our first meeting, I instructed you to inform me of any new connections in the Facility. Do you recall those instructions?"

"Yes." Seraphina bit her lip.

"Have you made any new connections, Ms. Lastra?"

"Sort of. Eoghan, the librarian, Caide, well, I'd run into him before, but I wouldn't say I interacted much with him. One of the security guards, Teddy. I don't know his last name."

"Teddy doesn't give me much to go on but noted." Sawyer searched through the papers before him and then jotted something down in his neat script. "Anyone else?"

Her mouth drier than a ball of cotton, she said, "And Sorcha, the one I play the game with."

"Did you inform me of these new connections?"

"I screwed up, Angwyndith. I should've told him all of this."

"Did he ask you to?"

"Yes."

"Hmmm. Then why didn't you?"

Seraphina answered Angwyndith's question to Sawyer. "I didn't think it was a big deal."

"You signed a contract with the Security Forces of the Free Folk for training and education, correct?"

"Yes."

"During your first day of class, did you also agree to an oath to uphold the rules and regulations of said Facility?"

Seraphina squirmed in her chair. She'd forgotten about that. "Yes."

"You mentioned you had classes on codes, regulations, and etiquette, correct?"

"Yes."

"Where the rules of proper conduct were discussed?" His words whipped her, every syllable landing hard upon her shoulders.

"Yes."

"And yet you thought a direct order from a senior officer was something you could disregard." His nostrils flared. "Do I have *that* correct, Cadet?"

"Yes," she whispered.

"I cannot hear you, Cadet. Do I have that correct?"

Every instinct screamed at her to curl into herself, but she clenched her teeth and zeroed in on the space between his eyebrows. "Yes."

Her response hung suspended between them, the air taut.

After a moment, he dropped his gaze to the paper before him as if reminding himself where they were. "This Sorcha you mentioned, that would be Sorcha Morgan, correct?"

"I don't know." The words got stuck in her throat and she swallowed to clear it. "We didn't exchange last names."

"You are doing fine, my Host."

"I'm surprised you're not crowing about his technique," Seraphina said, her voice tinged with bitterness.

"You have enough to distress you. I did not want to add to it."

The words took the bite off Seraphina's failure, but it still burned deep inside her.

"What did you exchange?" Sawyer asked.

"Nothing. We play video games together."

He glanced up at her. "She's given you nothing?"

"She gave me the name of the game and showed me how to play it." Her knee began its frenzied bouncing again. She let it.

"That is all?"

"Yes."

"Where did you first meet?"

"At the diner."

"How did that occur?"

Fear she would mess up again crippled her. *"Angwyndith, do I tell him what happened? That I just saw her there to only mention the first meeting?"*

"He most likely already knows when the first encounter occurred, my Host. Just answer his questions, but nothing more."

"She recommended a dish the first time I was there. The second time, she asked to join me at the table." That sounded bad when she put it like that. Did Sorcha use her as a shield?

"I do not think so, my Host."

"But you aren't sure."

"No."

The word dropped between them along with Seraphina's heart.

"Have you met in the Facility?"

"Yes."

"Where?"

"The cafeteria on her breaks."

His eyes scanned her face. "What did you discuss?"

"The game. TV shows." Seraphina pressed her tongue against her front teeth to stop from saying politics and the SF. Sorcha had shut that conversation down before it had even begun, so he didn't need to know about it.

A kernel of hope kindled inside her. Maybe Sorcha hadn't sold her out.

"How often did you meet?"

"A few times."

"And this afternoon?"

His tone slid under her skin, and she lifted her chin. "This afternoon? Yes. We met at the cafeteria, but she wanted to go out."

"And?"

"We ended up leaving the Facility to go to the diner."

"Did you enjoy your pie?"

She didn't know how to answer this question—either way implicated Sorcha and her.

"Keep to the point. Only answer what he asked."

"No."

He stared at her. She blinked back at him and wondered if this was why Demi blinked at her. To avoid telling her anything important.

Oh gods.

"What if Sorcha told him about Demi?"

"I do not think she could have made it back before you to do so. Nor has any new information arrived to indicate that she had."

"You spoke with no one else?"

Her leg jiggled faster. How did she keep him safe? He wouldn't like it here and Eoghan would eat him for breakfast. "No."

Sawyer picked up the tablet. He scrolled and then stopped, his gaze narrowing.

"He has a tablet." Seraphina's stomach sank. *"They could've messaged him the information."*

"That may be true. Or it may very well be a ruse. For such a subtle and controlled Shifter, his movements were dramatic."

"Is that the entire picture then?"

"It's not much of a picture because there isn't one to paint," Seraphina said. "I wake up, study, train, restore books, occasionally go into town, and go to sleep to do it all again. That's it, the sum total of my life." Her life was pathetic. Bleakness stole over her, and she sighed.

"I apologize if I upset you, Ms. Lastra. These are routine questions." A smile tugged at his lips.

"No. Your first set of questions were routine. These are definitely not." She sat back and crossed her arms.

"As you may have heard from people who do not know how to keep their mouths shut." His eyes glowed as his control slipped. "There have been a few security breaches and I am simply determining where they are coming from."

"I have no idea what the breaches are about, and I don't have access to anything that could be breached, so why are you talking to me?"

"Ms. Morgan indicated you know more than you are saying."

Bile surged in her stomach, snuffing out the kernel of hope. Her one friend had pushed her under the bus.

"If I understand that idiom correctly, he may be fishing. She may have said nothing."

"Did you read what happened in the woods?"

Pages fanned in her midriff, her stomach tightening to the point she felt her intestines might pop under the pressure.

"Ah. That is not good, but also not completely bad either."

"Ms. Morgan was incorrect. I know nothing. How could I do whatever it is that's happening here?"

"People are more ingenuous than they let on," he said.

"Not me. What you see is what you get."

"Really? And your conversations with the Bodach? Or the fact we were not told you would be restoring books while you were here? And the incident in the library, of which there is no record? Do you consider that to be us seeing what we get? Because from all accounts, no one received any information from those moments."

"Damn. He boxed me in."

"He did indeed." After a pause, Angwyndith said softly. *"I wish to take over this conversation. He is now encroaching on my territory."*

"I thought we were a team."

"We are, but I am more versed in these types of conversations."

"Fine. Take over. Let me tell him what's about to happen." She pressed her lips and said to Sawyer, "Angwyndith would like to speak to you."

Neither Shifter moved.

"The Bodach?" He frowned at his pad.

"Yes. The Bodach."

"Very well. Do you need a minute?"

Seraphina shook her head. Angwyndith's warmth slid up over her form, feeling more comfortable every time she did it. *"Go get him, Angwyndith."*

She closed her eyes and allowed it to happen.

24

BUREAUCRACY & BLUNDERS

(She Had Failed)

Angwyndith lifted the Child's head and concentrated her gaze on the Shapechanger opposite. His controlled aether field and the little movement in it told her what she needed to know. Not only was he good at what he did, he was also efficient at it.

"You spoke of me and so here I am."

"You do scary well, Angwyndith."

"Thank you." It never hurt to make them think their whispers brought her to life.

"Ms. Lastra spoke, not I. I merely asked a question about the information being withheld from the Facility. Information that may endanger everyone in it." No fear leaked through his voice or displayed in his aether field.

"Oh gods. He's not afraid of you. That is not good," the Child said, fear returning once more to her voice.

"He is a master at hiding his feelings. Do not be so quick to judge him unmoved," Angwyndith said, quelling the doubt that rose at the Child's words. While the Shapechanger across from them may have been unimpressed, the one in the corner was not so contained. The room reeked of his fear and his position had changed.

The lights in the Space Between blazed for a beat and then subsided. She did not need the Coda to tell her she needed to tread carefully. "Technically, that is true. But that is not what you wish to speak about, technicalities. Am I correct?"

He smiled. "No. It is not."

"What do you wish to know?"

"You and Ms. Lastra have had an encounter on this base of which we have no record. You have also had interactions with Eoghan of the High Vale. I wish to know what occurred during both instances."

"For someone hiding their fear, he sure is being nice to you," the Child said sardonically.

"It is called respect, my Host. You may want to learn what it looks like."

The Child snorted.

Angwyndith ignored the noise and chose to demonstrate one of her favorite interrogation tools in the hope the Child would learn from it, however unlikely that may be. "Can you not inquire of the High Elf that which you seek of those moments? He was also present and is more ingrained in the workings of this Facility."

His lips twitched. "We could, but he is even less forthcoming than you or Ms. Lastra."

"I can see how that is a problem for you. Had we known a High Elf ran the library, we may not have been so quick to agree to come to the Security Force domain."

"Wait, what? You only pushed it for the books?"

"You needed instruction, and I thought they would give it to you. I was mistaken on that point." Angwyndith paused to see if the Child would take offense at that. When nothing was forthcom-

ing, she continued, *"The books were an added benefit for me, on which I also was mistaken. But they do not need to know any of that."*

The Shapechanger said, "I had nothing to do with your negotiations of the contract, so I cannot speak to that." He glanced at his file. "Back to the issue at hand. On Thursday, October fourteenth, at approximately 13:02 hours, the wards of the floors above and in the library failed. What can you tell me about the incident?"

"Do you not have a full report from the team of Shapechangers in your employ?"

"I do. The team could not discern the reason, nor were there traces as to what caused the wards to fail."

"Fascinating. That is certainly a mystery," Angwyndith murmured as she pounced on the new information. She could think of no other creature who could remove and reinstate matter and aether as it passed through them, although her interaction with the higher phyla was limited.

She longed to scour the infinite bookshelf for any reference she may have overlooked but could not accede control back to the Child at this moment. Angwyndith did not want to show the Shapechanger the impact of his statement. "I do not see what our account of that incident would achieve. We did not interact with the wards, and they were reinstated seconds later, were they not?"

"The wards are the only alarm system we have. While we can and do use electronic devices and alarms, the never-ending high frequency whine that emits from them is distracting to most of the Facility's guards. If the wards fail, the health of everyone in this Facility is at risk." The muscles in his jaw clenched.

Finally a weakness she could work with. "There was no breach of your Facility nor of the measures in place to protect it. To that I can attest with certainty."

"While I appreciate your attestation, I only have your assurance and no other corroborating evidence to back it up."

He impressed her with his restraint and lack of tells; however, he did not impress her when he failed to respect her word. In any other century, they would be accepted as truth. That they were not galled her. "My word should be enough."

He shuffled the paper around in front of him, glancing at a line or two and then restacking the pile. Disgust rolled through Angwyndith at his obvious stalling tactic, but she stamped down on it. It would serve no purpose to antagonize him. Besides, she could control herself as well as the creature before her.

He pulled out a sheet and set it on top of the pile. "According to my team's report, and I quote, 'Ms. Covington's eyes were as black as pitch and almost as large as her face.'" His gaze bored into them. "What can you tell me about that?"

Angwyndith twitched her Host's lips up into a supercilious smile. "Nothing, as it does not concern you or this Facility."

His lips parted and showed the tips of his teeth.

She was not impressed. She had seen sharper teeth in Dullahan's severed head.

"That is for me to judge," the Shapechanger said.

"Angwyndith, maybe you should tell him something, like the Coda came by," the Child said, the fluttering of her pulse increasing.

"No. If I give him anything about that moment, he will use it to pry further."

"He already is."

The Child, as usual, failed to see the bigger picture. "There is nothing for you to *judge*." He should not forget to whom he spoke. "The wards did not fail; your security remained intact. The incident, as you call it, caused no harm."

"And yet, that is not enough. Not for me, nor for the people to whom I report, and most importantly, not for the safety of this Facility."

"Be that as it may, I cannot give you that which you seek."

His jaw clenched. "Very well. Let us move on to your interaction with the Librarian. I have a detailed report of your conversation from that day, October fourteenth, but I understand there was a second altercation," he checked his notes and then glanced up at them again, "a week later on October twenty-first. What was discussed?"

Her respect for him took another hit. Why must he continue playing games with them? He knew very well the dates on which they spoke. "Nothing more than what was promised in the original discussion on the fourteenth of October."

"And that was?"

"Is it not in your notes?" Not even his eyes twitched. Angwyndith shifted tactics. "Very well. We negotiated for more time in the library."

"As part of your agreement with the Facility, you already had acquired unfettered access to the library. What other access did you need?" He clasped his hands in front of him on the desk.

"What's the big deal, Angwyndith? Tell him what he wants to know."

"The big deal, as you so quaintly call it, is that they do not need to become aware that there is a secondary library to which they have no access or knowledge."

"I'm sure they know, or at least Carruthers' knows, about the books Eoghan doesn't put on show." The Child's tone was drier than the sands in the desert.

Irritation zipped through Angwyndith, inflaming the anger she held at bay. *"Oh? And how do you know that? Did you learn that in your little books?"*

"No," the Child snapped. *"It's a military organization. They want to know everything that happens in their walls, or they will figure it out if they don't."*

"Yes, they would. Would they not ask questions like the ones being put before us to do so?"

Considering the matter closed, Angwyndith returned to the external conversation. "It is of no matter. We did not receive it. Yet." Exasperation with the Child and the situation sharpened her tone more than she would have preferred. When the Shapechanger snuffed out a smile before it began, she knew he interpreted it as a weakness.

"If you share what it is you seek, I may be able to intervene on your behalf."

As if this Shapechanger would have any more luck with the High Elf than she. The very idea incensed her. "Thank you, but that is unnecessary."

"Let us move on to the next set of questions, then."

"I have nothing more of note to tell you."

"That is obvious," he murmured.

"He's playing you, Angwyndith," the Child said, adding injury to the insult.

"I am aware of what he is doing."

"Doesn't look like it to me."

The sting of the Child's words hit harder than Angwyndith expected, too close on the heels of previous statements to be ignored. *"You can barely understand the most basic of magic, Child. What you see and what you know are too vastly different things."*

"And you are not as great at negotiation as you think, Angry Death. Eoghan walked rings around you and Sawyer's doing the same. Maybe you should train more."

How dare the Child tell her what to do? *"I do not need training, Child. I AM the trainer."*

"Are you? You could've fooled me."

"That is not hard to do."

The Coda nibbled at her warmth, the lights dizzying her in their patterns, and Angwyndith struggled to maintain her position on the ladder. Leaving the conversation at this junction would cause irreparable damage. Mayhap mollifying the Child would ease the Coda's attack. *"I apologize, my Host. That was not a nice thing to say."*

The movement of the lights slowed as the Coda ceased its incursion.

"And yet, you don't deny its truth," the Child said.

Angwyndith could not lie to her; she chose silence to answer in her stead.

"That's what I thought." Bitterness darker than the coffee the Child drank flavored her words.

Having nothing to say in response, Angwyndith replayed the last part of the conversation with the Shapechanger. The Space Between worked differently with time. They could not have spent hours conversing, but a few minutes passed quicker here than out in the external space. It gave them an edge in battles and to strategize before engaging. She rarely needed to re-consult the track of the external conversation, however.

"Forgive me for asking," the Shapechanger said, "but as I am unfamiliar with how much information is shared between you and Ms. Lastra, let us start with the most basic of questions. What do you know of the security breach?"

Misgivings assailed her, much like the dancing lights of the Coda. It was as if he knew they had been conversing, but that was not possible. She studied him but saw nothing amiss. Choosing to dismiss him and her insecurities at the same time, she said, "Only that you failed to contain it."

"Angwyndith, stop," the Child wailed.

"It will be contained. Of that you can be certain." His fingertips pressed together hard enough to turn his knuckles white. "Do you have any knowledge you wish to share on the matter?"

"I do not know to what the matter pertains."

"I find that hard to believe." His voice took on an edge.

A lick of anger slipped from her grasp as he once again refused to believe her, but she wrestled it into submission as she composed her reply. Replaying what he had just uttered, she heard what he did not want her to—she was not the only one who struggled. Mayhap he would be unbalanced enough to tell her what she needed to know.

"Do you?" Angwyndith twitched the Child's lips up in an attempt at a smile. "Tell me what has been stolen and I can tell you if we have seen anything that would help."

His movement stilled as his mouth opened, the words hovering on his lips. The silence hung suspended between them, heady with the unknown. Flush with the rush of success, Angwyndith leaned the Child's body forward.

With a snap, he closed his mouth, and the spell broke. "That is not the way this works. I am not the one on trial." He straightened the already pristine pile of papers in front of him, his controlled mask slipping back into place as he did so. "I ask the questions and you answer them."

Angwyndith cursed herself for telegraphing her intent. An icy breeze snapped at her in the Space Between, and she gathered her warmth to her the way the Child did with the blankets she hid under.

"I knew it. They think I did this. Stop playing with him," the Child said. *"The Void, the library, Eoghan. Give him something, anything."*

Angwyndith did not need to be chastised nor told what to do. *"I will not tell him what I do not wish him to know. Especially since we do not know what the breach is about."*

"Who cares?"

"I do." Angwyndith's voice boomed out in the Space Between, a thundering silence washing in after the echoes of it faded.

A powerful arctic wind almost pushed her off the ladder to her place of rest as the lights blazed around her. She tightened her grip, determined to remain in control. The Coda battered her, but she would not give in. Not to it, nor to the Child, nor to the insolent creature before her.

She had had enough of disrespect. The fire of a fury too long restrained unfurled within her, and she pushed it out at the one across from her. "We, my Host Seraphina Lastra Covington, and I, the Bodach," snapping her teeth on the last word, "have nothing to do with that matter. We cannot answer your inquiries, nor can we give you information we do not have."

He did not flinch at her tone. "That is not good enough."

She did not care what he thought. Shrugging her Host's shoulders, she said, "Then we are at an impasse."

"Yes." He closed the folder before him and set the pen down. "Due to the unwillingness of both you and Seraphina Lastra Covington to share any relevant information into my investigations on a numerous amount of subjects, I am confining you to quarters. Meals will be brought to you, and you will be escorted to the bathroom facilities until further notice."

"*WHAT?*" The Child screamed.

"You cannot do this."

His mouth hardened into a line. "I can and I will. The safety of this Facility is my only priority. Section B clauses two through ten of the agreement you signed with Dr. Carruthers give me the power to do whatever is necessary to achieve that goal. You both agreed to these rules when Ms. Lastra signed the contract."

Angwyndith reached for the book with the contract, skimming it as fast as she could.

Coda be damned.

She should have paid more attention to that infernal agreement; that should never have been something to which they had agreed. The glacial air stopped swirling around her, the Coda instead encasing her in a blanket of ice so firm she could not move.

"How long do you plan on imprisoning us?" Angwyndith asked, keeping her tone polite, as if she were not being suffocated inside and out.

"Until I can rule out your roles in the ongoing security breach and you share with me some aspect of the incident in the library."

The icy blanket tightened around her in time with the tightness of the Child's chest as her Host struggled to breathe through her shock.

Angwyndith would not yield. "Then it will be a long time."

"*Stop talking. You're making it worse!*"

"*Do not dare speak to me in such a manner, Child. I know what I am about.*"

"No, you don't. You know nothing about this time, these people, and you never once thought to find out. You speak of knowledge and its power, and you failed to acquire any. You can seriously go fuck yourself." The Child's wrath rained down on her. Her emotions failed to move Angwyndith, but her words stung.

The orbs on the ladder to which she clung dimmed, creating a circle of the blackest night around her. This was an unfortunate turn of events.

He inclined his head. "That is entirely up to you. I can keep you for an entire lifetime."

The truth hit her harder than anything else that had been said at the table. He could, according to the agreement they signed, do just that. Granted, if a Bell rang, the Coda would ensure their release, but at what cost?

Shards of ice pierced her on the ladder as the darkness pressed in.

She had failed. Again.

The Shapechanger stood and gestured to the other Shapechanger in the room to approach them. She yanked herself free of her connections to the Child, the darkness and the cold nipping at her as she fell down the ladder. She only hoped they let her be when she arrived at her Rest spot. She had much to think about.

And none of it good.

25

THE LOCKDOWN

(SHE HAD A PLAN)

A sharp knock signaled feeding time. One of the many Shifter guards brought her lunch in and set it on the desk. Seraphina ignored him. They all looked the same, and they all refused to talk to her.

Just like everything they did here, her schedule was a tightly orchestrated exercise in monotony. Bathroom break, breakfast, lunch, bathroom break, dinner, bathroom break. Rinse and repeat *ad nauseam* for three days, and many more if Angwyndith had her way.

Anger and sadness took up much of the first day, once the hope that this was a joke wore off. The second day she spent restoring books and reading until she couldn't take it anymore. She had worked her way through three seasons of *Buffy the Vampire Slayer* since then. While she loved the show and found the main character a badass, the boredom of never leaving the four walls around her had its claws in her. She could feel her will to remain draining through its puncture marks.

Angwyndith tried to talk to her yesterday, but Seraphina met her words with hostile silence. They wouldn't be in this mess if not for her. Angry Death was the one to tell her not to say anything. She also was the one who told her what to do and Seraphina followed it every time.

And Sorcha. Seraphina clenched her jaw. Just thinking about Sorcha filled her stomach with anxious knots.

She clicked on a different show to stem the tide, but it was too late. As the new drama filled her screen, she closed her laptop and swung her legs off the bed. She couldn't just sit here anymore, she needed to move. There must be something that could distract her from the impossible closet in which she was locked.

There had to be something she could do to fill the time.

Struck by inspiration, she popped off the bed. She moved the clothes stacked on top of the trunk back into it and put her dirty clothes in the bag on the back of the door for the Facility to pick up on Friday. She moved the desk chair out of the way and then squeezed behind the end of the desk to push it forward. It shrieked as it moved a few inches across the concrete floor; the pitch amplified as it hit the four walls.

Her breath came out shallow as she leaned on it.

She straightened and grabbed a stack of books to toss on the bed. They scattered, some falling open on their own. She ignored the twinge she felt when the pages of one book bent. Not her book, not her problem. The lunch tray, however, was a problem. She didn't have enough space to put it where it wouldn't get knocked over.

With a shrug, she moved around to push the desk again. It moved another inch and then stopped. She got on the other side and yanked on it; the coffee sloshing on the tray, as it moved a mere two inches. This wasn't working. If she used her legs and the wall as leverage, it might make it easier. Two rapid knocks resounded on the door.

"Wait, I've got—"

The door opened, and it slammed into the desk, catching the edge of the lunch tray. The tray slid across the metal surface and crashed to the floor. Coffee splattered the concrete and the bed, brown droplets sliding down the shiny metal surface.

And, of course, the pizza landed pepperoni side down.

The guard squeezed his head around the door, took in the scene, and then removed himself.

"FUCK!" She didn't know who she was yelling at. Herself? The guard? Her head dropped and she sighed. On the bright side, at least she had something new to do.

Seraphina squatted down, flipped the tray over and picked up the food mess, moving the tray under the bed to keep it out of the way. She didn't have enough napkins to mop up the coffee. She skirted around it, climbed up on the desk, and squatted as she opened the door. "Excuse me."

The guard standing opposite glared at her.

"Can someone please get me some napkins? You spilled my lunch all over the floor."

He said nothing.

"Yo, dude against the wall," she yelled louder. "Napkins. I need napkins."

His eyes shifted to her, his expression unchanged.

"Seriously?" She slammed the door shut and climbed down.

Using the anger to fuel her, she planted her feet against the wall and pushed on the desk again. It screamed as it budged, and she screamed with it, the two tones weaving together in some painful, discordant harmony.

Once the desk was out of the way, she yanked her clothes off and threw them at the corner where the bed met the wall, hurriedly pulling on her leggings and sports bra. The ballet class video she wanted to watch was brutal and she'd be dripping when she was done, but who would smell her over the coffee, anyway?

She typed in the website address for the video and the cursor circled while it loaded. Her feet twitched against the cold cement beneath them, eager to dance.

And then her stomach dropped. A white page appeared. A clattering of keys filled the space and another white page appeared. And then another.

"Shit, shit, shit."

She pulled up the network settings and checked her connection. Her heart sank at the words on the screen. "No internet connection detected."

"Are you freaking kidding me?" she yelled as she punched the power button on the laptop and rebooted it. Her fingers pounded on the keyboard as she typed in her password and waited, her eyes glued to the little cone in the corner of her screen.

It flashed and the emptiness inside the outline of what should have been a Wi-Fi connection punched her in the gut. She slammed her laptop shut, scooted off the bed, and paced. It was fine. She was fine. She had no connection to the outside world, but that couldn't last long.

Her foot stopped mid-step, as if someone had turned her power off. Sawyer could keep her here forever and no one could stop him. Not even Angwyndith. Her foot dropped to the floor. She'd been right to be suspicious of the SF. She never should've come here.

The lights flickered and went out, plunging her into darkness.

"What the fuck?"

She stood stock still in the room, her eyes attempting to see the shapes around her, but it was empty blackness instead. Much like the time with the Void, but not nearly as mind bending. Her breath hitched, the swirling ball of emotions threatening to overwhelm her.

This wasn't the plan. This was never the plan.

Maybe this wasn't on purpose. Only one way to find out. She slid a foot forward toward the door and then another. So far, so good. She could do this. Lukewarm coffee licked her toe, and she pulled her foot back. Wrong direction. Heart thudding, her arms sweeping out in front of her, she took two more steps. The door had to be close. Her fingers brushed the wall.

Success went to her head, and she took a bold step forward, gasping as her toe slammed into the metal leg of the bed.

"Ow, ow, ow," she chanted while she held her foot in her hands, her eyes squeezed shut.

Her balance teetered to the left, and she hopped to get it back. She tilted sideways, her arms windmilling to stop the fall. Her hip hit the bed frame, and she bounced off it onto the floor.

Stunned, she stayed where she was, tears slipping down her cheeks. She had no power, no friends nearby, and no one wanted to help her. It was too much. It was all too much. She wrapped her arms around herself, feeling lonelier than she ever had.

What was she supposed to do now?

***

The tears had long since stopped when Seraphina lifted her head. Murmured conversation and shuffling feet penetrated faintly through the door. She wanted to press her ear to it to listen, but knowing her luck, she'd end up covered in tomato sauce instead. If she wasn't already.

She inched her way backwards until her butt hit the wall and pulled her knees up to her chest, hugging them despite their stickiness. The turmoil of the past few days seeped out of her, leaving her numb.

The darkness in the room and the bitterness of coffee were the perfect backdrop to shine a light on all the decisions she'd made since her master's graduation day. Or not made. Ro's words from their fight over the summer rang in her ears. "At least I make choices where I can."

Who was she kidding? This *was* her fault.

All this time she thought she'd taken control of her life when all she'd done was agree to someone else's decisions. Again. She hadn't wanted to come to the Facility. Angwyndith had pushed her to do so, and her aunt agreed with it. Seraphina signed the agreement without even a peep.

Angwyndith was the one who decided Eoghan didn't need to know about the Void. Seraphina not only lost that fight by not fighting at all but also lost the right to the books she needed to get out from under Angwyndith's arrogant thumb.

And the decisions Seraphina *had* made were a complete disaster. Trusting Sorcha. Not following procedure, multiple times, culminating in the stupidest decision of all—failing to inform Sawyer who she talked to or that she'd left the Facility. If only she'd told him, or sent him a note, she wouldn't be in this mess.

She leaned her head back against the wall, the cold rough concrete digging into her skull. She wasn't just bored with her room; she was bored with herself. There were so many things she could've done differently, but she didn't stop to think any of those choices through.

No more. It was time to make a plan. All this wallowing, hiding in books or studying, and expecting others to do things for her was over. It was her life, and she needed to own it, starting with finding a more comfortable place to sit.

The coffee was sticky on her legs as she pushed herself to stand. She bent over, her hands out in front of her and took small shuffling steps forward. She really didn't need to bang into the bed any more times than she already had.

Her fingers touched the edge, the roughness of the blanket sliding over them, and she inched forward. She sat, yanking the book out from under her thigh and tossing it toward the back wall. Her hands patted the bed until she found the sweats she had been wearing before.

Using her fingers to find the tag in the waistband, she set the pants down next to her and shimmied out of her coffee-stained leggings. She laid on her back, books digging into her spine as she pulled the sweatpants on.

She fished around behind her for the books she knew were there, coming up with three. Using the edges of the spines to guide her, she stacked them on her lap. The metal at the end of the bed hit her hand. She reached over it and placed the three books on the trunk, careful to make sure they weren't leaning over the edge.

Now all she needed to do was find the rest and stack them next to that pile. Easy peasy. She kneeled on the bed and began the slow process of feeling for the next book when the hard edge of her laptop brushed her fingertips.

She smacked her forehead. "Oh my gods, I'm a freakin' idiot!" The words bounced back at her as she pulled the laptop toward her and opened the lid. A warm blue glow lit up the room just enough for her to see. She squinted at the battery icon. She had a few hours' worth, enough to sort out the room, find her power cord, and plug it in.

If she had power.

One problem at a time. She reopened her browser to a blank page, the bright white illuminating the first few books she could see. At least the lack of the Internet was good for something. She snorted and then got to work.

Within ten minutes, she had all the books stacked at the end of the bed, her notebooks closed and piled up, and a few pens next to them. If she remembered correctly, her power cord was near the bookshelf. She only had a few hours of battery left; yet another decision made poorly. All the time she spent watching *Buffy* could've been powered by the wall instead the meagre laptop battery. But then she hadn't expected the lights to go out. She picked up the laptop and shone it on the floor.

The little green light on the main power block was lit, and her mood lifted. She plugged it in and shuffled back to the bed. At least she'd have light and something to do. It'd be tricky to study using the light of the laptop, but it was better than nothing until Sawyer turned the lights back on.

If he turned the lights back on.

As if by magic, light flooded the room, her eyes closing as the brightness burned her eyeballs. She opened one eye at a time, blinking until it no longer hurt.

"Oh, thank the gods for small favors."

A sharp rap echoed before the beep as the door opened. "All good in here, ma'am?"

"Well, no, but I don't think you care about that."

"I'm just checking in to see if you had any problems during the drill, ma'am."

She frowned. "The drill? Was that why the lights and Internet went out?"

"That was why the lights went out, yes, ma'am. You should have seen the notification of the drill on the intranet."

"Huh. Haven't checked it in days. I thought Sawyer was torturing me."

He swallowed a small smile. "No, ma'am. Just a drill."

His friendliness was a pleasant change from the wall guard she'd interacted with earlier. The guards must have changed after lunch. She made a spur-of-the-moment decision; the words spilling out of her mouth. "I spilled coffee all over the floor. If I could get extra napkins with the next food delivery, that'd be awesome."

"I'll see what I can do, ma'am."

She nodded, and he pulled the door closed. The emptiness of the Internet connection cone echoed the emptiness of her stomach. She didn't even have snacks to get her through until dinner, but then she couldn't watch a show either.

Her fingers typed in an address in her browser and the Facility's gray and black intranet page took over the screen. A red bubble in the corner indicated a few missed notifications, including the drill she'd just cried through.

She'd also missed multiple notices posted by her teachers with the assignments from class. She'd just decided to be more decisive. No time like the present. First decision, find a way out of here. There had to be something in the regulations to help her. If she still had time on her hands, she could study the wards. She didn't have the books she needed, but she had her notes. It would be enough.

She'd kill to be in the library right now. She'd actually kill to do anything as long as it got her out of this room, including talking to Sorcha.

Maybe not that. Yet.

26

THE MUSIC OF LESSONS

(SHE WAS NOT A GOOD TEACHER)

Angwyndith stewed at the foot of the ladder in the Space Between. Their predicament never should have happened, especially not to one such as her. Much of the respect for the Bodach had been lost during the hundred plus years she had been in her Dark Rest. Even worse, her Host, the very creature inimical to the completion of Angwyndith's duties, did not respect her.

Tamping down on her rising anger, she flipped the page of the memory book on the past few months of the Child's life that Angwyndith had been reading. The combat training proceeded better than Angwyndith expected, although the Child still failed to counter the most basic attacks.

Mayhap she should tell her. No, she'd only receive silence in response. And the Child would know it was to get her to talk.

The book fluttered before her, and she finished skimming the standard sections of code for how to engage with any manner of creature and the paperwork resulting from that. If this was the total of her education, no wonder the Child had failed to apply herself. Angwyndith was amazed the Child had stayed awake at all.

The infinite bookshelf appeared before her. She put the book away, hesitating as the next volume of the Child's life presented itself to her. Why bother catching up on codes, when Angwyndith would much rather read something entertaining she hadn't read yet that the Child had. Pushing the next volume back into its place, she pulled down the years in between, when Angwyndith hadn't been as present as she would have liked.

The pages flipped until Angwyndith found one where the Child read a book. She skimmed the pages, stopping on three different tomes the Child had read with enthusiasm. *Magic Bites, Rosemary and Rue, Dead Until Dark.* Disgusted, she put the memory book away.

Why the Child found any of these titles worth her time was a question Angwyndith would never answer. One of her favorite quotes came to mind. "It is not enough to have a good mind; the main thing is to use it well." The Child did neither, although she had some moments of good thinking.

Bored with what she had found so far, Angwyndith flipped further back. She reached for a book from the Child's younger days and flipped past the dancing, mindless show watching, studying, and sleeping the Child had done. Really, how she even graduated with the lack of attention she had paid to her studies was beyond Angwyndith. Scholarly standards were appallingly low compared to when she last was present.

As she passed a memory from the Child's earlier education after their Judgement of the Guide, the lights on the ladder blazed and the pages fluttered to a halt, resisting any attempt of hers to turn them. Heeding the message, she watched the memory play out.

Seraphina's eyes ached, but she gritted her teeth and kept writing.

"Ugh. Fi. What time is it?" a sleepy voice asked from across the room.

"Sorry, Ro." Seraphina fumbled for the clock. "It's almost time to get up."

"Have you slept at all?"

"No. I had to finish this essay. I still don't get the meaning of The Fox and Cat, *besides the cat outwitting the fox and the fox's arrogance killing him."*

"Who cares? It's one grade." Ro groaned and flipped over in bed, pulling the covers over her face.

"It's 50% of our grade, Ro. If I get this wrong, I could fail." Seraphina's voice shook with anxiety.

"But you won't."

"You don't know that. He shredded my last essay. I got a C." The pen left a gob of ink on the page, and she blotted it with a tissue.

"Cs are passing. Stop freaking out."

"He tortures the students who don't at least get Bs. He makes them stand up while he calls them stupid. I have

to get a B." Tears streamed down her cheeks, and she wiped them away.

From Ro's bed came the gentle sound of snoring. Seraphina was so tired. Maybe just twenty minutes of sleep would be alright. She'd finish the essay in time for class.

Angwyndith did not recall the memory, but the weight of the emotion in it surprised her. The Child had cared at one point about her academics. What had changed?

She flipped through the memory book, skipping past them both oversleeping and Seraphina yelling that she didn't finish her paper.

Seraphina trudged into class, her arms full of books, and sat down in her seat.

Mr. Grindler stood at the front of the class, watching her with a sneer on his face.

Students streamed in, laughing and talking. When the last bell rang, the teacher called for silence. Rustling paper and whispers followed. He held up their essays in his hand.

Seraphina's stomach cramped, and her gaze dropped to her desk.

"What is this dreck in my hand? Did none of you

understand the assignment? It is a simple fable. The meaning is clear and yet not one of you grasped it." He moved around his desk and dropped the papers one at a time on the students' desks. "One step up from trash."

Plop. "Somewhat closer to gibberish than Pig Latin." Snap. "You were the closest and yet if it were a goalpost, you'd have missed it by a mile."

Snickers erupted from the jocks on the right. They stopped abruptly when he glared at them.

Slap. "Absolutely missed the point."

Seraphina could see his feet coming closer to her desk. She squirmed and hid her face under her arms.

"Not bad. You at least know how to string a sentence together," he said one desk away. "And then there's this."

She could see his feet from under her arms. Her hands clammy, she sat back. He towered over her desk and waved her paper around for people to see. Across the top was a C- in thick red pen. Angry marks slashed across the words on the first page.

"Tell me, Miss Covington," his voice sharpened. "How exactly do you get dressed in the morning? Do you have instructions next to your bed of what to do first? Get out of bed, pull your shirt over your head?" A few of the

students tittered. "No? Then explain to me how you not only completely missed the point but submitted such dreck as to be incomprehensible."

"I did the best I could," she whispered.

Everyone in the room watched, the tension growing. Some smiled, happy not to be his wrath's next victim, while others enjoyed the bloodshed to come.

"The best you could? This," he dropped the paper onto the desk as if it was disgusting, "is the best you can do? Really? I could do better reading and writing in Russian, which I do not speak. This absolute piece of crap you turned in I wouldn't even use to wipe my ass if I was desperate."

The color drained from her face and her nails punctured her palms.

"Take note, everyone." He turned and gestured to the other students. "She is not who you want to be in my class. She set the bar low, so it shouldn't be too difficult for you to pass it. But just in case your addlepated brains missed it, do not ever turn in another paper such as the one Miss Covington did."

He grabbed the paper off her desk before she could stop him. "In fact, I'm going to put this on display. I want you all to read it. See where she failed to be even mildly coherent. You can judge for yourself where her intelli-

gence failed her, if she even has any."

Her mouth dropped open as he strode to the bulletin board, ripped the first page off and stapled it to the wall. He mounted her pages like trophies next to the first page, each staple blasting out like a shot.

A tear slid down her face and she wiped it while everyone watched Grindler. Drawing on the many times her grandfather had yelled and humiliated her, she forced her face into a neutral expression.

He turned around and smiled at her. "Please, everyone, come and read the unintelligible drivel and learn from it."

She stayed where she was, face forward, as her classmates brushed by her desk, eager to view her failure.

That did not appear to be a good way to teach someone how to think properly. Angwyndith scanned the memories from that year and noted the Child increased her frequency of admitting to her stupidity or calling herself an idiot in her conversations.

The lights around her bobbed and weaved and she stopped to give the thought more attention. Had she done the same? Treated the Child as if she were incompetent? No. She may have been arrogant at times, but nothing as bad as this.

The lights flickered, their brightness ebbing and flowing. The infinite bookshelf spun and stopped, specific tomes tipping out and then sliding back into place, each one lit up by a ball of light. The shelf moved backward. Again, more books tipped out and then slid back in. Repeatedly, until it looked like a song played on a pianoforte in a dizzying array.

Every single one of them was past Host memory books.

It was not as bad as all of that.

The movement of the shelf sped up, moving forward this time, the books and lights moving so fast she could barely follow them. When she could not take much more, the bookshelf stopped. One tome floated toward her, the pages flapping open to different moments in the Child's life since they had arrived at the Security Forces domain.

Every single one was an interaction between them where Angwyndith called out the Child's inability to focus or failure to train. She cringed when she rewatched the Child asking for her guidance and getting hostility instead.

I understand. You can stop now.

The shelf disappeared, only low-lighted orbs hanging in the space around her. She *had* left all the training to the Security Force, who appeared to teach the Child regulations and paranoia. None of it was of any use in the field where they were to Judge. She had not taught the Child anything. All her knowledge, all her experience, and she treated the Child like she treated the Security Forces—with silence and excuses.

Could they have been further ahead if she had? The Child used what she had learned effectively with the High Elf as a shield to protect what little books were left to her.

Angwyndith had not even put up a good fight. Both the High Elf and the Shapechanger had outwitted her. She failed to negotiate the items she sought or hide those things she did not want them to see. She also failed to use the Child's own knowl-edge about this time and space to their advantage.

No wonder the Child failed to respect her. Angwyndith hadn't given her any reason to do so.

This modern world differed from the time before. While she had maneuvered successfully around other military figures in the past, she had not faced one as organized and structured as this Security Force appeared to be. Mayhap she underestimated their abilities and overestimated her own.

And mayhap she needed to train as well. No, there was no need to be harsh. But she could help the Child more than she had. She gathered her warmth and climbed the ladder.

It was time to do things differently.

27

BREAKTHROUGHS

(SHE WASN'T INEPT)

Seraphina's fingers tapped a rhythm on her leg as she repeated the combat regulation on the page in her head. Around her lay the debris of her studying.

Day five of captivity. Still no Internet, but she'd learned a lot over the past two days. She now knew every single code section in her textbook, and she'd used them to get the guards on the door to provide her with food that wasn't just breakfast, lunch, or dinner. At least she wouldn't starve.

Boredom came and went like the tide. She either slept or danced through it, using routines from her memory to guide her. She also restored two more books for Finn and reread every book she brought with her. Occasionally, she got a guard who would say more than just one word, but mostly silence reigned. Even Angwyndith hadn't visited, and Seraphina wished she had. Her anger had cooled with the coffee on the floor. They both had made mistakes.

Angwyndith's warmth pooled in Seraphina's stomach, as if she knew Seraphina was thinking of her. *"Good day, my Host,"* Angwyndith said.

Guilt spiraled out of Seraphina. Angwyndith never sounded less sure than she did right now. A spike of anger chased the tail of the guilt. Guess she wasn't completely over it yet. *"Hey."*

Angwyndith's warmth splayed out as she stretched and settled back in. Seraphina's head tingled. *"It appears, my Host, that you have been redecorating."*

All the words Seraphina hadn't said bubbled up from inside. *"Captivity sucks, Angwyndith. No one will talk to me. Sawyer took away the Internet, taking away any form of entertainment and the only means to reach anyone on the outside. They also won't clean up the mess I made moving the desk nor let Caide in to do so, which is insane since he lives for it."*

Seraphina had seen him outside the door a few times, his enormous eyes drooping and a mop in his hand as he stared at the puddle on the floor. It had occurred with more frequency over the past day. How they were stopping him from coming in when she showered was beyond her.

"I do not think he lives for it, but it may well be his purpose."

"I don't see the difference."

"The Elf was not made to clean, but it is something he is good at and something he can do to contribute. He may well be beholden to the High Elf, and cleaning could be his way of paying it back."

Irritation gnawed at Seraphina at Angwyndith's condescending tone. Did Angwyndith always have to be right? *"No, I don't think so. He's focused when he's cleaning."*

"That may be as well."

Seraphina's irritation morphed into resentment as she felt the pages of her memory book tickling her ribs. *"You know, you could just ask me what I've been doing."*

"I apologize. It is an old habit now that I am spending so much time away."

"It's annoying, right up there with never talking about anything you say we will."

Angwyndith sighed, the warm air brushing against Seraphina's throat. *"My Host, I realize I have been lax in my duties toward you and will take steps to ensure that it does not occur again."*

"What does that mean?" Seraphina drawled out the words, unsure where Angwyndith was going.

"I failed to train you in a way that would have been useful. I expected the Security Forces to handle it. Instead of sharing my knowledge, I expected you to learn it from them. I misjudged their capabilities and the overall situation. I am not used to military as organized as this."

It was the longest almost admission of being wrong Angwyndith had ever said. Seraphina's dropped. *"I did too. But their training isn't all bad. I have learned a lot about the MC that I didn't know and wouldn't have gotten from you. The library, even its current limited form, is still useful."*

"We should not have had to beg to receive access to it. Now that I know the High Elf feels the library is part of his domain, it makes a bit more sense as to why we did not receive what we negotiated for."

Seraphina rolled her eyes. *"You sure are good at spinning things to make yourself look good. I don't see why you can't do that with Sawyer."*

"I do not spin things," Angwyndith said, her voice tinged with frost. *"And my interaction with Sawyer came after he had already cornered you."*

"Of course. It's my fault you failed," Seraphina replied, the words tinged with a bitterness so old it felt familiar.

"My Host..." Angwyndith paused. Seraphina braced herself for one of Angry Death's truth bombs. *"I have been reviewing things. I have concluded you are not unintelligent. You can learn when you*

put your mind to it, but you choose not to. Unlike the Elf, you just lack focus."

Her teeth came together with a click as Seraphina kept her mouth and her mind quiet. The silence stretched out between them.

Angwyndith continued, *"I fear your quiet means that you mistake my words and my meaning. I have been researching that as well and I believe it is because of your experiences with your teacher, Grindler. After that moment, your insecurity increased and your focus dropped."*

The bite of that memory burned like the acid swirling in Seraphina's stomach. *"Taking a walk in my memories?"*

"I had not intended to. I wished to find a memory of you reading a book I had not yet read. You have read an inordinate amount of unfortunate books."

Seraphina choked out a laugh. *"Sorry about that. I went through a phase where I wanted something easy and light while I studied."*

"You certainly have done that. I do not think I can read another book with vampires falling in love with humans." Angwyndith's tone changed, and Seraphina braced herself for a lecture. *"The Cold, from which the myth of vampires derive, would never see the value in human life. Humans are an energy source; nothing more, nothing less. To say nothing of the age difference. Whatever would a thousand-year-old soul want with such a young one with no actual experiences to share?"*

"Potato, po-taught-o, Angwyndith."

"Whatever do you mean?"

Seraphina found it hard to believe Angwyndith didn't see the correlation. *"You, me, separated by thousands of years."*

"We are different, my Host. We did not choose one another; the Coda chose for us. In those books you read, the characters choose to be together. It is nonsensical and would never happen in this reality."

"Ro said the same thing when she saw what I was reading. I was in high school, and everyone was reading them. I wanted to know why." Seraphina shook her head, a smile creeping across her face as she remembered Ro's rant. It put Angwyndith's to shame and had a lot more hand waving and shrieking. *"It also gave me something in common with the other students."*

Her smile faded as she remembered the looks and the whispers that had followed her around for the next two years. Much like how they did at the Facility. She groaned. *"That's why it bugs me so much."*

"What does?"

"The way people treat me here. The looks, the dismissals. It smacks of what happened after Grindler's class."

"My Host, your teacher was wrong for what he said and what he did. And you were wrong to believe him."

Seraphina grimaced. *"My paper sucked. I didn't finish the analysis, and I didn't get the true meaning of the fable. While what he did was harsh, it wasn't unfair."*

"What he did was stifle any of your own initiative and capabilities by being cruel because of his own insecurities. And you were not far off with your analysis of the fable."

"I was too, Angwyndith. I analyzed it again in college."

"I knew the Grimm brothers, and my previous Host and I discussed this fable at length with them. You were on the cusp of being correct. You just saw the cat's actions in the wrong light."

Seraphina mimicked the sound of a buzzer. *"That's not the only fable I got wrong."*

"My Host?"

"A few weeks ago, the Coda pointed me to another, The Hart and the Hunter. I had never realized how much I hated fables until that moment."

"I did not see that memory. You do not see the message the fable expresses?"

Seraphina had to give Angwyndith props for her restraint. Not only did she not feel the fan of pages, but her voice remained neutral with a tint of curiosity instead of derision. *"If it means don't stop to admire your good traits, then sure. But I'm guessing not."*

Angwyndith sighed. *"Not quite. We have had many conversations since we arrived at this place about your humanity and how you despise it."*

"I don't despise it. I just recognize it as the weakness it is." The words came out defensive, coated in the darkness of her pain. *"What does that have to do with the fable?"*

"That is what the fable is all about. Our greatest weaknesses can also be our strengths. You despise that which is intrinsic to who you are, and that which is also most useful to you."

"What's useful or strong about being human? We can't do magic, and we sure as hell can't measure up to the other phyla." Moynihan's comments in the gym echoed through her head, followed by the argument with Sorcha. *"All we can do is breed."*

"That is not true. I cannot speak to all humans, but the few I have known had more heart than any other creature I have met. They valued the life they lived, loved deeply, and, for the most part, do not see as starkly the differences between them. In fact, they value uniqueness."

Seraphina scoffed. *"No, they don't. Didn't you just read my high school years ? If you were different, or stupid, you were a target. The Community is no different, except that it's not about fashion or intelligence, but about ability and skills. And I apparently have neither."*

"That is not true. You underestimate yourself and your phylum. You do not lack ability; you just use your humanness as a reason not to try something that may be difficult."

Hurt blossomed, poking the old wound like a dentist with a sore tooth. *"Yep, that's it exactly. It has nothing to do with my inability to wield aether, my ineffectual body or its shorter lifespan."*

"You are speaking of the physical traits. But are there not physical differences amongst humans?"

"Of course, there are." Seraphina got up and paced, avoiding the sticky brown stain. *"But this is different."*

"No, my Host, it is not. Your brain knows you can do it, but your beliefs stop you from following through. Humans are not weaker than Wielders; they are simply different from them. They have different strengths and different tools to wield."

Seraphina stopped and yanked on her hair. *"What tools, Angwyndith? Our cars? Our technology? A car or a phone won't help me out of this situation. Our brains? Wielders have those too. What then makes me so special?"*

"Your thirst for knowledge. Your eye for strategy. Your ability to think outside of the box. It is why humans are the only Bodach Hosts." Angwyndith paused, as if there was something else to that sentence she didn't want to share. *"Wielders only ever review a situation from their magical perspective. They pursue knowledge of spells and aether manipulation, but little else. Shapechangers review it from a predator's perspective. How can they get this creature to go in that direction so that they may close it in, or what is the best way to move forward and capture this space?"*

"Humans do that too, Angwyndith. Pursue a specific field of study or determine battle strategies on the field." Seraphina paced again.

"But that is not the only thing they do. They also have hobbies. What hobbies does your Wielder family member have?"

"She gardens."

"And what does she do for employment?"

"She... gardens." Seraphina sat on the bed, thinking of all the people in the Community she'd met over the years. Ro partied or studied marine biology, which was where her people thrived. The teachers in Merricott taught various subjects at the high school, but they pivoted around aether, construction or strategy based on who was in the class. Only Finn did something outside the strengths from his phylum.

"There are outliers," Angwyndith said after a pause, as if she heard the thought. *"For instance, some Shapechangers study philosophy, but they study it for a specific purpose."*

"To understand the enemy," Seraphina said, the words trickling out as she thought about it.

"Exactly."

"Except Sorcha plays video games and writes computer codes for a living. How does that fit?" A small burn of anger flared at the thought of Sorcha. Some friend she was.

"The focus of her attention is on the building blocks of the game and the various aspects she can use to achieve success. The Motion phylum is continually in motion. Knowing the pieces in play is how they use that aspect of themselves they cannot control to win the field or avoid injury or obstacles."

"And the coding?"

"If I understand it correctly, is that not using different building blocks to create a winning strategy?"

Seraphina frowned. *"Maybe, if you stretch it."*

"No stretching is involved. Humans are of value not because of their multitude, but because they have the freedom to pursue what-

ever endeavors they wish, and they do so," Angwyndith said, sincerity warming her tone. *"They can be a strategy-focused being or a creative-focused being. They can produce goods or services or neither. They can choose to understand the heaviest of the sciences while having a skilled trade as a hobby. They are more well-rounded than the other phyla. That is their gift."*

"Huh. I never thought about it like that before."

"The Grimm brothers shared their fables with humans because they felt humans received more value from them. The Magic Community is too old, too powerful, and too set in their ways to change how they view the world. Humans are not."

Seraphina slumped back against the wall. *"What were the Grimm brothers like?"*

"Chatty. Inane. But a good way to pass the time." Angwyndith's voice was light with humor. *"But that is not the point. You are not stupid or weak. Nor are you inept. When you focus, as you have been doing, you achieve a better understanding than even I of how the world functions."*

Tears came to Seraphina's eyes, the sincerity of the statement piercing through the wall of inadequacy she held inside. *"You actually mean that."*

"I would not attach myself to a stupid human."

She wiped her cheeks as her eyes narrowed to slits of mock severity. *"Wait a minute. I thought you said you had no choice."*

"The Coda would not attach me to a stupid human," Angwyndith replied, her tone mimicking her earlier inflection.

Seraphina laughed; she couldn't help herself. Angwyndith obviously had at one point thought she was stupid, inept or both. She probably would again, but nothing could take away this moment when she said Seraphina was neither.

She could work with that.

28

THE FRIENDSHIP DANCE

(One Step Forward, One Step Back)

A familiar chime rang in the small space. Seraphina pounced on her laptop, a smile blooming across her face as she saw a solid network cone in the corner. Her fingers flew across the keyboard as she typed in her password and opened a browser window. The beautiful splash of tabloid headlines filled her with a glee she'd never thought she'd have for trash news.

"Alright. Now we're cooking with gas."

"I do not know what that means," Angwyndith said, her words stilted.

"The Internet is back up. I can finally do something other than study."

"But you are making such progress."

"And I will again, but people are out there. People I can talk to. People who could spring me from this joint."

Seraphina scanned her email and cheered when she saw Finn had responded. She'd sent him an email as coded as she could before the Internet died, detailing why she could not send the book she promised. Hopefully, he understood what she meant by referencing the title, *The Prisoner of Zenda,* since it wasn't a book he'd given her to restore. It was, however, a book about being held prisoner.

> Ms. Covington,
> Thank you for your note. It was good to hear from you at last, as it had been longer than anticipated. I understand your dilemma with *The Prisoner of Zenda*. I truly hope it will not be long before you can send it on. However, do you have any plans to restore *The Count of Monte Cristo*? It would be a good book to work on next. I await your response eagerly. I trust it will come sooner rather than lat-er.
> Yours,
> Finn Hanes

He understood it! And he was concerned enough to not only inquire about her escape plan but also let the SF know, if they were reading her email, that he was waiting for a response. It was an empty gesture, but it touched her, nonetheless.

"Of course, he understood your message. He is a highly intelligent creature, for a Troll."

Seraphina scowled. *"Why do you do that?"*

"What, my Host?"

"Qualify his intelligence based on his species."

"You sound hostile when my approach is based on quantitative data. I have known a great many Trolls and they are good with geometric imagery and mathematics, logic, but they are not as good at novel thinking," Angwyndith said in her most smarmy school-

teacher voice. *"Your friend is not good at the one he should be but is good at the other. It is an unusual trait among their phyla."*

"People who build bridges and buildings are just as smart as people who are creative. Some would say more so. And second, there are some amazing Troll artists, Angwyndith." Seraphina paused, biting her lip. *"I think your information is outdated."*

"Hmph. Knowledge in all its forms is the sign of intelligence, including logic, but the ability to take that base knowledge and apply it in unique and novel ways is a true sign of intelligence." Angwyndith paused, as if reluctant to say whatever was on the tip of her tongue. *"But my familiarity in some things may be outdated, my Host. It was outdated regarding the Security Force. You can never stop learning."*

Seraphina suppressed a smile. She dashed off a quick response to Finn to keep him informed, mentioning she was working on *The Count of Monte Cristo,* but it was slow going and she may need some help.

"Speaking of knowledge... I thought I had an inspired thought about ward creation, but it turns out I didn't. I don't think I think the right way, Angwyndith. I think I'm an example of a Finn-like Troll; different, but not completely useless."

"In what way do you think you need to think? This turn of phrase is not concise. Finn is still a Troll regardless of his use of logic versus creativity," Angwyndith grumbled.

"I know. I just said that." Seraphina ran her hands through her hair and tugged on the ends. Frustrated, she gathered her hair up into a messy bun at the back, stabbing it with the glass chopsticks laying near her leg. She tried again. *"I figured out what runes were on the floor of the lab and what they mean. I thought that sealing a ward was because of the intent of the Wielder, but that seems impossible. It would make the wards unbreakable."*

"*That is correct. It would preclude another Wielder from breaking any of the wards that were placed before they arrived.*"

"*What about anyone else with aether abilities? I've recently read that every phylum has inner flames with more power and strength than the last. What is stopping Gabriel, that Shifter in the lab who comes from a phylum higher than Wielders, from breaking the ward?*"

"*The cage he is in, presumably, and that he is of The Moon and not The Seasons.*"

"*I don't get it.*"

Angwyndith sighed but didn't elaborate.

Frustration zipped through Seraphina. "*This is part of the training you said we'd do together. No one's told me this because they already know it. I don't and the books aren't clear. I am asking for your help. Please, Angwyndith.*" Seraphina slipped in the "please" to butter Angwyndith up. If Seraphina had more time in the library, she would've figured this out already.

"*Hmph. Very well. While those of The Moon can wield aether, their power and strength are drawn from their inner flame, rather than the aether surrounding them, as they have no need of it. Those of The Seasons have weaker inner flames to draw from, which means they must use some other aspect of the world, aether, to practice their magics. That is why they are trained from birth to wield it, so that it becomes as like the magic that occurs when a Shapechanger changes shape.*"

"*Okay. So, let me break this down.*" Seraphina scanned the notes she took on the phyla. "*Some of the phyla have stronger flames than others, which means they use pieces of themselves to do the magic things they do. Like Eoghan and the books in the library. Right?*"

"*In its most basic form, yes.*"

"*So, when a Wielder casts a spell—*"

"Wields aether, my Host. Really, those books you read did you no favors."

Seraphina rolled her eyes. *"Fine. When they wield aether, they draw more on the energy around them than within them."*

"Yes."

"So then, how are they creating the wards? By weaving the aether in a specific pattern?"

"Yes, and no. When a Wielder creates a ward, the runes are impor-tant, but they are only one part of the puzzle. The other piece is the order in which they placed the runes. The Wielder then uses aether to trace that pattern into the runes to create a solid seal."

Seraphina tapped the pen against the notebook, her brain whirring into overdrive. *"I get that. How do I know what ward comes first? From what I've read, the first rune is the strongest and then the runes are applied in decreasing strength and meaning. How do I know what rune is stronger? They're all the same."*

"No, they are not." Angwyndith said in her most patient tone, which always held a note of condescension. *"When you are crafting a ward to keep people out, different wards have different strengths than when crafting a ward to keep people in. The intent of the ward is different, thus, must the runes used be different in focus within the pattern."*

Her computer pinged.

"Oooh, it's Ro."

"My Host, you were just focused."

"I know, but I haven't talked to anyone in days besides Grunt the guard. I'm dying for interaction."

"I did not realize I was not anyone."

Seraphina winced. *"She could help get us out."*

"Very well. I beg you to be discreet."

"We've got a whole code thing happening to get past the censors in this place. Don't worry."

Angwyndith sighed.

"You have no faith in my ability to be sneaky," Seraphina said.

"Because I have seen no evidence that you can be," Angwyndith fired back.

"Touche." Before Angwyndith could distract her anymore, Seraphina clicked on the instant messaging app.

Ro: Hey, hey. We're finally sorted and settled in NC. How's it hanging?

Seraphina: Oh, it's hanging. It's hanging so still I could be a statue.

Ro: It can't be that bad.

Seraphina: How's NC? Do you like it?

Ro: It's that bad? How?

Seraphina: Can't say. Can't do much of anything.

Ro: NC is good. Different from NYC.

Seraphina: Oh, less freedom of movement then?

Ro: ??? No. I have a car.

Seraphina: Good. I'm glad you can go where you want to go when you want to do that.

Ro: I always could. What's with you?

Seraphina: Nothing, just bored. Stuck in my room with nothing to do.

Ro: I thought you were playing video games.

Seraphina: I was. I'm not now. I'm not doing anything at all right now and my room is boring.

Seraphina had left all the clues she could. Her fingers drummed on her legs while she waited for Ro to figure it out.

"An imbecile could figure it out. If you think this is fooling the people monitoring your activity, you are sadly mistaken."

"Shush, Angwyndith. If they didn't want me talking about it, they wouldn't let it through."

"That is not why they 'let it through' as you call it," Angwyndith said drily.

Ro: Do I need to call in the big guns?

"If by big guns she means Beatrice Griffiths, the answer is no, my Host."

The finality in Angwyndith's tone cut through Seraphina's glee that Ro understood her meaning. *"What? Why?"* Seraphina asked, exasperated. *"She could get us out of here. You've seen what her name does to people when it's brought up."*

"While I do not deny her power, I want you to consider carefully how you use it. Boons are high-cost items."

Ro: Fi, you there?
Seraphina: One sec. Ang is yapping.

"I am not a little dog," Angwyndith said, her voice vibrating with irritation.

"It's an expression, Angwyndith. Relax."

"I will not relax. Do not be indebted to Beatrice Griffiths. You will not like the consequences."

Seraphina squinted at the screen. *"It sounds like you've met her. I know from the Mythology book that she's a cruel taskmaster within in her phylum, but what else am I missing?"*

"The obvious."

Seraphina rolled her eyes.

"Yes, I am familiar with Beatrice Griffiths, although she was young when last we met. Even then, the Griffiths were unusually powerful. From what I've seen in your memories, they still are. That sort of dedicated power gathering means only one thing: Beatrice Griffith and her progeny are not to be trifled with."

"I'll give you Beatrice. She's one scary lady. But what does Ro have to do with it?"

"Your friend is being raised to take over the family dynasty. She cannot do that if she is not as fully invested as her elder."

"Dynasty?" Seraphina scoffed. *"Ro's going off to be a marine biologist. Yes, she's a part of the family, but that's it. You're seeing things that aren't there."*

"And you are missing things that are. You would be well-met to remember that whenever you renew your bond with her."

Seraphina blinked. There was a lot to unpack in that sentence.

> Ro: Fi, I need to bolt. Do you want me to make a call or what?
> Seraphina: No. Not yet. I'll let you know.
> Ro: K. Speak soon.
> Seraphina: Enjoy your new space.

Seraphina set the laptop to the side. "Renew my bond?"

"Yes. When was the last time you initiated contact?"

Her brow wrinkled. *"A week ago."*

"And before that?"

"I don't know. What are you getting at?"

Angwyndith sighed. *"You have a pattern. You rarely speak and when you do, she initiates, you complain, she cuts you off. You say you love her. Repeat."*

"That's not how it goes."

"Are you certain of that?" Angwyndith asked.

"Are you trying to piss me off?"

"No. You wished me to be present more and train you. This is part of it. In recognizing your shortcomings, you can address them."

"That's not the training I need, Angwyndith."

"Are you positive about that? I am attempting to open your eyes to what is in front of you. It is larger than a dwelling and yet you never see it. It will cause problems for you, and thus us, later."

As if Angwyndith knew how friendships worked. And why was this about her? *"I think I'm done with this conversation for now. Thank you for your help."*

"I will not be dismissed like some errant child."

"I'm not dismissing you. I simply no longer want to talk to you," Seraphina snapped.

"That makes you the child in this scenario."

"Well, you keep calling me that whenever I don't do what you want me to do, so maybe I'm just meeting your expectations." A hostile silence filled the Space Between. Seraphina groaned and plopped back against the pillows. *"I don't want to fight with you, Angwyndith, which is why I'm trying to shut this conversation down."*

"This is you running away from the hard discussions, my Host, rather than stopping an argument."

"Maybe. Oh my gods. Please, just stop talking about whether I'm a terrible friend, okay?" Seraphina pleaded.

"We can address this another time, when you are open to it and I am more patient."

"Like that's ever going to happen."

"'She wanted to complain, not to be consoled; and it was by exclamations of complaint only, Emily learned the particular circumstances of her affliction.' You would do well to think upon this."

"Thanks, Angry Death. Maybe I will."

Angwyndith pulled her presence away, but her warmth remained, pooled like a hot spring in Seraphina's stomach.

Seraphina stared at the ceiling as thoughts tumbled around in her brain. Flames and souls. Aether and wards. Secrets and lies. Great titles for a book, but not helpful, since she wasn't writing one. Great for avoiding the big topic, though. She grabbed her laptop and pulled it to her, scrolling through her and Ro's past conversations, hoping to prove Angwyndith wrong.

The more she scrolled, the more the pit in her stomach grew. Seraphina's comments were littered with negative tones, but Ro's stayed light. In fact, Ro rarely spilled the beans about any of her drama. If it weren't for the summer they spent together in the Hamptons with all of Ro's family, Seraphina wouldn't have even guessed at how bad it could be for Ro. But did frequent visits and Beatrice's domination over the family equate to Ro being groomed?

No. Ro lived her own life and made her own decisions. Something Seraphina wanted to emulate. Something she couldn't do if she didn't face the hard decisions. Just like Angwyndith had just said. She flopped back on the bed with a groan. Angwyndith had been all doom and gloom about her friendship with Ro for months. Finally, they had discussed one of the many things they had said they would, and Seraphina shut it down before it even began.

"*Angwyndith, are you there?*" The warmth seeped up her chest, but the silence lingered. "*I'm sorry. You were doing what I asked, and I didn't like the message, so I shot the messenger.*"

The quiet within shifted as Angwyndith's warmth swirled around her throat and then her head. "*You were correct as well. Patience is not my strong suit. But I must learn it if I am to train you more.*"

"*Uh, did you just admit to a flaw?*"

"*No.*"

"*I think you did.*"

"*I merely pointed out an area for improvement. That is not a flaw. A flaw is something that cannot be fixed. This can.*"

Angwyndith could talk her way out of any situation where her imperfections were at the center. If only she was that good with negotiations, they wouldn't be in this mess. A tendril of anger unfurled within her, but she refused to feed it. They couldn't change the past, only how they moved forward.

The usual knock plus beep at the door forestalled any comments Seraphina planned to make. After checking the time, she sat up, frowning.

"*Is there something wrong?*"

"A guard's coming in. Now's not the normal time, not even for snacks."

"*Mayhap the Shapechanger has changed his mind.*"

"I'm not that lucky," Seraphina said, her eyes peeled on the door as it swung open. Her jaw dropped.

Maybe she was, after all.

29

BATHROOM BREAKS

(She Missed Something Important)

Overjoyed with her good fortune, Seraphina grinned. Teddy stood at the door, his arm badge crisp and his uniform pressed. If she didn't know better, she'd think he was attending an official ceremony.

"Hey, Teddy! You're looking fancy. What's the occasion?"

"Ms. Covington. It will be lunch soon. Do you need to use the facilities?" Teddy's tone was as sharp as the crease in his shorts.

Disappointment nibbled at her grin and it melted like the last of her fro-yo at the bottom of a cup. He was either just doing his job, or he thought her guilty of the leak. "Yes, sure."

"My Host, did you not just say it was unusual timing? Something else may be afoot."

Seraphina closed her laptop and set it aside. *"Maybe, but if it means getting out of this room, then I'm all for it."*

"I do not think this is a good idea. It reeks of manipulation."

"And you should know." Angwyndith didn't rise to the bait, although the sharp swirl of warmth near her face said she wanted to. Seraphina bit her lip. *"Maybe it is. But what if we used his tactic and turned it back on him?"*

"What do you mean by that?"

"We use Teddy to get a message to Sawyer to see if we can renego-tiate the terms."

"What would you wish to renegotiate? We are not giving him anything of which he asked. We cannot." Angwyndith sounded firmer than the hard mattress on which Seraphina now sat.

"Maybe we should rethink that. Give them something small to open the door. I'd like to at least attend classes and gain access to the gym. It'll be better than staring at these walls." When Angwyndith said nothing, Seraphina pressed her point. *"If we show them we're trustworthy, this could end sooner rather than later."*

"Mayhap."

While not an enthusiastic endorsement, Seraphina would take the win. "One sec," she said to Teddy.

She grabbed a ponytail holder and shoved it on her wrist, so she could braid her hair. They didn't rush her when she was in there, but she needed something else to do to draw her time out besides the necessities.

Teddy grunted and said to the guard across the hall, "I've got this. Why don't you grab lunch and then bring hers back with you when you're done?"

"That's not protocol."

"What's a few minutes? No one will know."

The Shifter across the hall gradually nodded. "It'd be good to stretch my legs and get some grub. I'll clear the bathroom before I go." With a glare at Seraphina, he pivoted on his heel and strode away.

"What's his deal?" Seraphina asked.

"He's bored. Guarding you isn't as much fun as guarding the guys on level fifteen. They make more noise." Teddy gestured to her to continue.

She closed her door, and they sauntered down the hall. "Really? Why's that?"

"Because they're not happy to be caged up."

"I'm not happy about it either."

"It's your own fault. All you have to do is tell the Master Chief what he wants to know."

"Are we good to talk to Sawyer, Angwyndith?"

"Yes, but we need to be clear as to what we will share."

"Understood." Seraphina stopped and faced Teddy. "Okay. Let him know I'm open to chat again."

He blinked. "Just like that?"

Not really. "Yeah. Just like that."

Down the hall, Teddy's counterpart guard barked out, "Bathroom's clear. Be back in twenty."

Teddy lifted his chin in agreement and yelled, "Take thirty. I'm good for it."

The guard lifted his fist in acknowledgment but didn't turn around.

"Are *we* good, Teddy?" When he didn't respond, her need to make him believe her had her blurting out, "I didn't have anything to do with the breach. I didn't do anything. I don't know what it's about or how the leak works or... well, anything." She winced at how similar her words were to Sorcha's confession in the clearing. No wonder Sorcha had been such a mess. Seraphina hadn't even bothered to say she believed Sorcha.

"No?" A dark look flashed upon his face, too quick for Seraphina to catch.

A heaviness filled her limbs. He didn't believe her. "No." If someone who knew her didn't believe her, what could she say to Sawyer to make him believe her?

"We'll find a way, my Host. It's a good plan," Angwyndith said gently.

"Thanks, Angwyndith." At least they had a plan. Feeling slightly bolstered, Seraphina swiped her badge to the bathroom.

As she opened the door, Teddy tapped her shoulder, his breath heavy on her neck. "You can just tell me instead. I can pass the information on without him ever needing to talk to you."

She turned to face him, her grip tight on the door handle behind her back. "I need to talk to Sawyer directly. Besides, I'm done with letting other people speak for me."

The strength of his gaze increased, and she shifted her eyes to his forehead. She pressed her lips together, determined to wait him out. Seconds passed like minutes, and the desire to put a door between them intensified.

He leaned away from her and threw out a fake laugh. "Of course you are. Why would you tell *me* when you could go straight to the top?"

"It's not that, Teddy."

He rolled his eyes and checked his watch. "Are you going in or not?"

With a curt nod, she slipped into the first chamber of the bathroom, making sure she shut and locked the door as soon as it closed. *"That was weird."*

"He is a guard. His duty is to give whatever information he observes. Mayhap he is eager to be seen in a good light."

"He's always been friendly before."

"Hmm."

The flickering glare of the overhead lights in the mirror over the sinks gave her a ghostly pallor. *"What?"*

"His friendliness did not seem genuine to me."

"What are you talking about?"

"He only ever approached you when no one else was around. If he was just being friendly, would it matter who saw?"

"He talked to me in the cafeteria and..." Seraphina thought back to all the times he talked to her. Angwyndith was right. Even those moments in the cafeteria were quiet times, after his crew had left or when only a few Wielders who had remained were involved in an intense discussion about Samhain celebrations. *"Huh."*

She pulled out the glass chopsticks she'd been using to keep her hair off her neck, the red and orange patterns looking like blood in the dim light. Ro had given them to her for her twenty-fourth birthday after an Asian-themed celebration, complete with chopstick lessons. She set them on the shelf. When they rolled forward, she caught them and shoved them in her back pocket.

"It doesn't matter. I'm not telling him anything, anyway." With deft fingers, she pulled her hair back and braided it.

"I do not trust him."

"You don't trust anyone."

"True."

The rubber band strained against her hand as she tied it off. She had just finished smoothing out the wispy hairs sticking out around her face when the lights went out. *"What the hell?"*

"What is wrong?"

"No lights."

She groped for the door, smashing her hip into the last sink when she miscounted how many there were. "Ouch."

The door handle rattled, followed by Teddy's yell. "Seraphina, we need to get you back to your room."

"What's going on?"

"We have a situation. Unlock the door. Now."

Prickles of fear slid up her spine. *"I didn't see a notice for a drill, Angwyndith, and I've been checking. This is something else."*

"It may be wiser to stay here, my Host."

"Ms. Lastra. I need you to come out. Now. Unlock this door immediately." A thud followed, as if he just bumped the door with his shoulder.

Seraphina hesitated, the need to keep space between her and Teddy getting stronger. In the hall, the pounding of feet and random shouts rang out. "Lockdown Level Fifteen! All teams converge."

The voice sounded familiar, but she couldn't place where she'd heard it before. She shook her head and focused. *"This is bad. I need to get to my room."*

"You do not know what is on Level Fifteen."

"Based on how everyone talks about it, I never want to. I'll be safer in my room."

A deep voice boomed in the hallway. "We have breach. Converge, converge, converge."

"Ms. Lastra." The handle rattled again. "Either open this door and come with me now or be stuck inside until the emergency is over."

Seraphina really didn't want to be stuck in the bathroom for hours, but none of this made sense. She cracked the door open a few inches. The hall had small glowing emergency lights tracking along the ceiling, giving it a blood-washed look. Teddy stood in front of her, his eyes glowing red.

"Close the door," Angwyndith urged.

Seraphina's breath caught in her chest. She rushed to close the door, but it bounced off the foot he shoved in the jam. He shoved the door into her, and she fell backwards, slamming into the stall. Her arms flailed for purchase, her hands grabbing nothing but air as she slipped to the floor. The chopsticks snapped in her back pocket, the sting of one piercing her skin making her gasp.

The last of the rouge-tinged light seeped away around the borders of Teddy's body as the door closed and the lock clicked.

30

DANGER, SERAPHINA, DANGER

(A ROCK & A HARD PLACE)

The darkness in the bathroom absolute, Seraphina sidled on her hands and feet like a crab away from Teddy's glowing eyes. At least she knew where not to go; if he'd been better trained, she wouldn't have.

A nervous giggle escaped her lips.

He snarled in response.

"My Host."

"Sorry, can't help it. I'm trapped in a bathroom with a Shifter who may just be a bit unhinged."

"All you had to do, you stupid human, was tell me what I needed to know." He stalked closer.

"Say nothing."

"I didn't plan to. Now what?"

"You need to get him away from the door. Is there nothing you have to defend yourself with?

She winced as she pulled out the glass piercing the skin of her butt. *"A broken chopstick."*

Angwyndith groaned. *"That will not be enough."*

"You think?"

Seraphina left the chopstick in her pocket and slid to the left.

His eyes followed the movement. "I can see you, human. There is nowhere to run. Just tell me what I want to know, and no one gets hurt."

Seraphina drew in a shuddering breath. "Why would you want to hurt me? I thought we were friends."

"I would never be friends with someone like you. I thought when she told me to get close to you, I could do it, but you turn my stomach. Your whining. The way you smell like oil and coffee. Your needless focus on your problems."

Her fingers dug into the cold tile, his eyes mesmerizing her like a deer in headlights. *"I can't escape him. He's bigger and stronger than me."*

"You have no choice. No one else is coming to save you."

"Can't you help me?"

The silence was deafening inside her head.

"Fall back on your training." Angwyndith finally said, her voice taut. *"You can get out of this if you use your head and what little combat training you have."*

"I can't flip a Shifter in a bathroom this size."

"It does not matter, my Host. Keep him talking. Use his weakness, his ego, to negotiate your way out of this room."

"I can't negotiate a lower price on a knock off purse in Chinatown, Angwyndith. But I'll try." She stood, careful not to move too fast and bump into something she couldn't see, and balanced her weight between her feet. "I don't understand," she said to Teddy.

"You don't think I'd willingly talk to you, do you? No." His voice changed pitched as he mimicked someone. "Get close to her, Davies. Make her think you like her. She'll spill all her secrets then."

"They don't know me very well then. But you do." She clenched her hands into fists, tucking her thumb out of the way. "I won't tell you anything in here. Let's go back to my room and we can talk. I'll tell you what you need to know."

"No." He barked out a laugh. "I'm not stupid. You're trying to escape. You can tell me everything here and now."

"What do you want to know, Teddy?"

"Everything." He drew in a sharp breath. "You're my ticket out of guard duty. I'm combat material. If they only knew what I knew, they'd be down on their knees, begging for more. But they won't even give me the time of day. No, instead I'm babysitting some cockroach who can't even focus on the big fucking picture."

"At least he does not have room to change forms," Angwyndith said, her voice even.

"He's short and bulky. He has room." Seraphina inched closer to where she thought the sink was. She had one shot to get away.

He rushed her and shoved her into the back wall. The impact sucked all the air out of her, her head slamming hard enough to see stars. She lost a moment in the pain. The sound came rushing back, the words breaking in and out like the tide.

"...me...information."

His breath was hot on her cheek, his claws digging into her left shoulder as he pressed her into the wall. Pain consumed her; the world colored in red.

"He is out of control, but at least he pulled back right before he touched you. Otherwise, you would be dead from the blow. This is not good, my Host."

Angwyndith's voice came from far away, like an echo down a long narrow chamber. The tingling in Seraphina's head grew stronger, overriding the pounding and slowing the swimming of her eyes.

"I am fixing what I can, but you need to leave this room before he kills you." A pause. *"I cannot fix that."*

Seraphina closed her eyes to focus. The room smeared behind her eyelids and the nausea overwhelmed her. Bile rose and she vomited before she could stop herself.

He switched hands, the wet splash of her puke hitting the floor as he shook it off. "Fuck!"

The world slowed down as if she were in a stop motion film. In her head, she heard Moira's voice giving her step-by-step instructions. "When you're smaller and weaker, use all the tools available to you—gouge his eyes, pull on his ears, step on his instep. Use your momentum in your favor but do whatever is necessary to give yourself room."

She let her training take over. She moved her free arm between them, hitting his arm holding her somewhere near the elbow. The pressure on her chest eased. With the free space she created and the momentum of her swing, she grabbed the broken chopstick out of her back pocket and stabbed him in his side. His rush of breath told her she did some sort of damage.

Emboldened by her success, she shoved him as hard as she could. He stumbled back and the stall door smashed into the wall. Water sloshed on the floor as he fell into the toilet. She used the room he gave her, her hand trailing the sinks to her left, suddenly grateful for the moments she'd spent locked in utter darkness in her room.

Fumbling for the lock, she heard Teddy swearing behind her as he untangled himself from the metal stall.

Fuck, fuck, fuck.

"You can do this. Unlock the door and run to the nearest place where others will be. He cannot attack you there without considerable problems. Do not go to your room."

"Why not? My room is safe."

"Did he not unlock it to bring you here?"

"Right. You're right."

The click of unlocking a door had never sounded sweeter. She threw the door open and ran. A brief moment of satisfaction filled her as Teddy thudded against the bathroom door. The emergency lights danced around her as she neared the stairwell. She pulled the door open and stumbled down the stairs.

She missed a step, and her shoulder wrenched behind her.

Keep moving.

She reached the floor with the lab and burst through the door. Down the darkened corridor she ran, sliding around the corner and out of sight. Her chest heaved as she gasped for air. *Too loud.*

She slowed her breathing down but could do nothing about her racing heart. The slam of the stairwell door against the wall made her jump. She couldn't outrun him; he was too fast, too strong, and his senses were better than hers.

"Keep moving," Angwyndith said, her voice strained.

More tingling warmth covered the back of Seraphina's head. Ahead, she could see her goal. Once she was in the lab, the Wielders could shield her. She tiptoed to the door and tapped her badge to the scanner. The door remained locked.

"No." Her breath caught. *"What do I do? What do I do?"*

"There is a pin pad next to the scanner. Insert the code."

"I don't know the code." A fanning of pages thrummed through her. *"Angwyndith, hurry."*

"1002392018."

Relief flooding her as the door clicked open. She opened it enough to slide through and closed it softly behind her. She moved away from the hall door to the metal door between her and the Wielders who would save her.

One down. One to go.

"Is the code the same?" she whispered in her head, even though no one could hear her.

More fanning of pages. A pause.

"Angwyndith?"

"You have watched no one open this door. I do not have it."

"We'll try the first one. Read it out to me," Seraphina said.

"1002392018, but it will not work."

The sound of claws scratched on the wall made her freeze. "Little cockroach, where did you scramble off to?"

Oh gods, oh gods, oh gods.

"Input the code, my Host."

The lock clicked red. She froze, not daring to breathe as the scratching sound stopped as well. Her ears strained to hear what he was doing.

The squeak of his clothes gave him away. He was inches from external lab door.

A sign in front of her face captured her attention. She pulled it down and slid to the floor, making herself as small as possible. In the dim emergency lights, she read the paper. Her heart sank.

"They are not here, Angwyndith. It's Samhain."

"Coda be damned," Angwyndith snarled.

A thunderous clang hit the metal door between the antechamber and the lab, a dent forming like an iceberg surfacing in the sea.

31

MAKING A MESS

(A Broom Just Wouldn't Cut It)

Seraphina tucked her feet in even closer, ignoring the stinging sensation in her butt. Her head throbbed worse than any hangover she'd ever had, but she had bigger problems. The metal door bent further as something in the lab hit it again.

"It appears the Shapechanger specimen in the lab is no longer contained."

"You think?"

"Our only hope is for that door to hold and the Shapechanger in the hall not to come in."

Seraphina put her head on her knees. *"Hopeless then. I'm trapped between an insane Shifter and an equally insane Shifter."*

A laugh bubbled out of her, but she held it in.

"There is always another way, my Host. How can we get help to our position? Will not the Security Forces know of this Shapechanger and come to ensure he does not escape?"

"Maybe, but they have a bunch of prisoners on Level Fifteen, which apparently are higher priority than this guy."

A scream of metal pierced the mental fog of Seraphina's thinking as the door bulged further.

"I don't know what else to do."

"Find a weapon and be prepared to use it."

Her stomach cramped. *"Even if I had a weapon, it'd be useless. Moira disarmed me in thirty seconds flat. Teddy had the same training."*

"You have no other choice."

Seraphina scanned the room in the dim red emergency lights. A long brown shadow stood in the corner. She groaned. *"There's a broom. I'm fucked, but at least I'd go down fighting."*

"That is the spirit, my Host."

She slid along the wall. *"Too bad Demi wasn't here to distract Teddy."*

"He would be of little help although his poisonous spikes would get a revenge of sorts."

"Demi..." Seraphina's voice trailed off. *"Caide."*

"Caide? I do not understand."

Seraphina eased the glass door open, her eyes scanning the shelves. *"If I make enough of a mess, Caide will come."*

"The Brownie will be of less help than the Boobrach would be."

"Caide can fetch help or Eoghan."

Angwyndith's breath drew like Seraphina's had when Teddy threw her against the wall. *"You will not owe an Elf a favor, my Host. You will never be able to repay it."*

"What other choice do I have, Angwyndith? It's death or death right now. At least I'd be alive to figure it out."

The metal door rattled again, the hinges stretching away from the wall echoed by the door handle to the hall.

"Do it."

Seraphina yanked the box of bicarbonate soda toward her, all pretense of hiding gone. She pushed the box over, smearing it on the floor. *"It needs to be bigger. I need to grab his attention in a big way.*" She shoved other boxes out of the way and found the payout. "*Yes. This will work.*"

"*Vinegar, my Host?*"

"*It fizzes when mixed with baking powder.*"

"*You could also throw it at the Shapechanger at the door.*"

"*Good idea.*"

"*I was joking.*"

Seraphina yanked the top off the bottle. "*Still a good idea.*" She poured the vinegar on the floor and in the box. It fizzed and grew, reaching the far corners with its bubbles. The door slammed open, and Teddy stood in the frame, his hand holding it open against the wall. She scooped some of the fizzing mess out of the box and threw it at Teddy, scrambling out of the way when it hit his chest.

Fuck.

He stalked toward her, the red wash of emergency lights casting the room in an eerie light as the door caught on the magnet behind it.

She flipped on her knees and surged to her feet, grimacing when the throbbing in her head increased.

"You shouldn't have run. It made it so much more fun for me." He cackled like a hyena.

Shivers ran down her spine as she scrambled for the broom. Her fingertips brushed the wood handle, but it was too late. He grabbed her by her braid, and slammed her into the wall. Stars erupted, and the skin on her cheekbones scraped the wall. She bit her tongue, blood filling her mouth as she slid down the wall. Doom filled her as the broom clattered to the floor out of reach.

A high-pitched squeal followed by quick chittering filled the air behind Teddy's bulky form.

Caide.

"Get help," she mumbled, unsure if he understood her.

Teddy spun around and swiped at Caide, but he dodged the blow, blinking in and out of existence before her eyes.

Caide appeared in the door and bowed. Enraged, Teddy lunged after him, tripping and landing on his face in the doorway as Caide disappeared from view.

Seraphina coughed out a laugh. "No wonder you're still a guard." Her face felt like it was melting on one side.

Teddy pushed himself to his feet and growled at her.

"It'll be too late, won't it?"

"Hush, my Host. Have faith."

A warm tingling cascaded over her face. She laughed again, a bubble of blood popping on her lips. *"You're trying to fix me right before I die?"*

"Get up and face him."

"Why?"

Angwyndith was so quiet, Seraphina wasn't sure if she'd respond.

"So that you die with honor, my Host."

Seraphina's breath caught in her throat, but she pushed herself to her feet. The room reeled around her. Too many knocks to the head for Angwyndith to fix.

"What do you think you're going to do? You can't fight me."

She spit the blood in her mouth out. "No. I can't. But I won't cower either." Her heart pounded, her legs shook, and her head ached so much it felt like it was cracking open. "You're going to have fun explaining all this. You think your dream of being in combat will be helped by killing me?"

"I can't kill you. She won't let me. She wants that honor. But I'll just say you were trying to escape. They'll believe me, I'm well-respected. Unlike you. They'd never believe you."

"*She?*" Angwyndith queried.

"And I went down instead of up? Sawyer may be biased, but he isn't stupid," she said, her breath wheezing out.

His fists clenched and he took a step toward her. "You're still nothing in his eyes."

"*Keep him talking. If help is coming, it will take time. Who did he mean when he said she?*"

"Who is she? Carruthers?" Seraphina said, bracing herself to dodge the blow.

He cackled again. "As if I'd ever trust the Aetherhead who throws Shifters away like they're garbage. No. You'll find out soon enough." He took another step toward her and the metal door to his right blew off its hinges.

Gabriel pushed the door into Teddy, slamming him into the opposite wall. Teddy groaned and slid to the floor, the door smashing him flat. Gabriel faced her, his eyes glowing red, his mouth making sounds no human ever could.

"*This really couldn't be a worse way to die.*"

"*You do seem to have all the bad luck,*" Angwyndith said.

"*Can you help with him?*"

Angwyndith sighed. "*I cannot. I have used most of my energy healing you enough to keep you on your feet. And if I announce myself, the fear will drive him to attack.*"

"*Awesome. I'll stall as long as I can then.*"

Time to appear harmless and small. It seemed to stop Peter whenever he was in his aggressive mode.

"Hey there," Seraphina said, her hands out in front of her. "I'm not here to hurt you. I'm not a threat to you or your freedom. You can just go out that door and I will do nothing to stop you."

He half-moaned and snarled at the same time, but didn't move.

"I'm just a human. That's all."

He sniffed the air. "No, not human."

"What did that mean?"

"I do not know, my Host. Mayhap he senses me," Angwyndith said, fatigue evident in her voice. *"Try to pacify him."*

Teddy twitched under the door. Gabriel cocked his head and stepped on it. Teddy moaned, but made no further movement.

She licked her lips, her hands shaking. "I'm sorry for what they did to you. I'm sorry you've been locked up. I know what that feels like and it sucks. Bu you have a chance. You can leave. The power is off in the building, no one will stop you."

"Not for long." Teddy whispered. "It'll come back on real soon, minutes even. But you have time to kill her and leave before it does. She's just like them, just like those who left you and your team to rot at Crater Lake. James, Nolan, and Levin died for nothing. All because of someone like her."

Seraphina stared at Teddy in horror. She felt the compulsion in his voice. "You caused the power to go down."

"Of course I did. I couldn't question you with another guard around, could I? It worked perfectly, until you stabbed me."

Gabriel's eyes glowed brighter, his snarls increasing.

Oh gods.

"You don't have to kill me. I'm not like them. I had nothing to do with Crater Lake or what happened to you. I'm so sorry," Seraphina said, the words falling out of her mouth as she shuffled backward until she bumped into the wall.

Gabriel cocked his head.

"Oh crap. I said the wrong thing."

"There was nothing right you could have said, my Host."

"I'm not a threat to you. I'm not a threat to you. Please, don't do this. You have a choice." Her voice died out on a whisper.

Gabriel squirmed, like a cat about to pounce, but stopped. His head swiveled to the hallway outside.

"Fuck. It's too soon," Teddy mumbled under his breath.

"Oh gods, I think help has arrived."

"Let us hope it is more than just an Elf. There are too many variables for the Elf to focus on."

"You always know just the right thing to say as I'm about to die."

A canister spewing fumes of gas bounced off the metal door and rolled on to the floor between them all. Gabriel roared and surged toward the door.

The gas filled the room and she could no longer see anything beyond her own hands. As her vision blurred with tears, she sagged to the floor and crawled under the sink, one inch at a time. Dimly she heard people yelling, some snarls, and the impact of someone hitting the wall above her.

She'd just reached the broken doorway as the gas overwhelmed her.

And everything went dark.

32

THE RUNDOWN

(THE TRUTH WOULDN'T SET HER FREE)

A squeak of the chair near the door broke through Seraphina's nap in the medical unit. They must've been quiet coming in. She blinked her eyes open, the glare of the lights making her wince.

A smooth pale wall faced her; nothing marring its surface. A blank canvas, much like the one she'd like to have with the SF. Since she'd woken up from the gas, she'd been thinking about how she'd like to start over again and do it right this time.

But she didn't think it was possible anymore.

"Ms. Lastra, I know you're awake. It's time we talk." Sawyer's voice was calm. The edge he had the last time he had interrogated her missing.

Passing out and waking up to hard questions was getting old. *"Angwyndith, I need you."*

Angwyndith's warmth swirled around her torso. *"My Host, I will be here to help."*

"Thanks. I think it's time to come clean."

"Come clean of what?"

Seraphina pushed herself up with one arm so that she didn't trigger another dizzy spell. Dr. Liesl had said the concussion was healing, but the headache and nausea lingered like the horrid aftertaste of the tea the doctor kept making her drink.

"Tell them enough to show we will share information and they can trust us, but not so much that they know everything."

"Mayhap," Angwyndith finally said, her tone touched with frost.

"You're right. It is." Seraphina reached for the water on the table next to her, taking a long sip. Her stomach rumbled. She hoped a nurse would bring lunch soon, but Sawyer's presence told her she wouldn't be so lucky.

"Focus, my Host."

"I am focusing. Being hungry and in pain makes it difficult."

She faced Sawyer. He sat on a wooden chair, his legs crossed, with a clipboard and file on his lap.

"I need you to tell me, in your own words, what happened the day of the power outage." His gaze pinned her in place as if he expected her to refuse.

"I got a knock on my door that was early. Teddy—"

"Guard Davies, you mean?"

"Yes." She swallowed the lump in her throat.

"How early was the knock?"

She frowned. "Early enough for me to notice it wasn't to schedule, so maybe half hour?"

He motioned for her to continue.

"Teddy, um, Davies knocked on the door and said it was time for the bathroom break before lunch. He told the other guy—"

"Guard Manning."

Seraphina sighed. "—that he had this and that Manning could go get my lunch. Manning cleared the bathroom and then headed down for a thirty-minute break."

"Thirty minutes? Are you sure?"

"Yes. Davies told him to take the extra ten." With the help of Angwyndith, she had dissected every sentence from her conversation with Teddy since she'd arrived. She'd also connected him to the guard getting yelled at in the stairwell after the Eventon tragedy. All his comments about being just a guard clicked into place after that.

Pages fluttered within. *"That is correct. He said exactly that."*

Sawyer raised his eyebrows but said nothing.

"As we walked to the bathroom, he told me I could tell him what I knew, and he'd pass it on to you. We reached the bathroom, and I used the facilities. I had finished braiding my hair when the power went out. I heard boots in the hall and someone yelling about Level Fifteen lockdown."

His jaw clenched.

"He did not like that you know about that level. I wonder what is down there."

"Focus, Angwyndith."

"Hmph."

Seraphina hid her smile and continued her tale. "Davies yelled through the door that we needed to get back to my room. I opened the door to see the hall dark and the emergency lights on. Davies' eyes glowed red."

He shifted in his chair. "Are you sure? The emergency system has a red light and can cast a glow."

"He's not my first encounter with an angry Shifter, Sawyer." She glared at him, daring him to rebut her statement.

"Very well. Continue."

"I knew then something was wrong. I tried to shut the door."

"You tried to shut the door?" Sawyer opened the folder on his lap and made a note.

"Yes. I thought I could hole up in the bathroom. It had a lock on the inside. Davies shoved me backwards, and I fell against the stall. He stepped in, shut the door, and locked it." Her fingers clenched the soft white blanket across her knees. "He threatened me and told me to give him what he wanted."

"What did he want?"

A spike of anger at Teddy's next words eased the lingering fear from the memory. "He said he was told to be nice to me, get close to me, to put me off guard and find out information. Was that true?"

"Were those his exact words?"

"Basically."

His gaze bored into her.

"He does not know this part, my Host. And I do not think he gave those instructions." Angwyndith's tone was tentative; more tentative than Seraphina expected.

"I've been thinking about this, and I think he did. I don't know if he chose the person or just assigned someone, but there were always guards lurking about." It didn't explain why Teddy spoke to her before her first conversation with Sawyer, though. Seraphina's fingers played with the blanket, a sourness churning in her stomach that had nothing to do with food and everything to do with not having the friends she thought she did.

"That may be, but it does not quite connect, especially with this Shapechanger's behavior."

"What do you mean?"

"He is very good. From what I can tell, he stares straight at you when the information you provide is unexpected and his hands twitch."

"Huh. I'll watch for that then."

"Continue," Sawyer commanded.

"We spoke. I tried to get him to bring me back to my room. I wanted to get out of the small, enclosed space. I thought I'd have a chance to get away from him." Her shoulder throbbed where his claws had punctured the skin. "He slammed me into the wall and held me there. I don't remember much about the conversation."

"Dr. Liesl mentioned there was evidence of a concussion, although much of it had dissipated by the time we brought you in."

"Do not tell him I healed you." Angwyndith warned.

"I have to tell him something!"

"Very well. Mention that your being a Host provides some immunity to damage. It is more than I wish to part with, but it cannot be helped."

"I have some… side effects as Host. I'm not as fragile as a normal human."

The click of the pen shot through the room as he asked his next question. "To what extent are you not as fragile?"

She shook her head and regretted it as the room swam. "I can't give you a scale, Sawyer. I just don't get as damaged as someone my size and shape would."

"What happened next?"

"I threw up on him and he loosened his grip enough for me to remember what Moira taught me. I hit the elbow of the arm holding me and then stabbed him with the broken end of a glass chopstick."

Sawyer shifted in the chair and opened the file, scanning it.

"That is also new information."

"You think?"

"A chopstick?" He raised his eyebrows.

She flushed. "Yes. My best friend gave them to me. They were in my back pocket. When he first pushed me, I fell, and they broke."

"You stabbed him where?" He squinted at her.

"The side, I think." She lifted her hand and gestured toward her ribs. "It was dark."

He nodded. "And then?"

"And then I unlocked the door and ran. I wanted to be where the people were. I headed for the lab. There's always someone in the lab."

"On Samhain?" he murmured.

"I forgot what day it was. Being locked in your room will do that," she snapped.

"How did you get in the lab?"

"*I know, Angwyndith. Don't tell him,*" she said before Angwyndith could warn her again. "I watched a Wielder input the code and I have a really good memory." She tried not to squirm as she held his gaze. At his nod, she relaxed. "And then I was locked in the antechamber. I didn't have the code for the other door, which turned out for the best."

"You didn't open the door and let the Shapechanger, who was locked in a cell, out?"

"No. I didn't leave the antechamber."

"And then?"

"I was trapped. Davies was in the hall, sliding his fingers down the wall, hunting me. Something slammed into the metal door to the lab. I had no weapons but a broom in the corner." She shivered, the panic and red-filtered light of that moment rushing in to push out the calm white room in which she sat. After a moment of clenching and unclenching her hands, she said, "It was the broom that did it."

"Did what?" He cocked his head to one side.

"Reminded me that a mess would bring Caide and Caide could get someone to help me."

"Caide?"

"The Brownie who cleans up the offices. You do know about him, right? His name is in your files?"

"It may be mentioned somewhere, but since I do not interact with him, I do not need to know his name."

"He's staff in this building. You are building security. You should know his name." Seraphina said, her anger at everyone always dismissing the little guy leaking through.

"Careful, my Host. You do not want to create a hostile environment with him over something inconsequential."

"For the love of the gods, Angwyndith, lesser Elves are NOT inconsequential."

"I did not mean the Brownie. I meant his lack of information about the Brownie."

"Anyway. The metal door took a beating. Davies got into the antechamber and slammed me into the wall." She put her fingers up to her cheek, remembering the pain exploding across her face like her skull had shattered. "Gabriel broke through the door and hit Davies with it and then stood on it and him." She smiled at the memory. It was not a nice smile. "Davies tried to compel Gabriel to attack me. After that, you guys showed up."

Sawyer leaned forward, his eyes intense. "When did you learn Chief Gabriel's name?"

"I first heard it in a hall as his team left for the mission…" she frowned as she swallowed the sadness of all that was lost, "the one that ended badly. But it was confirmed by a Wielder in the lab, Dr. Myers. I asked what had happened to him and why they caged him. He seemed sad."

Sawyer's jaw clenched. After a moment, he leaned back in the chair and made a note in his folder. "So, you weren't trying to escape when Davies brought you to the bathroom?"

"No. There were guards from my door to the outside. I'd already thought about it and ruled it out."

"My Host, no. Do not hint at the idea."

"You thought about escaping?"

"You see?"

"Hush, Angwyndith. I'm going for total honesty. Mostly. Except for what you don't want him to know. Which is most of it. Gods."

"Hmph."

"I'd been locked in my room for a week. I was bored and annoyed. Of course, I did. But then I ruled it out."

"And yet, according to Davies, you kicked him when you opened the bathroom door and then ran. All his actions were trying to bring you back to your room."

Her blood boiled. "Are you kidding me? He told you I was trying to escape?"

"You just said you'd thought it through." Sawyer paused. "The blackout was oddly convenient."

"He planned it. He told me he caused it to question me. He couldn't have another guard around while he did so."

"That too seems convenient, and I only have your word for it."

"This is where you need to be clear. You cannot prove any of it."

"Neither can he."

"But he can imprison you."

A sick feeling rose in her stomach. *"You're really not helping, Angwyndith."*

"I am doing the best I can in the situation in which we find ourselves. It is the only way forward."

Angwyndith was right. This situation sucked. She needed to stick to the truth. "Ask Gabriel. He was present when Davies mentioned he caused the blackout."

"The subject of which you speak is currently sedated. He will not be talking to anyone."

Her gut twisted, guilt flooding in. "Is he okay?"

"Who? Davies?"

"I don't give a fuck about Davies. Gabriel. Is he okay?"

She'd confused him. He looked up at her, his brow furrowing, and then down at his notes. "He is as okay as someone in his position could be."

Fluttering pages tickled her and Angwyndith said, *"In one of your conversations with this Davies Shapechanger, he mentioned being responsible for the tests. He had the means to make it happen."*

"Davies also mentioned in one of our numerous conversations that he ran the practice drills in the building. Wouldn't that give him the means to cut the power?"

Sawyer ignored her question. "Why the lab?"

"I've already told you. It always has people in it."

"It wasn't to set the subject free and cause havoc so that you could escape?"

"No. I went to the lab to find people who could protect me from Davies. If I wanted to escape, I would've gone up the stairs, not down. Besides, I couldn't open the door. And even if I could, I couldn't break the ward containing Gabriel."

"And yet you opened the outside door by memorizing the code."

He had twisted her terrified flight to make it sound as if she had planned it. Dread tightened Seraphina's chest, and she fought to keep her breathing even. What else could he twist?

"Whatever he wishes, my Host, to achieve his aim. He is excellent at what he does."

Angwyndith's ability to see the positive in dire situations never failed to amaze Seraphina. *"He's using my words against us."*

"I learn from every encounter. I can appreciate the methods even if I do not like the results."

Sawyer cleared his throat.

"I told you. I have a good memory."

"You also had drawings of the ward encasing Gabriel's cell in your room." He clasped his hands over the clipboard.

Seraphina seethed. *"This could've been avoided. Had you just told me how wards were created, there'd be one less piece of evidence against me."*

"It is a weak claim. You studied the ward and have shown no ability to wield aether. He is fishing."

"I came to the Facility for an education. The drawings of the wards were part of that. Besides, I can't wield aether, either to create a ward or to break one."

"And yet, you broke a ward in the past," Sawyer said, his voice soft. Dangerously soft.

Seraphina grit her teeth. *"I* didn't break the ward, Angwyndith did on our way to a Judgment. And Gabriel could've broken the ward himself."

He glared at her.

"What?" she said. "I've been doing research, and it came up." He didn't need to know how it came up.

"We have only your word for either of those two events." He frowned at his notes. "Shifters have some abilities, but those particular wards required a Wielder to break them."

"I'm not a Wielder."

"But you know someone who is. Someone who has walked these halls before."

Seraphina scowled. "I haven't spoken to my aunt since I left the house. She got a little spooked when she met Angwyndith. Check your records if you don't believe me. Ask Summers or Bradley. They can accurately describe the experience to you." Seraphina spit the words out, her head throbbing in rhythm to her pounding heart.

"I have spoken to both and am familiar with the accounts of that day. That does not change the fact that you know a powerful Wielder and have checked out many titles from the library on wards."

"Because I was trying to figure out how they worked."

"My Host..."

"Precisely." His teeth snapped down on the word, just like his judgment on her involvement in the breach and Gabriel's escape.

Davies was right.

No matter what she said or did, he'd never believe her. The weight of that hit her, and she slid down further on the bed, her cheek throbbing. "I've told you what happened and how."

"Let's go through it again."

"Why? It won't change. Davies attacked me and hunted me down like an animal. If it wasn't for Caide or Gabriel, I'd be dead and then you could believe whatever you wanted." She closed her eyes, the fight completely drained out of her.

Everything was such a mess.

A knock on the door preceded it opening and Dr. Liesl's sharp, "Sir."

A murmured conversation followed. Seraphina couldn't hear it, but it didn't matter. She'd always be the outsider, the other. Just like Sorcha.

Except he hadn't used anything Sorcha may have told him against her. Did that mean anything, or was Seraphina reaching for anything that redeemed that friendship?

The door opened again, and Sawyer said, "You are tired and still healing. I will return tomorrow, and we will discuss it again."

"I'll tell you the same thing tomorrow," Seraphina mumbled to the wall.

"Then we'll discuss it again the day after that," Sawyer said in a matter-of-fact manner.

She heard the door close, and the lock clicked.

New prison, same sentence. Would it never end?

33

THEY HAD TO STOP MEETING LIKE THIS

(SHE HAD FINALLY LEARNED)

Seraphina's stomach churned as she forced the last of the bland oatmeal into her mouth, swallowing it with minimal chewing. She set the banana and hot tea on the side table and pushed the tray away, no longer hungry. As if he prowled the corridors, waiting to pounce, Sawyer had arrived every day within minutes of her breakfast tray being removed.

It had been three days of nonstop visits, the same interrogation each time. He varied the way he asked the questions, trying to catch her out. She stuck to her truth, but there were times when she didn't know what her truth was as he twisted her words back at her.

Dr. Liesl had pronounced her fit to leave the med bay, but Sawyer had ordered her to remain. He enjoyed having her without the fake protections of her own things. With no computer, TV, book or phone to distract her, she spent her days staring at the ceiling.

At least that was what they thought she did.

Instead, she and Angwyndith had spent whatever time Seraphina wasn't counting ceiling tiles to train. Long marathons of storytelling, and drills and repetition exercises to ensure Seraphina had remembered everything she'd been taught. They had made more progress in the past three days than in the five months of being officially together. It too had its moments of torture, though; bombarded by other words, words she couldn't escape even when she told Angwyndith to shut up.

She'd also spent some of it rethinking everything that had happened so far. Most of the hostility aimed at her had been because the people at the Facility had thought she'd betrayed them. Or because they were already hostile to anyone not them.

Adept Stanton blamed someone for decimating the Wielders at Eventon. Myers blamed Gabriel for his situation. The Shifters blamed the Wielders for their injuries. The digs, the jabs, the derogatory slang—there was so much more going on than she'd ever be able to see.

The Community's contentions ran deep, scars from past hurts obliterating any potential for unity. The combat teams should have been immune from the division, the danger they were in requiring each person to rely on the others. But Eventon cracked that false belief wide open.

It was open season in the MC, and the outsiders, like her and Sorcha, were the first victims.

The only good thing to come out of it was that Seraphina no longer believed Sorcha had sold her out. Too many hours with Sawyer disabused her of that, especially since he never brought up Demi and he would've hammered her with it if he'd known. The promise of their friendship remained a light at the end of a dark tunnel, which she clung to like a climber on a ledge.

Seraphina wanted to leave this room, where nothing ever changed except Sawyer's questions, the words beating at her like hard rain. She thought imprisonment in her room was a punishment, but it was nothing compared to this. A pressure valve pushed to its max, her screams tickled the back of her throat. She wouldn't scream for them, though. It was the one thing she had control over, and they would have to wrestle her cries from her cold, dead hands.

A knock on the door signaled the start of today's torture as a nurse came in and took her tray. Seraphina smoothed out the blankets across her knees and sipped her tea. She grimaced but smoothed it out when Sawyer entered the room.

The tea was all the Wielders would give her, even when she told them her headaches were because of the lack of caffeine and not the concussion. If he'd bothered to do any research, Sawyer would've brought her coffee. But he didn't. He thought he knew who she was.

He was wrong.

Sawyer sat in his usual chair, his leg casually crossed. One thing was different, however.

"Where's your handy dandy folder? I didn't think you could go somewhere without your security blanket," she said, derision coating her tone.

The beginnings of a smile crossed his face, but it died before it reached full maturity.

Much like her if she stayed in this room any longer.

"Good morning, Ms. Covington."

That was new. He always started with a question. What new tactic was he trying out on her today?

Angwyndith's warmth surged upward, and Seraphina felt a sense of detachment about it, no longer needing her support.

"You seem remarkably chipper today. Had a good breakfast of torturing innocent souls again?"

"My Host, I know you are upset, but try to remain polite. Something has changed."

They could all go fuck themselves.

He picked imaginary lint off his perfectly creased shorts. "We have been making some inquiries about your statement."

The door opened and Dr. Carruthers walked in. The dread turned to a hard fist in her stomach. They were going to kill her.

Would that be so bad?

The thought surprised her. That was hiding, not living; giving in, not choosing. And that was not the plan.

She lifted her chin. "Dr. Carruthers, to what do I owe this, I would say pleasure, but it doesn't feel like that kind of visit." Her lips tight, Seraphina radiated controlled calm. She had learned more than Sawyer had over the past few days.

"You have survived their questioning remarkably well, my Host. Trial by fire was not my first choice for you to learn control, but it was effective."

"Too bad it was all for nothing."

Angwyndith said nothing. There was nothing to be said.

"I understand you are upset with the way you have been treated here. But you must understand our position as well," Dr. Carruthers' said, her gaze steady.

"Oh?" Short and sweet, it never failed to piss them off.

Sawyer shifted in his chair and Seraphina fought to keep the small smile of victory off her face.

Dr. Carruthers' smooth forehead creased into a tiny frown and then rippled back to its marble-like consistency. "We have, still, a serious security breach in our facility. We also had an incident that involved damages to a state-of-the-art laboratory, for which there appears to be no explanation and a power outage that was not an accident. Because of that, we have had to be vigilant in our investigation to find the culprits."

Seraphina sucked in her cheeks to stop the scowl threatening to emerge. "You've certainly been vigilant in questioning me."

Dr. Carruthers frowned at her clasped hands.

"She does not like that part of the Facility's task. Interesting," Angwyndith mused.

A light bulb went off. Angwyndith only found something interesting when it didn't fit into her known experience. And she said it a lot.

"After further investigation, we have concluded that you were not responsible for the events last Saturday," Sawyer said, as if he were discussing the weather.

Seraphina's hands clenched on her knees, and she swallowed down the words that rushed up. When she had control, she asked, "What led you to that conclusion?"

Sawyer flicked his eyes to Carruthers, who nodded.

"Little inconsistencies in the other account of the events."

That could only mean one person. "Davies?"

"Yes. But what sealed the nail on his coffin were the shards of red and purple glass we found embedded in his side, which matched a broken stick we found in the bathroom. He had healed around it. He also failed to mention it in his original report. It was the crack we needed to get to the truth."

"This is good news, my Host."

"Maybe. They still don't trust me, and I don't trust them. All this means is that they don't blame me for Saturday."

"That is a fair assessment."

Dr. Carruthers shifted, her gaze more intense than it had been when she walked in the room. "We have not, however, determined the cause of the leak."

"See?"

"Hmmm."

"As such, we would request you remain at the Facility while our investigation continues."

Seraphina glanced at Sawyer. A muscle clenched in his jaw.

"This was not his decision," Angwyndith said.

"Nope."

"They made it a request, my Host. You can leave if you would like."

The urge to run screaming from this room, scoop up all her possessions and drive away, cackling as she did so, was strong. But she wasn't going to. "Fine. Will I be able to leave the Facility whenever I choose if I remain?"

"Yes. You will not be... confined to your room. You will, however, still be brought in for any questions Master Chief Sawyer and his team may have."

Sawyer's stare turned to ice, flaying the sore skin on her cheek. She flicked a glance at him, her lips pressed together into a hard, straight line. If nothing else, they were in agreement about their dislike of each other.

"If at some point you wish to leave the Facility for good, there will be a final debriefing before you do so," Dr. Carruthers said in an even tone.

Seraphina knew exactly what that debriefing would entail. And she'd be ready for it. "And training? Combat and classroom instruction? I'd like to continue those."

"Are you sure? They cannot teach you anything that I cannot as well."

"Yes. I'm going to milk this institution for all its worth and wring out whatever information I can. I'm done with being in the dark."

The warmth within stilled. She'd confused Angwyndith. *Good.*

Dr. Carruthers blinked.

"*She did not expect that. You have surprised her.*" Angwyndith's warmth swirled in her throat, like a snake waiting to strike. "*Good.*"

One corner of Seraphina's mouth lifted at the echo of their thoughts.

"Of course," Dr. Carruthers said. "The full agreement we have with you still stands."

"Great."

Sawyer stood. Apparently, the meeting was over.

"What happens next?" Seraphina asked, her tone leeched of any feeling.

"You will be released back to your quarters to enjoy the weekend. Instruction will resume on Monday morning."

Sawyer moved toward the door.

"Before you leave, I'd like to be very clear," Seraphina said.

Sawyer pivoted to face her, his face as neutral as his pants.

"Yes?" Dr. Carruthers asked.

"I had and have had nothing to do with the security breach you are currently facing. I came to the Facility under the agreement we made as a gesture of trust. Trust that you would treat me like any other recruit. That trust has been broken." Dr. Carruthers moved to speak, but Seraphina held her hand up. "But not just for me. I failed to be as open with you as I might have been, given the circumstances."

"*My Host, what are you doing?*"

"*Opening a door to an easier relationship without giving them anything. If we don't rebuild the trust, Angwyndith, I'll always be threatened by imprisonment and interrogation.*"

"*They would do that, anyway.*"

"Yep, but at least this way, they'll think I don't believe that anymore."

"I do believe that you have impressed me far more than I ever expected at this point in our relationship."

"I'm a quick learner." A ping of sadness hit her. She used to want to impress Angwyndith, but not anymore. "Not that you will know everything that I know or that we know. But I will share what I am able to share."

"Able or willing?" Sawyer asked.

"Interpret it however you want. You will anyway." Seraphina locked eyes with him, this time her challenge unmistakable.

He quirked one bushy eyebrow and then nodded. Challenge accepted.

None of them understood, though. Not even Angwyndith. There was no challenge here. Survival was her goal, nothing more. She'd be damned if she died at their hands.

She almost had.

Dr. Carruthers clapped. "Excellent. I feel confident we are about to embark on a stronger relationship."

"Did she always sound like a life coach, and I just missed it?"

Angwyndith chuckled. *"If that profession is what I think it is, yes. I would compare her to a traveling snake oil salesman. They were very charming and yet said nothing of value whatsoever."*

"Sounds about right."

"We'll leave you in Dr. Liesl's capable hands," Carruthers said as she followed Sawyer out the door.

The show over, Angwyndith's warmth swirled away as she murmured, *"We'll continue our studies later, my Host. After you are free of this place."*

"Okay."

As the last of Angwyndith's warmth trickled away, a deep darkness unfurled to fill the space inside her. It wasn't the Void or the Coda, but from within. The darkness colored her view of the world and everyone in it. No longer would she rely on others to make decisions. She'd use the tools available to her to learn everything she could about the SF, the MC, and herself.

She wasn't going to study just because they told her she had to. She was going to study as if her life depended on it, because apparently it did. Seraphina wouldn't say her position was stronger, but she would walk into it with her eyes open.

For once.

34

MOVING FORWARD

(FREEDOM NEVER SMELLED SO GOOD)

Now that freedom was just a few steps away, Seraphina itched to get out of the med bay. She slipped out of bed, the cold of the stone floor seeping through the thickness of her borrowed socks. Her sneakers were the lone survivors of her encounter with Teddy; everything else had either been ripped or reeked of the gas the guards had thrown at her. She rushed to pull them on before someone stopped her.

Dr. Liesl appeared in the door, blocking Seraphina's escape. "I want to see you in four days. That's Tuesday—in case you've forgotten what day it is—to see how your cheek is healing." Seraphina made a move to leave, but the doctor stepped in front of her. "Eh, eh. I am not finished yet. I promise, it'll be quick. While you can train, I don't want you to do any hand-to-hand combat for the next week at least. I will tell you when you are released from the restriction."

The pinch in her gut as Seraphina rebelled against someone telling her what not to do must have shown on her face, because Dr. Liesl said, "Moira will be given these instructions as well, and she does not break the rules." She kept her gaze on

Seraphina, although it was softer than the ones Seraphina had just endured.

"I understand."

"Good. Your brain needs more time to heal before you subject it to being slammed on a mat. Now, eat well, sleep as much as you can, and try not to be so hard on your body. It's been through a lot."

Seraphina's foot tapped the floor.

"Go. I'll repeat this the next time I see you." Dr. Liesl waved her hand and Seraphina shot off like a rocket, desperate to get out. "Tuesday. I'll see you on Tuesday," she yelled at Seraphina's back.

Her legs were shaky, but stable enough to hold her, and she took the stairs two at a time. She unlocked her door, slid inside, and was dressed and back in the hallway in under five minutes. Her fingers beat a steady rhythm against her leg while she waited for the elevator.

When it reached the top floor, she bolted out of it and headed toward the gym and the outside yard. She didn't want to deal with the guards in the lobby, especially since Davies was associated with them, and she didn't trust herself to drive yet, anyway.

The doors slammed into the wall as she pushed through them. Her gaze focused on the doors to the outside, she ignored the clanking of the weights near the mirror.

"Covington!" Moira yelled.

She made it to the doors before Moira yelled again, closer this time. Her stomach sank as she faced the doors. "I'm just going for a walk," she squeezed out between clenched teeth.

"That's fine. I just wanted to give you a heads up. There's a drill on the west side of the grounds. Stay to the left of the path and you'll be fine."

"You're not stopping me from going outside?"

Moira's frown shimmered in the reflection of the glass. "No."

The weight in Seraphina's stomach lightened. "Great. That's really great."

"I'll see you on Monday, eleven hundred hours sharp. Be prepared. I won't go easy on you."

"I don't expect you to." The emotions choked Seraphina, but she held them at bay.

"Good to see you back, Covington. Now go get some fresh air. You look like you could use it."

Seraphina charged through the door, the chill fall breeze slicing through her jeans. Her footsteps quickened, the need to put distance between her and the gym urging her into a run. She ran until she couldn't run anymore, and the sounds of the drill were a muffled blur of shouts and bangs. Leaves crunched underfoot as she left the path, seeking somewhere even further away from the Facility and the people within it.

As she walked, she stumbled across a little clearing, a dead tree blocking off one side, and the outline of the campus fence looming fifty yards away. The richness of decaying plants contrasted with the crispness of the air as she breathed in deep, like a drowning man who'd surfaced from beneath a murky lake.

She finally understood Sorcha's need that day to roll down the window and escape the confines of the car. If only Seraphina had learned it some other way than the weeks spent confined to a room, but that didn't matter now. No more looking back; she'd only look forward.

A shower and a meal of her choosing called. Seraphina was no longer at the mercy of whatever the guard on duty chose for her. There would definitely be frozen yogurt involved, maybe even a tub of it.

The combination of a growl and someone gargling water brought her to her feet. Frozen in place, her ears strained to determine from which direction it came. She approached the fence, peering through the gloom. Just on the other side of it, outside of the border of the ward, stood a naked brown Elf, his tongue hanging slack between his teeth.

Feeling as if the world brightened, a grin broke out on her face as she picked up her pace and stopped short of the fence. "Hi, Demi."

He chittered at her, his words smashing together in his haste to tell her about his adventures while she'd been away. She missed most of the details but understood the gist. Smiling constantly through it all, she let him ramble about fighting off badgers for his dinner as the chilly air made her nose cold.

"I'm glad you like it here. I'm going to be staying on for a bit. I don't know how long, but at least another month or two. It'd be good to see you while I'm here."

He nodded and asked her why she had sat there for so long.

"My world is changing. I resisted it for a long time, but I can't anymore. It won't let me. There are more dangerous things in these woods than badgers."

He promised to show her how to beat them off, mimicking his words with his spear.

She laughed, and the world brightened even more. "I'd love for you to show me. There's a lot I don't know, but it's time I do." The daylight seeped from the land, shadows rushing to fill the void left behind. "I have to go back now, Demi. I'll see you around, though, right?"

He nodded, wagged his tongue, and then streaked away.

Still smiling, she headed back for the path. Her phone buzzed in her back pocket and she pulled it out. The boundary of the fence or the distance from the gym must've given her the reception denied to her nearer the building.

Six missed texts from Ro. Three emails from Finn. And two missed voicemails.

She fired off a text first to Ro.

> Seraphina: Hey. Things got a bit hairy, but I'm fine.
> Ro: Hairy? How hairy? Did you get a BF or something?
> Seraphina: No. I had an adventure. I'll tell you about it sometime.
> Ro: Sounds ominous.
> Seraphina: It's fine. I'm fine. How's NC?
> Ro: Definitely ominous. NC is good. I love it and the program is amazing. Talk soon?
> Seraphina: Yes.

She read her emails, her head down. The phone pinged again.

> Ro: You ok?

The tightness in Seraphina's chest eased. Angwyndith was right. She needed to be a better friend.

Seraphina: Yep.
Ro: I'm here if you want to chat.
Seraphina: I know, and I appreciate that more than you know.

A bevy of hearts threw up across her screen. She went back to her emails. Finn was worried; he'd sent increasingly more grave emails the longer it took for her to respond. She didn't feel like talking to anyone, so she sent him a brief response to let him know she was okay and that she'd send him the latest book after training on Monday. He'd understand what she meant by that.

She clicked over to her voicemails and listened to the first one. It was her aunt, her voice concerned after she'd received a call from the Facility regarding her injuries. Tristana didn't say much more, but asked if Seraphina would come home for the Harvest festival at the end of November. Seraphina frowned when the message ended.

Classes didn't end until December, and Seraphina wanted to complete them. She also wasn't ready to face her aunt or her aunt's fear of her just yet, although she understood it a lot more now since she'd survived Davies' attack. She'd send Tristana an email later when she was more certain of her decision.

The lingering sunset slipped over the horizon, the last of its rays winking out behind the Facility wall. She listened to the last voicemail, her footsteps quickening as the cold seeped into her bones. Finn's gravely voice rumbled through the phone. After a minute, her footsteps stalled.

Her brow furrowed; she replayed the message.

She fired off another short email, this time with a request. She needed to decide about it soon. One way kept her where she was, and the other moved her into a position she didn't necessarily want. Angwyndith would be good counsel, but ultimately the decision was Seraphina's.

The outline of the gym came into view, the windows emitting a warm glow of light, but concealing everything that occurred beyond them. Sort of like her now. She stepped inside the gym, smiling at the familiar sound of a body hitting the mat.

Monday. It all began again on Monday—after she bought a decent coffeemaker for her room. She was done drinking crappy coffee.

Author Notes & Appreciation

Thank you reading Seraphina and Angwyndith's experiences with the SF. I hope you enjoyed it!

If you're excited to see what comes next, the story continues in the third book publishing in March 2024. If you'd like to stay updated on when it will publish and want to get the free prelude, *The Prior Space Between*, please sign up for my newsletter: cassandracstirling.com/spacebetween-book2.

In *The Prior Space Between*, Seraphina navigates six snapshots from five years of her early life (ages 8-13), where being barred from entering her family's library or being bitten by a frightened Elf were the worst things that could have happened to her. Until they weren't.

Last but not least, something I never realized until I became an author is how important book reviews are. If you enjoyed this book, I would love it if you could take a few minutes to throw a few stars at it and leave a comment about what you liked and didn't like.

About the Author

Cassandra Stirling is all about books. She reads them, edits them, writes them, reviews them, and throws them at the wall when they frustrate her. They also appear as key features in all the series she writes, whether as jobs for her protagonists, a love of reading as a hobby, or as literary quotes to teach someone a lesson. You could say she is immersed in them in all the ways that count.

You can sign up for her monthly newsletter on her website: cassandracstirling.com/spacebetween-book2.

Or hunt her down on social media:

f facebook.com/CassandraCStirling

instagram.com/cassandracstirling

g goodreads.com/cassandracstirling

Also By Cassandra Stirling

Space Between Urban Fantasy Series
The Deep Space Between
The Dark Space Between

Merryton Mews Cozy Mystery Series
Poison and Pens (Kindle Vella)
Holly and Havoc (Kindle Vella)

Works Cited

Epigraph

Robbins, Anthony. *Unlimited Power: The New Science of Personal Achievement*. New York: Free Press, 2008.

Chapter 7

Choderlos de Laclos, Pierre. *Les Liaisons dangereuses*. Trans. P.W.K. Stone. London: Penguin Books, 1961.

Chapter 15

Choderlos de Laclos, Pierre. *Les Liaisons dangereuses*. Trans. P.W.K. Stone. London: Penguin Books, 1961.

Descartes, Rene. *A Discourse on the Method*. Trans. Ian Maclean. New York: Oxford University Press, 2006.

Kant, Immanuel. *The Critique of Pure Reason*. Trans. Norman Kemp Smith. New York: Palgrave MacMillan, 1929.

Twain, Mark. "Disappearance of Literature." 1900. In *Mark Twain's Speeches*. New York: Harper & Brothers Publishers, 1923.

Chapter 26

Descartes, Rene. *A Discourse on the Method*. Trans. Ian Maclean. New York: Oxford University Press, 2006.

Chapter 28

Radcliffe, Ann. *The Mysteries of Udolpho*. New York: Oxford University Press, 1966.